INTENTIONAL
CHANGE

0643 STEP

INTENTIONAL CHANGE

Personal and Professional Coaches Describe Their Work and Lives

John S. Stephenson, Ph.D, Editor

To order additional copies of this book, contact:
Xlibris Corporation
1-888-7-XLIBRIS
www.Xlibris.com
Orders@Xlibris.com

CONTENTS

DEDICATED TO THE COACHING COMMUNITY.

PREFACE

While attending the annual conference of the International Coach Federation in 1998, I was struck by the wide applicability of coaching. People were describing their work with individuals, couples, small businesses and multi-national corporations. Their approaches to coaching were equally varied; some pragmatic, some spiritual. Some coaches were taking a systems perspective to coaching, others an individualistic approach. All had one thing in common; a dedication to the profession of coaching.

In creating this book, I sought to bring together a varied group of coaches who would describe their work, their lives, and their thoughts on coaching. The reader may find approaches to coaching with which they agree, others may seem difficult to relate to. Coaching is a new, innovative and exciting profession, and as such defies being simplistically labeled or pigeonholed.

When I decided to take on this project, I contacted coaches who's work exemplified the vast world of coaching. I was a stranger to most of them, but they all eagerly agreed to become a part of this project. No contracts were exchanged; there were no long negotiating sessions. They eagerly agreed to my invitation to write a chapter. The chapter authors demonstrated a great faith in me and this project, and I am sincerely grateful to them all. This speaks well of them as individuals; it also says a great deal about people who become coaches.

I would like to thank my classmates, buddies, and class leaders at Coach University, as well as my own students. You have provided me with friendship, ideas, and, like good coaches, have cheered me along the way. A special note of thanks to my mentor coach, Bill Thomas, whose guidance and belief in me and my work as a coach has been a great support. My family gave me the space I needed to work on this project, often sacrificing "family time." Finally, a special thanks to my wife, Dawn. Her editing of the book was a great help, and truly an act of love.

COACHING
CREATIVE GENIUSES

Madeleine Homan

Let's just say it right up front: I am not a nice person. I am judgmental, harshly critical, contemptuous of inferior intellects and tough. My standards are ridiculously high and most of the time I am unable to live up to them. I am often shocked by how mean my thoughts are. Why am I telling you this? Because I am a coach, and my job is to see the best in people. My mission is to have people connect to the parts of themselves that they love and value most, and to have them find a way to at least enjoy those parts, and at best profit by them. Does this seem like a paradox to you? A wonderful client who is as tough as I am and recognized it instantly, asked me recently what I do when I really don't like a client. My answer was news to me: " My job is to find something about them that I can love."

When I find that something, all the harshness, meanness and critical judgment falls away, and I am in a state of grace. All that matters is that the client be served, and that they find something in our communicating that will be essentially useful to them; that is, useful in a way that moves them forward, dissolves a block, or has them see a situation in a brand new light.

Who I am, and the things that are right or wrong with me are completely irrelevant. I'm in the zone. All that matters is that by some genetic fluke or miracle, I am able to do this "trick". I always felt compelled to do it, though it took a lot of time to get good at it. It also took time to figure out how to translate this service to a completely clueless public. I saw such an obvious need in the marketplace. All my friends were going to therapists and getting nowhere, when what they really needed was some inspiration, clarity about what they really wanted, structure, accountability and some goals. Don't get me wrong, I'm a big fan of therapy. It has helped me a lot, but it offers something very different from what coaching offers.

I have such a strong memory of the moment I became a coach. Henry Kimsey-House, my mentor and teacher for years, called me and said "I've become a coach and you are a coach also and you need to hire me to help you do it." I said, " OK." When I heard the word and put it all together it was absolutely clear as clear could be that a coach was who I was and coaching people was what I was going to do. I had no fear and no doubts even though I essentially had no idea what I was doing. Henry gave me some cool tools to use, and I had some great consulting training and a ton of school of hard knocks experience. Off I went. I sat on my bed — I don't think I even had a reasonable desk — and called every one I'd ever known to tell them what I was doing. My husband, bless his heart, also told people and quite of few of my first clients came from his talking about me.

What makes me feel a little sorry for coaches today is that there are standards and training programs and lots of experienced coaches now. Therefore there is a strong notion that there is a "right" way to do coaching. This may be true, but it doesn't mean that there is any real way for a new coach to learn to coach "right" by any other method than we old timer coaches used: by doing it and making mistakes. All the training I got later definitely made me a better coach, and I continue to train myself but I am grateful to all of the clients who took a leap of faith with me in those first years and showed me how to coach well.

Why Creative Geniuses?

When my practice started to get to the point that I wanted to treat it like a business, the time had come to understand who my customers were. A lot of newer coaches feel pressure to choose a niche, if only because it's one way to distinguish oneself from the coaching crowd. It was my experience, however, that you don't choose a niche; rather a niche chooses you. When I approached the question of what I was passionate about, what interested me most, it appeared as though I would end up with a practice that specialized in female entrepreneurs with young children. The fact was that at least half of my practice has been men. So I looked at what they all had in common, and it became immediately clear that they were all highly creative and had obstacles and problems that stemmed mainly from that fact.

I have the ability to understand where these people came from, while gently teaching them to apply the pragmatic, linear thinking that's necessary to create a life that works. How did I know how to do that? I attribute living with my husband who is an actor, singer, director, writer, composer, professor, talented artist who likes to sit around talking about Nietzsche and going winter camping. I learned a lot about what creative people like him need just by observing him all these years. You might be wondering if I coach him. The answer is never, ever, ever. But I have used my experience with him in everything I've done with clients over the years.

Highly creative people tend to require a little more patience, and a special touch. They need to feel that I really understand them and that it's OK for them to be the way they are, which often has been defined as flaky, irresponsible, flighty, dramatic, etc. What I understand, because I'm the same way, is that they have to get through a regular day just like anyone else, with the added handicap that they are constantly firebombed by great, interesting ideas. It can be a total nightmare, and they need to learn how to accommodate it and stick to their program. They need to know that they are not defective, that the way they are is neither good nor bad, but simply the way they are. They need to know that whatever value they derive from all of their ideas depends strictly on their ability to translate them in a way that others will be as entertained by them as they are.

People sometimes ask me how I ended up coaching creative geniuses. My answer is that they chose me. How do I know that I should work with a client? I only work with people who laugh at my jokes. Simple huh?

Coaching allows me to combine all of my talents and use fully all of my quirky attributes. People have always come to me for "advice." I learned early on that no one really wants advice, they just want you to ask the questions that will allow them to access their own wisdom. When friends call me to talk about a problem, I get to voice my opinions and give advice. This is a luxury and allows me to indulge my natural bent toward being opinionated. One of the things I get paid to do when I coach is to lay that particular trait aside. Sometimes I'll have such a strong opinion that I will voice it with caveats and disclaimers, but I try to do this as rarely as possible. What guides me as a coach are what I perceive to be universal, and physical laws. Often clients will think that I am giving advice, when all I am really doing is pointing out a universal law and asking them how it applies in their particular situation.

The following are some of what I call universal laws, that guide me:

If you don't ask, the answer is always no.

People are terrified to ask for what they want. I include myself because I catch myself shrinking back whenever I am afraid that I might be overreaching. Is this just a human thing or is it cultural? Are we just horrified that people will not be able to say "no," and then hate us for asking? Or that they will say no and then feel guilty every time they see us? Or that they will think we're needy, or pathetic in some way? When I do ask for what I want, I find that people generally are happy to help as best they can. Being specific helps. This brings up an important point: we often aren't really that sure what it is that we really want, which makes asking for it tricky. So, I get clients to figure out what they want, and to ask the right people for the right information, help and favors. Sometimes they get a no, but they always get some yeses too.

Any commitment you make will be tested.

It's hard to know when we've committed to a course of action whether the Universe is saying stop, cease and desist, or if we are simply being tested. This can be a very hard call to make. My general experience has shown me that if a client can stick with a new venture or endeavor for 18 months, then it is a keeper. No major decisions should be re-thought until a good chunk of time has been put into it. A certain amount of bad luck in the form of mishaps, errors, acts of God is to be expected, but a good plan and a strong commitment should be able to get us through. It is also important to recognize what we are actually committing to.

I was working with a client who had an extremely successful training business, and he was on the verge of losing a huge client. He had made the classic business error of spending all of his waking hours satisfying the client instead of making sure that this client wasn't his only one. This is an understandable and extremely common business error, that is usually made by entrepreneurs who are gifted at delivering their service or product, but have very little interest in actually building the business. These kinds of entrepreneurs hope that doing good work will naturally build business, which it sometimes does, sometimes doesn't. My client was sounding very strung out and betrayed by his big client, and put a lot of energy into trying to salvage the relationship (which was ending thorough no fault of his own because of a new company policy). At a certain point I asked my client if he might want to consider finding another way to use his talents, as it seemed that he had no commitment to his business. He almost hung up on me. Though I knew I had taken a risk, I was surprised at how angry he was. He thought I had questioned his commitment to his work, which I wasn't, but I did question his commitment to his business. Once he understood the difference, he immediately understood how he was misplacing his energies, and got to work marketing.

Talent and $.25 gets you a phone call.

Don't get me wrong. Talent is important once you get where you want to go, but alone it is worth less. Gifted people who understand that they need to develop skills, and who understand the value of relationships will probably stay in the game long after the prodigies have fallen away. I have worked over the years with some true geniuses who had to understand that without the strong support network of people who knew, understood and loved them, that their talent would die on the vine. Ultimately, people care about people, not about raging talent. People hire their friends, those they know they can count on.

When you are upbraiding someone else for something, look to yourself.

This rule is as old as the hills, and for the longest time, I didn't understand it. And then I saw the most extraordinarily clear example. A very dear friend, whom I'll call Linda, had done a huge favor for another mutual friend, Mary. This favor resulted in an unexpected and extraordinary change in Mary's fortunes. Linda never felt that she had been appropriately acknowledged for the role she played in Mary's rise to stardom, and hasn't quite forgiven her. Well wouldn't you know that yet another friend has recently done Linda quite a nice favor? And wouldn't you know that he has heard not a word of thanks or acknowledgment. All I can do is laugh, and ask myself next time I'm complaining about someone, what behavior do I see in myself that I find it so upsetting in others?

Lie only at your own peril and only as a complete last resort. If ever.

I really used to think of lying as a black or white issue: you don't and that's that. Well, that's what I thought until my ever watchful ("Mom, wasn't that a stop sign?") children started to catch me in minor, little white lies. I realized how much I lie, or "spin the truth" to keep my life smooth, to maintain relationships, to save time, to protect someone's feelings. There is a lot of pressure for coaches to have flawless integrity, but I have to admit that I sometimes do not have the courage to tell the whole truth. Often I feel that I don't have the correct language to tell the truth in a way that won't cause damage. I lie rarely and badly and almost always as a way to keep the peace. I have watched my children learn how to do this and believe it to be a basic social skill.

I have two problems with telling whoppers: I get a terrible tummy ache when I tell them, and I have a terrible memory so I forget to whom I've said what and mess everything up. Most of clients who lie often find that there is a physical toll to pay, and find it to be a huge relief when they stop.

Ignore reality only if you can afford to, and let someone else run the numbers.

The summer I graduated from college, I went to work for a wonderful, brilliant man who was starting a brand new summer theater company. Things went pretty well at first, and then certain "done-deals" started to fall through. It turns out that these deals were in fact fantasies and that a lot of what the theater was built on was myth. With a ludicrous amount of hard work we actually managed a season of theater, but when it came time to mount the last show we were all completely exhausted. Our leader was also completely played out, and was behaving erratically. He was going to borrow more money to mount the last show, and was throwing around numbers to prove that he could make it work. I knew what the existing debt was, and I'd been manning the box office before each show (I was also in the shows which gives an idea of how understaffed we were) so I knew that his numbers were hogwash. And, I'm no whiz with numbers. I pointed this out to him and after some ranting and raving, it was agreed that the theater would close. It was like a Mickey Rooney—Judy Garland movie without the happy ending. My friend never forgave me for pointing out the truth, and to this day blames others (mainly me) for the demise of his theater. I have seen this scenario played out now with clients many times. They all think they're Han Solo flying through the asteroid field yelling at Chewy: "Never tell me the odds." Yikes. I love a good challenge, and I sob harder than anyone does at the movies when the underdog pulls it out and wins the day. I also know that if the numbers aren't working, that all the energy needs to go into finding a way to make them work.

Fear makes you small. Love makes you bigger.

When I started singing professionally, I was so terrified that I got myself into all kinds of scrapes. For me the higher the stakes, the more scared I was, the less able I was to hear the accompanist and start on the right pitch. Now, pitch is not a problem for me, unless I can't HEAR, which is what used to happen. I always wonder: if that particular faculty is so affected, what happens to the rest of them? Ones that are much harder to assess? I know fear makes me hear poorly, think badly and generally stupid. The only antidote known to me is generosity and love.

Anything worth doing is worth getting help with.

(If you want it done right do it yourself vs. If you want it done right delegate well.) I grew up in a culture that taught me that I should be able to do it by myself, whatever it might be. That if it couldn't be done by me alone, I shouldn't attempt it at all. I've come to realize that there are armies of brilliant, talented, over-achieving members of control freaks anonymous who cannot ask for help, and can't bear to delegate anything. However, I've learned to coach my clients that if they want it done right, delegate well. If a client leaves coaching with a strong circle of 10 people who love and support him/her, and an increased skill at asking for help, I feel that's a job well done.

Write thank you notes, and remember that anything good that happens to you is the result of many people.

One of my favorite exercises to give clients is to ask them to write an "Oscar acceptance speech." I tell them to pretend that they have won the highest award available in their field (and if there isn't one, make one up). What would they have done to earn it? Who would they thank along the way? This exercise does two things: It has people get clear about what they see themselves capable of doing, which is important, and it also clues them in to who their supporters are. I ask my clients to identify and cultivate their heat sources, and to thank them often.

I don't happen to subscribe to any one particular religious dogma, but it can't be an accident that certain things crop up in all religious teachings. These laws have made it on to my books because I have seen repeated evidence of their existence. I take absolutely nothing on faith and I don't expect anyone else to either. I always ask clients to look to their own experience when they need to decide on the criteria by which to make a big decision. If a client can show me evidence that one of these laws has been untrue for them, I don't argue.

The following are some physical laws that guide me:

Nothing is wasted.

People get scared that they will waste time by going down a certain path. But I've found that unless people are completely unconscious, they generally make choices that they need to make to develop the way they need to develop at that moment. People make choices because they have to get a need met, or they need to have certain experiences. When people are making a big decision they can only make a big mistake if they ignore their gut feelings and do what they think they should do. Even if they end up changing their minds later, whatever it is they decided to do was not wasted.

Time is fixed.

At always amazes me that smart people rationalize themselves into thinking that they can manipulate time. That they are somehow above the law that says, "If you must be there on time, the subway will break down." Or the law that says, "It takes 3 hours to write a proposal." I have seen many otherwise successful people who are so over-stressed by lateness that their quality of life is reduced to zero. And they actually believe that they are powerless to stop the madness. I believe a person can get hooked on adrenaline. The kissing cousin of adrenaline addiction is powerlessness addiction. People addicted to powerlessness who can't say "no" to their bosses, their spouses, their in-laws, their kids. They start to play fast and loose with the reality that there are in fact only 24 hours in a day (one hopes that 7 of those are spent sleeping). I hear constantly, "I don't have any time", or "I don't know where the time goes." We act as if its Time's fault and we are just like bugs pinned to its crazy vagaries. But the fact is that time is fixed. It ticks by ever so consistently. We don't want it to be that way, so we pretend it is malleable and then complain when it's not. The truth is, if we want more time, something has to go. Period. End of story.

I finally learned this the easy way when I was working with a wonderful coach named Dana Morrison. I was coaching full time, I had two adorable small children, my husband traveled often for months at a time, and I spent a lot of time trying to figure out how to make it all work. One day I was in the throes of a very regular bout of "Oh-my-god-I-don't-have-an-advanced-degree-how-will-anyone-ever-take-me-seriously-itis," and had been filling out graduate school applications. Dana pulled me up short by asking me if I was tired. Of course I was, my baby had been up all night. She asked me how I thought I was going to make it all work when I added grad school to the mix. I figured I would just power through, but I hadn't thought about the cost to the rest of the family and about how my new-found quality of life would suffer. She asked which I wanted more; the validation of a degree or a successful business. I said, I want a degree so that my business will be more successful. I had no evidence to show that my business would be less successful if I had no advanced degree. She pointed out that what I need to do to make my business successful was build it — not take my focus off of it. In retrospect, I am glad that I was forced to prioritize so strictly. Now it is clear that focusing on the business was the right thing to do. An advanced degree was a luxury I could not afford. It was one of the first times in my life that I bowed to reality, and it served me well.

My personal rule is that everything takes twice as long as I think it should take. If it involves computers or the government make that three times. With home renovations multiply estimated completion time by a factor of four and you're safe. I have been testing this rule for about eight years now, and it is almost always true. The good news is that if its not, your life is much easier than if you hadn't acted as if it were in the first place.

Our psyches are just as affected by inertia as any other matter; the same goes for momentum. If you've ever watched W.W.II movies, you've seen fighters taking off from a ship. They have so little space to gain momentum that they get the engines going on all burners, hurl themselves off the boat, and out across the ocean. You can see the plane leap off the deck and then dip slightly. Most humans do the same thing. When our mental/creative/psychic energy has stopped flowing, it takes a massive amount of energy to get it moving again. This is normal and should not be cause for concern, but a lot of people interpret it as a message to stop. Wrong.

It is just ramping up time, which requires constant application of energy to push things into the flow and to build momentum.

When a new client begins coaching, they almost invariably follow a pattern that goes roughly like this: They get all excited, wanting to fix everything about their lives, and they launch into action. They go like gangbusters, and then around the second month they have complete breakdowns. They almost always get sick, or have small fender bender. Though it is completely predictable, it is hard to warn clients without feeling like you are creating the breakdown. Only the rare soul doesn't go through this. Almost everyone does, and I am convinced that it is simply burn-out from the incredible energy required to get the plane into the sky. If you watch modern planes, they don't dip visibly. My goal is develop myself and others to be so well tooled that there's no dip when we hurl ourselves into the blue.

The human soul growth pattern is a spiral, which is why we always seem to come back to the same place. OK. This is my own personal belief, and I have zero scientific evidence to show that this is true. I feel that this is the case, and I constantly gather evidence to support it. I have to admit that on a purely rational level it is indefensible. It is comforting though, so I'll throw it out there. If our souls' journey were to take the shape of a spiral, starting in a very tight circle at the bottom of the page and widening out as it winds its way up to infinity, that would explain why no matter how much work we do on ourselves, no matter how enlightened we are, we often seem to find ourselves in the same spot, just with a slightly different landscape. The wider the circle, the less often we have to deal with the fact that we are essentially who we are and that certain aspects of us do not change. By growing up toward infinity, or God, we change the landscape enough for ourselves so that we can enjoy the parts of ourselves that we value most and love. We are still going to have to deal with the little ruts in the vertical continuum, no matter what. I've seen this be true among people addicted to certain types of sabotaging behaviors, or substances. No matter how "recovered" or restored people get, those ruts do not go away.

My View On What Makes A Coach Successful

People who ask me about the profession of coaching often want to know what it takes to be successful coach. I'll outline here what I believe has made me a one. I think there are a lot of different successful coaches who succeed with specific types of clients for different reasons, so this is not a statement of what I think it takes for every coach to be successful. It is what I believe has made me successful.

First and foremost I am entertained, amused and engaged by people's stories. I want to hear it all. I want to know what makes them tick, what lights them up, what they're going to say next.

Second, I have a passion for learning, so I am constantly looking for different types of clients to work with. I've learned more about the law than I'd ever dreamed through working with attorneys, and about the body by working with health care practitioners. I am an expert in small business because of all my small business clients. I've learned about photography, painting, sculpture, writing, and flying. New clients ask me how much I know about some aspect of their lives, and my response was always: the less I know the better, because we will be so much more creative and unrestricted, plus you'll fascinate me.

Third, I am rigorous about my self as an artist. I see coaching as both a science and an art. To me that means a combination of craft, skill, discipline, inspiration, and accessibility. I devote time to developing skills, practicing, and talking with colleagues who inspire and challenge me. I am always looking for ways to apply coaching technology, and to translate concepts to clients easily and effectively. I am always looking for ways to expand what coaching can do. I love looking for ways other arts and sciences can apply to coaching.

Fourth, immediately apply everything that I learn from clients to my own business. I am learning and growing as fast as my clients. The minute I start working with a client who is more organized, technologically savvy, or systematized than I am, I bring myself up to their level as soon as I can. My clients often know that they've inspired me to upgrade, and they love it. Fifth, I have never, ever made a client wrong. Even when they behave badly, I take the highest possible road, refund money, make apologies. Sixth, if I can't find a way to love them, I let them go.

Madeleine Homan is president of Straightline Coaching, a firm devoted to the profitability and personal balance of creative geniuses since 1990 (www.StraightLineCoaching.com). She is raising two children and Australian shepherd puppy named Indiana Jones with her creative genius husband in Dobbs Ferry, New York. E-mail : MHoman@StraightLineCoaching.com

COACHING WOMEN

Elyse Killoran

*Feminism is the articulation of the ancient, underground cul-
ture and philosophy based on the values that patriarchy has
labeled 'womanly' but which are necessary for full humanity.
Among the principles and values of feminism that are most
distinct from those of patriarchy are universal equality, non-
violent problem-solving, and cooperation with nature, one
another, and other species.* — SONIA JOHNSON

When you ask a coach how he/she got into coaching, you'll often
receive this reply, "Oh, I've been coaching all of my life." Although
it sounds like a cliché, this statement certainly rings true for me. I
view coaching more as a way of relating to other people than as a
specific profession. When I am in coaching mode — whether I am
coaching a client, a friend or one of my children — I am consciously focusing on the best that is within the other person and
intending to bring their attention to that place as well. I've done
this in just about every job that I've ever had — as a teenage camp
counselor, a high school teacher, and in my own business. I now
refer to myself as a Life Coach and my professional responsibility is
to help my clients get what they really, really want out of their
lives.

For me, the best thing about my current profession is that as I
focus my energy on helping clients get what they really want, I
increase my own ability to attract what I really want. I'm not talking about a prestigious executive title, a luxury car or a designer
wardrobe. What I've acquired is a deep-seated sense of peace and

satisfaction — with myself and with my life. I wake up feeling energized and optimistic about the day ahead. When I retire, I can look back on a day well spent.

I love my job, every aspect of it. Especially because I outsource all the components that do not suit me. I love the flexibility of my schedule. I am able to teach, to write, to work on my personal and professional development, and to serve 20 clients/week while taking Wednesdays and Fridays off to be with my kids. I love the fact that I chose a specialty that is very meaningful to me — coaching women — and that I have clients of every age, race, career and income level. I love the fact that having a high standard of living — mentally, physically, spiritually and financially — is a requirement of my job. Finally, I love that fact that I am surrounded by extraordinary people every day, in the form of clients, colleagues and teachers, who provoke me to continue learning and expanding while fully appreciating me for who I am right now.

I couldn't have said any of this about my life before I began working with my first coach. In fact, if someone had told me 15 years ago that I was going to find my ultimate career satisfaction by enrolling in a training program offered by a virtual university, and that I'd be earning a rather nice income "coaching" an international clientele over the telephone from an office in my home, I'd have had a good laugh at the absurdity of it all. Even ten years ago I was controlled by such limiting beliefs (among them: it takes hard work to earn an income, the "helping" professions don't pay well, I am worth whatever an employer says I am worth) and restricting fears (among them: fear of the unknown, fear of failure, fear of success) that I would not have been able to imagine such a fulfilling future for myself. (Coach's note: fortunately, those fears and limiting beliefs are a part of my past and I now have access to tools and methodologies to rid my clients of such blocks).

Coaching And Right-Livelihood

Your work is to discover your work and then with all your heart
to give yourself to it. — Buddha

In *Do What You Love and the Money Will Follow: Discovering Your Right-Livelihood*, Marsha Sinter writes, "We are not born to struggle throughout life. We are meant to work in ways that suit us, drawing on our own natural talents and abilities as a way to express ourselves and contribute to others. This work, when we do find it — even if only as a hobby at first — is a key to our true happiness and self-expression." When I first read this book in 1987, my heart resonated with every word, but my logical-rational mind told me that the promise of the book was too good to be true. Now that I have been on both sides of that equation — stifled by jobs that did not allow me to fully express myself and, today, psychologically, emotionally and spiritually fulfilled by my current profession — I must share my deeply held belief: that the process of dedicating yourself to uncovering and surrendering to a call from inside yourself about the work that you are meant to do can (and will) transform your life.

I can write that coaching is my "right-livelihood" with some conviction because I had already had numerous careers by the time I entered a coach training program. I had experience in public, private and not-for-profit organizations and I had even begun my own small business. A casual observer reviewing my job history would be hard-pressed to see a theme — much less a valid direction. But looking back I can see all the threads in my life that have brought me to this point. I feel a great deal of gratitude for the journey and for every teacher and every experience that has shaped me along the way.

Searching

> *We must be willing to get rid of the life we've planned, so as to*
> *have the life that is waiting for us.* — JOSEPH CAMPBELL

I experienced my first career crisis when I was a senior majoring in psychology at Franklin and Marshall College. I was, as were most of my peers, fixated on graduate school. Although my professors were urging me on to a career in academic psychology, I felt no attraction to that route. Doing research and publishing articles that would only be read by other academics seemed pointless to me. I was primarily interested in how the knowledge that emerged from such research could be used to help people live happier lives. For example, my senior research project was a study of how male-female friendships are impacted by how men and women interpreted sexual signals.

My plan was to go on to graduate school for a Psy. D. degree in clinical psychology. I was a very driven student and I stood a very good chance of gaining admission into some very competitive programs. Mid-way through my senior year, after all of the applications were out, I seemed to "snap." I began to question whether I wanted to go to graduate school at all. Was I sure that I wanted to be a psychologist? Could I commit myself to staying sheltered in school until I was 27? Did I feel that academic psychologists had the answers that I was looking for? I had no rational explanation for why I began to feel that I would miss something important if I took this route. When the acceptance letters came I seized on the excuses that "I didn't get into my first choice school" and that I "wanted to take a year off and apply again." I was trying to extricate myself from this path.

The years after college became an important learning ground for me, because I wasn't as good at real life as I was at academe. Had I continued on the track that I was programmed to follow I would have been successful by many standards. However something inside of me demanded that I look further outside my safety zone for a career that would offer true fulfillment. I began my search with the book, *What Color Is Your Parachute*, which is a guide to finding an ideal career from the inside-out. The author, Richard Bolles, has been on a mission since he first self-published this wonderful book in 1970, to eliminate under-employment by expanding his readers' perspectives on careers and employment. This book is truly a coaching manual for job-seekers and the central theme (that we are all "gifted" and that it is up to us learn how to lead with our gifts) impacted me at a very profound level.

Readers of *What Color Is Your Parachute* are guided through a series of exercises to uncover their future ideal job. Here are some of the points that I have written in my 1987 edition:

> My future ideal job will involve educating and improving the lives of others using new approaches and problem solving. I wish to work with women, young adults and children on such issues as self-esteem and relationship skills. The people skills that I will emphasize in my work will be: communicating, sensing/feeling, and training. The information skills that I will utilize will be: creating/synthesizing, planning/developing and analyzing. The only technical skills I'd like to use would involve a computer. My ideal co-workers will be bright, well educated and enthusiastic. I will work in a room with windows and my own desk in a small company of less than 100 employees within a short commute from home.

I emerged from hours with this book with a description that did not fit any job that I had ever heard of. Still, I tried every job that I could think of that came close. I tried social work but found that the high responsibility/low control and pay did not suit me. I tried the life of a public school teacher but I became frustrated with the bureaucracy. My next idea was to leave public service and go for the financial rewards of private industry. After working in training for a small communications company, and while my job performance always met with approval, I started to think that maybe there was something wrong with me.

I was always the one to leave my previous positions, I couldn't understand why everyone else seemed content to work their way up in one company. I was still looking for someplace that could hold my interest and challenge me to bring out the best of myself on a daily basis. Now, as I work with women who are seeking to shift careers, I find that the range of my experiences and my expanded view of the job search process has prepared me to be an especially good partner and ally to women in any phase of career transition.

Motherhood Metamorphosis

> ...there's a lot more to being a woman than being a mother, but there's a hell of a lot more to being a mother than most people suspect. — ROSEANNE BARR

In 1993 my company downsized and eliminated my department. Instead of looking for a new position within the company I jumped at the chance to take a severance package because, as luck would have it, the timing coincided perfectly with the birth of my first child. Like most women, I had no idea how much my life would be altered by the birth of my son. I knew that my activities would have to be modified, but I was completely unprepared that "I" would be different once I became someone's mother. Today, as a coach, I am fully cognizant of the power of this transformation and I coach new mothers to honor this period of metamorphosis. We don't talk a lot about becoming a parent in this culture. Mothers-to-be spend months preparing the nursery and weeks in classes preparing for the labor without devoting much (if any) time to preparing themselves mentally and emotionally for their new lives. Elizabeth Stone's words in *The Quotable Woman* ring true, "Making the decision to have a child — it's momentous. It is to decide forever to have your heart go walking around outside your body."

I wish that I had a coach or had participated in group coaching during the early months of motherhood. While I did meet many mothers in similar situations, the truth is that new moms who are meeting in social settings are often so fixated on social approval that they don't let down their masks. We'd talk mostly about the children — how they are sleeping, what they are eating, what they are wearing, what tremendous new feats they have accomplished. Only rarely did a new mommy acquaintance make a foray into touchy territory to discuss how the advent of the baby affected her sex life, how her image of herself changed since the birth of her child or how she was sometimes overwhelmed by fears that she would not measure up as a mom. To became more appreciative of the complexity of this transitional period, read Iris Krasnow's *Surrendering to Motherhood* and Susan Maushart's *The Mask of Motherhood.*

Becoming an at-home mom after spending so much time in the workforce was a shock to my system. The images that I had of motherhood, garnered from the media, had me believing that nearly every minute spent with my new bundle of joy would be peaceful, joyful, and fulfilling. Yet caring for a child is difficult, emotionally demanding, and frequently boring. I was surprised to find that I was not enamored of this new role. I found myself feeling frustrated by the repetitive nature of the tasks (for as soon as I had diapered, clothed, and fed the baby, it was time to repeat the cycle). I missed the social interaction that I enjoyed at the office and the intellectual stimulation of my job. Now, as a coach I tell my clients who are first-time moms: No matter how much you love your child, it is perfectly normal to admit that you dislike some aspects of full-time baby care. The key here is to focus on the positive while admitting to, and growing to accept, the negatives. A woman who can admit that she is sometimes frustrated, annoyed, tired and/or bored being home all day with a baby is a woman who can tell the truth. And having such feelings doesn't make her a bad mother.

After six months I was ready (actually eager) for some adult conversation and intellectual stimulation. I found the ideal part-time position as the Educational Coordinator in a nursing home. The position required me to work four days a week from 12:00 - 4:00 PM. I'd play with Brett all morning, feed him lunch and drop him off with a sitter in time for his afternoon nap. He'd sleep until 2:00 or 3:00 and play for and hour or so until I picked him up. We were both very satisfied with the arrangement until I became pregnant with my second child. The only drawback of the position, which I so enjoyed, was the low pay. After considering the cost of daycare for two children I was going to bring home around $5/hour. There did not seem to be much point keeping the job after Justin was born, so I considered other more financially viable options.

The Entrepreneurial Mom

> *Challenges make you discover things about yourself that you never really knew. They're what make the instrument stretch — what make you go beyond the norm.* — CICELY TYSON

I have always had an entrepreneurial bent. I've come up with notions of ways to improve current products and ideas for products that did not currently exist but that often appeared on the market a short time later. Knowing that my independence had been a major source of my employment challenges, I sensed that working for myself while being at home with my kids might be the ideal solution. After considering all of my talents I decided that I'd be most marketable as an SAT coach (helping high school students increase their college admission test scores) and I began to advertise my services. I found it easier than I expected to get my business started. Within the first four months of the year I was able to earn almost $10,000 while only working 4:00 to 9:00 and a handful of hours over the weekend. In the next four months business slowed to a standstill. SAT fever is seasonal and during summer and late winter there is no demand at all. I needed to find a way to optimize my earning potential year round so I decided to add college selection advisement to my client offerings and embarked on a quest to create a brand new business on top of my SAT coaching.

I had a strong sense from my SAT clients that parents and students needed more support during college selection than school guidance counselors could provide. I spent countless hours after my kids were asleep studying college brochures and typing at my computer. I was not bringing in any income so I found it impossible to justify paying for child care or help around the house. This is a clear example of how not to start a business. After pushing myself to the limit, I found myself in a depressed state; totally exhausted and at a loss for what to do next.

It was at this point that I first came upon a book written by a coach; Azriela Jaffe's *Honey, I Want to Start My Own Business*. It is an essential guide for home business owners. I began to see that my business success was heavily impacted by every other dimension in my life. This seemed to reinforce information that I had seen in an article in my local paper. Digging up the article I found links to web sites dedicated to the emerging field of personal and business coaching. After surfing the sites over the period of a week I decided that it was time to hire a coach.

The Power Of A Coaching Relationship

> We do not believe in ourselves until someone reveals that deep inside us something is valuable, worth listening to, worthy of our trust, sacred to our touch. Once we believe in ourselves we can risk curiosity, wonder, spontaneous delight or any experience that reveals the human spirit.— E.E. CUMMINGS

Although I hired my first coach for financial and business reasons, she helped me to confront the bigger picture of my life. I had become exhausted trying to care for my children all day and working non-stop in every "free" moment. Because I was home all day I had decided that I should be fully responsible for all of the things that made family life tick: housekeeping, doctor appointments, grocery shopping, bill paying. I made certain that everyone in the house got just what they needed but I had no time or space for myself. I had been putting off projects, letting things go and, when things slipped through the cracks I would blame myself. After my initial coaching session it became very clear that my external reality was a mirror of my treatment of myself. I resolved to turn things around.

My coach listened to me and then took me beyond the words. She encouraged me to tell the truth about every aspect of my life without judging or criticizing myself or others. The goal was to be clear about what was and was not working in my life and to take positive actions to bring about desired results. I began to own up to my predisposition towards perfectionism, self-criticism and playing the victim. Unlike a therapeutic focus, my coach did not encourage me to dwell upon why I had developed these tendencies. Instead, we focused on how, with my newfound awareness, I might do things differently in the future. I learned that these characteristics were not deep personality flaws but simply examples of habits that I had acquired that did not serve me. By becoming aware of the situations in which I would habitually demonstrate one of these "unskilled behaviors." I became empowered to choose to take a different action in order to bring about a more appealing result.

Coaching was a transformative experience for me in so many ways. I learned and began to live according to critical life lessons that no one had shared with me before. Simple shifts in perspective such as:

- We teach people how to treat us;
- If we don't take care of ourselves no one else will;
- you can't give to others what you don't have yourself;

led me to institute improvements in every area of my life. My coach taught me a kinder, gentler way of accomplishing everything that I had set out to accomplish. I was actually getting more done with less effort. I learned that instead of pushing myself and viewing the business as a place of struggle, I could focus my energy on my greatest talents, on the most important aspects of my business, and allow opportunities to come to me. I was so overwhelmed by the changes that I had experienced that I did the only rational thing that I could do. I signed up for coach training and never looked back.

Becoming A Coach

> *If you want joy, give joy to others; if you want love, learn to give*
> *love; if you want attention and appreciation, learn to give*
> *attention and appreciation; if you want material affluence,*
> *help others to become materially affluent.* —DEEPAK CHOPRA

By the time I began taking coach training classes, my personal life transition was already in full swing. I, who had lived all my life as an achiever in the thinking/doing/striving mode, had to learn to honor a completely foreign way of life. As I went through the classes and began connecting to my new colleagues, I found myself fascinated, challenged, shocked and often overwhelmed. Few people in my life understood exactly what I was trying to do. I became more and more appreciative of the new community that had embraced me.

While some shifts happened effortlessly, it took longer to release some ineffective ways of being. For example, I continued to do SAT tutoring while studying coaching in the evenings. It took some time before I was willing to pay for child care so that I might have personal time and space. I read coaching related books voraciously. But I had a hard time making myself stop reading in order to do the recommended exercises which would make the learning more effectual. I made some significant changes in my lifestyle and my relationships but I continued to avoid certain things in my environment and in my relationship with my husband. It took a bit of time before I was really "practicing what I was preaching."

I found as I achieved greater integrity between my thoughts, words and deeds, my ability to have a positive impact on other people increased.

Being a Mommy-Coach

Any mother could perform the jobs of several air-traffic control-lers with ease. — LISA ALTHER

The hardest part was trying to balance my studies, work and family responsibilities with the time necessary to work on my personal development. I've kidded some of my mentor coaching clients who are trying to build coaching practices simultaneously with being parents that the mommy-coach track offers many "best of times, worst of times" scenarios. As the vast majority of coaches do not have primary child care responsibility for young children, we must hold ourselves up to different standards. It is easy (and, I suppose, natural) to be envious of other coaches who have reserves of personal time and space. I consider envy a positive emotion in that it makes us aware that we want that something. Jealousy occurs when envy becomes twisted by negative energy. We feel a sense of pain because someone has something that we want. However, it is incumbent upon mommy-coaches to remember that the choice of building our practices when our children are young offers numerous benefits.

I have been able to plan my work schedule around my kids and I take time off during their school vacations. I have been able to integrate coaching skills into my parenting repertoire. I have been able to model for my sons that it is essential that a woman consciously design a life that fills her needs and values instead of trying to fit someone else's mold or trying to be "supermom." Most crucially for my clients, many of whom are wives and mothers themselves, I have been able to ascertain, through direct experience, which strategies, tools and techniques work best for women who want to effect positive changes in their home environments.

Attracting Coaching Clients

*To build the life you want — complete with inner satisfaction,
personal meaning and rewards — create the work you love. By
this I mean invent a way to earn an income doing what you do
best, while serving others, becoming an authentic, fulfilling the
highest standards of your vocation. This is spiritual work. It's
life's assignment. And most of us are well-equipped to do it.*

— Marsha Sinetar

In many training programs, new coaches are encouraged to "hit
the ground running" by attracting a handful of pro bono clients to
coach as part of the training. I, like most coaches, chose people
who I knew well and who I felt could really benefit from coaching.
Because coaching holds little appeal to a majority of the population (and because these people were coming to coaching mostly as
a favor to me), these early relationships were frustrating and not
terribly rewarding. If I was to have judged my future career by
these experiences I would have turned in my headset immediately.
Fortunately, my personal experience with coaching had been so
powerful that I could not hold my enthusiasm back. I offered everyone with whom I came in contact a free month of coaching to
"see how it fit." A large percentage of my first real (not relative)
clients stayed on with my after their free month were over. I was
actually in business making money as a coach.

The need to attract clients is typically the most challenging
aspect of becoming a coach. When I mentor new coaches I advise
them to lead with their gifts. Great writers most easily attract clients through their writing. People with tons of charisma are most
attractive when rubbing shoulders with people in person. Coaches
with teaching in their blood need to do seminars. Most of my
current clients come to me via referrals or through my web site.
This works nicely for me because my web site is very representative of who I am.

The most important thing about marketing to clients is the

energy in which the communication is sent. When I needed clients in order to pay my bills, the fearful, constricted energy behind my marketing efforts drove clients away. It was only after doing a lot of inner work and releasing my attachment to the outcome of all my coaching calls that my practice really began to blossom. For those people who have been trying to do what they love but who have not seen the money follow, there is a lot more to this philosophy than meets the eye. In order to operate in synch with these principles it is essential that you rid yourself of negative beliefs and emotions that might block the flow of good into your life. A coach who is well trained in metaphysical processes can help you move past such blocks.

Choosing A Niche: Coaching Women

> *The great question ... which I have not been able to answer,*
> *despite my thirty years of research into the feminine soul, is*
> *'What does a woman want?* — SIGMUND FREUD

> *I feel there is something unexplored about woman that only a*
> *woman can explore...* — GEORGIA O'KEEFE

Amazingly enough, although two of my first pro-bono clients were men, all of my regular clients were women. I began to notice the kinds of books that I was attracted to, the kinds of coaching situations that peaked my interest, and the kinds of seminars that I had an interest in developing. Within my first six months it had become clear to me that, intrinsically, I wanted to work exclusively with women. When I told others that I wanted to coach women exclusively, I was met with surprise and resistance. One coaching buddy asked my why I would, voluntarily, cut off half the population as potential clients. To my peers, delving deeply into some niches obviously made sense; if you are a specialist you are going to be able to attract more of those kinds of clients and command higher fees. But women? Why, asked one coach, would anyone have a greater desire to work with a coach who specialized in working with women? I did not have the answer at that point. I just knew that I was moving toward something, and I had faith that it would reveal itself at the appropriate time. I believe that having the faith to follow that inner urging was a critical piece of the puzzle for me. Once I had affirmed that large numbers of women could benefit tremendously from the partnership of a coach, synchronistic things began to happen. Every book that I read, every person to whom I spoke, seemed to have a valuable insight about my new direction. There is no question that an awakening is occurring. Women everywhere are feeling the responsibility for, and the promise of, creating their own health, wealth and happiness. And who better to partner with women on this journey than a sensitive, empathic coach who has experienced many of the same challenges and who has rekindled her own authentic power?

There Has Got To Be A Better Way (Or, Choosing The Heroine's Journey).

> *Many women today feel a sadness we cannot name. Though we accomplish much of what we set out to do, we sense that something is missing in our lives and — fruitlessly — search 'out there' for the answers. What's often wrong is that we are disconnected from an authentic sense of self.* — EMILY HANCOCK

Clients come to me wanting to become better protagonists, or heroines, in their own life stories. Many feel tired and worn out from pushing and striving to succeed in the world. They come with the hope that there might be a better way. As members of what Anne Wilson Schaef calls, "the addictive system," these women have been taught: that success requires striving, struggling, suffering and sacrifice; that in order to succeed one must compete, prove his/her worth, and be vigilant in protecting the territory he/she has acquired; that happiness comes from acquiring status symbols, possessions, and from gaining positions of power; they must become slaves to the Protestant work ethic, the win-lose mentality, and the mind/body split. Whether or not they do achieve by following this "success at all costs" model, they are left feeling disconnected from themselves and others, prone to addictions, drained of energy, and suffering the effects of damage to their relationships and their self-esteem.

Women who choose to work with me are attracted to the notion that they can tap into an inner reserve of personal power in order to get what they really want out of life. I present them with an alternative model of how to attract success by directing them to: engage the flow, lead with their gifts, monitor their energy, follow inner guidance, practice cooperation, let go of the need for external approval, work to support a life and not a lifestyle, unleash the power interdevelopmental relationships, create win-win partnerships, focus on wellness and holistic health, adopt an abundance philosophy, and work towards integration of mind/body/soul. I call this model "Success from the Inside-Out."

The Practice Of Coaching Women

We cannot teach people anything; we can only help them discover it within themselves. — GALILEO GALILEI

The model that I use in work with my clients is cyclical and consists of the following five steps:

1. Shifting to an Empowering Paradigm (adopting the Heroine's Code)
2. Doing the Mental work (releasing limiting beliefs and replacing unskilled behaviors)
3. Doing the Energy work (freeing energy trapped in the past, focused in the future and other-directed)
4. Doing the Emotional Work (reclaiming the wisdom of the body and the heart)
5. Doing the Spiritual Work (tapping into inner guidance and living an illuminated perspective.)

Even with the use of a model, I have found that coaching is more of an art than a science. Although my formal training emphasized use of a series of pen and paper tests, I found that, although these work splendidly for other coaches, they did not suit my personal coaching style. I have since abandoned the use of assessment tests and rely instead on an eclectic toolkit which includes journaling, progressive affirmations, the introduction of archetypes, role-paying, guided imagery, the use of chakra clearing and metaphysical techniques, nurturing through nature, forgiveness work and exceptional self-care. I have seen wonderful results on all levels (career, financial, health, relationships, happiness) when women take the necessary steps to reclaim their personal power across the full spectrum of their lives.

Women In Community

> *Talks with women friends and in women's groups ... both are situations in which women mirror aspects of themselves to each other — we see ourselves reflected in another woman's experience, and we become conscious of some aspect of ourselves we were not aware of before, or of what we women have in common.*
>
> —JEAN SHINODA BOLEN

I love to talk about all of the above themes with women in groups. The most amazing aspect of these gatherings is the overwhelming sense of relief (and release) that most women seem to feel when they hear their own stories mirrored by the life experiences of another. One of the saddest trends in society today is the fact that women are disconnected from one another and only have rare opportunities to share their deepest truths with each another. In a recent survey, 66% of American women reported feeling lonely and finding it difficult to build relationships with other women. Where women used to meet in consciousness raising groups or across the back fence, women today feel they do not have the time to devote to friendships.

As we are relational by nature, a woman's sense of isolation is a serious matter. Women who have a large social network are healthier and live longer than those who don't. Friends are not a luxury — they are a necessity.

It is essential, for our own health and well-being as well as for the health and well-being of our society, that women begin to put the "busyness" of our lives into proper perspective. We need to begin to nurture those relationships which support and sustain us. Women need to talk to other women. We need to break down the barriers between us and to confront myths, such as, "You can have it all," and "Perfectionism and guilt are proof that you care," head on. As relational creatures we naturally view the world as a web of mutually enhancing relationships. The difference between the heroes of old and contemporary heroines is that the hero's story always ends when he has slain the dragon or rescued the fair maiden and received his reward. In stories featuring heroines, the story is never complete until the heroine returns from her adventure armed with wisdom and gifts, and proceeds to share bounty with the others.

As I began to deliver seminars and workshops for the purpose of attracting new coaching clients, it became very clear that there was magic inherent in gathering a group of women together and acting as catalyst, as facilitator, while they shared their truths. I saw that I could simply create a safe environment and set a conversation in motion and the group energy would develop a life of it's own. I became more and more intrigued with the notion of coaching women in groups around a basic theme. As a mother at home with two young children, I became a devoted fan of the teleclass system. I could put the kids down for the evening, grab my coziest robe and slipper-socks, and connect to a group of like-minded adults for stimulating discussion and a true experience of community. "Every woman needs this!" became my mantra. I was convinced that whatever was working so well for me in live seminar format could work equally well on a telebridge. The teleclass notion provided me with the opportunity to offer a class with a very narrow appeal while still attracting a fair number of participants, thanks to the lack of geographical restrictions.

Gifted Women: Embracing Our Gifts

Self-recognition is not to fuel egotism or elitism, but to align with a more powerful, creative part of you that will let your heart, your knowledge, your talent loose on the world.
                                                        — MARY ROCAMORA

The first teleclasses that I developed were designed for "Gifted Women." These classes provided me with an ideal opportunity to test whether I could draw forth the same experience of synergy in a class over the telephone as I was able to evoke in a live format. Forty women enrolled in the first two-session classes (I had to split them up into two sessions to allow for interaction) and the results were every bit as magical as I had anticipated.

From my research to become more aware of my own processes I had learned that my "giftedness" (which for me was just a term bandied about by teachers and guidance counselors), has had a far greater impact on my life experience than I had ever anticipated. While most people are aware that gifted individuals possess a high degree of intelligence, few, including gifted people themselves, are aware that there is a personality profile associated with giftedness. A cluster of personality traits (which includes: divergent thinking ability, excitability, sensitivity, multi-potentiality, perceptivity, introversion, and perfectionism) correspond with high I.Q. Amongst most gifted persons, commonalties of experience abound.

When I lead classes for gifted women and question whether participants have experienced such things as: a sense of alienation and loneliness; conflicts between needs for self-actualization and maintaining traditional relationships; feeling out of step and on a separate path; relentless curiosity and heightened creative drive; compulsion to hide abilities in order to "fit in," I am met, in every instance, with a group-wide sigh of recognition. The testimonials that I've received from participants in these classes provide further evidence of the impact and value of these sessions. "I'm not sure that I can put words to how I have felt since the call tonight. You have done a very wonderful thing by opening this door and creating this environment! I know I am not alone in feeling very, very grateful to you....It kind of filled a huge gap which was really enhanced with a connectedness in tonight's call." "Thank you so much for making this work available to me and all of us. I very much appreciated the teleconference. I hadn't realized how much this awareness of giftedness has been pervasive in my life. How it is a major drive in my pursuits and even in the activities or people I avoid. I love the "community" forming here and would want to continue." "I have been at a loss for words regarding everything that began opening up for me after last week's get-together. So much is unfolding for me!"

I continue to offer these free programs for gifted women out of the belief that they must come together, not to fuel egotism or elitism, but to gain an awareness of how our processes have impacted our lives. In doing so, each woman enables herself to challenge her perceived limitations and to encourage the women around her to shine more brightly.

Women's U

> *I've always felt that one woman's success can only help another woman's success.* —Gloria Vanderbilt

My enthusiasm about teleclasses grew and, along with it, my conviction that women could benefit immensely from having a safe, convenient space where they can learn, grow and connect. My interest in creating such a space led me to put out feelers among my coaching colleagues to get a sense of how many other coaches were inspired by the same notion and how many of my friends would want to participate in the building of just such a community. In May of 1998 Women's U. was launched on the world wide web. The site featured 40 teleclasses in categories such as: Personal Development; Career Enhancement; Business Building; Financial Prosperity; Mothers and Parenting; Spirituality and Transitions. All course are led by trained professional coaches or published authors, and a membership program has proven to have appeal. The site also features free newsletters, a women's bookstore and free "quote-cards" to send across the internet. The mission and purpose of Women's U. is as follows: "The Women's U. Community is a virtual one — it exists in the hearts and minds of the women who have found their place in an interdevelopmental web of teachers, students, collaborators and friends. We come together from all parts of the globe to embrace our similarities, to celebrate our differences and to make significant changes that will positively impact our lives."

What's Next?

I do not believe that I will ever reach a stage when I will say, 'This is what I believe. Finished.' What I believe is alive and open to growth.. — MADELEINE L'ENGLE

As I continue to grow and develop as a coach, I find that my interest is now totally taken with the idea of helping women learn and grow within a community. Women's U. provides elements of that, while my newest project, The Women's Reclamation Project, takes this vision to its ultimate fulfillment. The mission of The Women's Reclamation Project is to draw together a network of women — to weave a women's web — in the conscious awareness that, as we transform our own individual thoughts, feelings and perceptions, we will, simultaneously, transform our world.

As many futurists, historians and scholars contend — it is time for women to come forth to midwife a new era on this planet. We must be prepared to use what Margaret Mead calls our "age-long training in human relations" to pull the world out of the trouble it is in. But first we must look at our own lives and take action to make the necessary improvements in our relationships, finances, health and professional endeavors. We must "reclaim our power" so that we'll have the energy we'll need to fulfill our roles in the greater cosmic drama.

This "paradigm shift" is not an easy shift to make. The essential elements of this mindset run counter to everything we have been taught since childhood. To reclaim her power a woman needs to unlearn limiting beliefs, disentangle herself from energy that is draining her, learn to see through fear and doubt, effectively let go of the past, become adept at interpreting the messages in her emotions, listen and respond to her body wisdom, develop a new understanding of "reality" and begin to surrender to the possibilities of the present moment. When she has done these things she will find that changes in her inner world are accompanied by changes in her outer world. She will see evidence of her new connection with her power reflected in her relationships, finances, health, and her power to create her own reality. It is time for all women to reclaim their power.

Cultivating An Attitude Of Gratitude: My Most Powerful Recommendation To Help You Get What You Really, Really Want Out Of Life.

> *If the only prayer you say is a prayer of thanks that will be enough.* — MEISTER ECKHART

As Oprah Winfrey credits keeping a gratitude journal as the most powerful thing that she has ever done, I know that my clients and I are in good company. Every night, before I go to sleep, I write notes in my gratitude journal. I am continuously amazed at how much I have to be thankful for. Much of what I include are things that have always been present. Yet, in the past, when I was stressed out and I felt empty, I could not pause my inner chatter long enough to take note. I have since discovered that when you take time to reflect upon the things that are working in your life, the universe conspires to bring you more of what makes you truly happy. I am grateful for the gifts of love, peace and joy and for the creative energy that flows through me. I am grateful for the wonderful people who have been attracted into my life and for the wisdom that they share with me. I am grateful for my health and for the health of those I love. I am grateful for the lessons that I am learning from my children. I am grateful that I have learned to say "yes" to life and that I am truly open to whatever the future holds. I am supremely grateful that I have uncovered my right-livelihood and that my investment of energy in my career is now returned to me in a way that exceeds my grandest expectations. As a personal coach deeply committed to the notion that, through coaching we can heal the world, one person at a time. I can think of no more rewarding role to play than the one I have chosen.

Elyse Killoran is personally, creatively and spiritually fulfilled by the integration of her key roles: personal coach, president and "steward" of Women's U., and, most significantly, primary caretaker, guide and playmate to her two young sons. She can be reached by phone at (516) 851-1192, by e-mail at Elyse@ Womens U.com and on the web at http:/ www.womensu.com.

Recommended Reading

Aburdene, Patricia and John Naisbitt: *Megatrends for Women*. NY: Fawcett Books, 1993

Beck, Martha N.: *Breaking Point: Why Women Fall Apart And How They Can Re-Create Their Lives*. NY: Random House, 1997

Bolen, Jean Shinoda: *Goddesses in Everywoman*. NY: Harper and Row Publishers, 1993

Borysenko, Joan: *A Woman's Book of Life; Biology, Psychology, and Spirituality of the Feminine Life Cycle*. NYC: Riverhead Books, 1996

Breathnach, Sarah Ban: *Simple Abundance*. NY: Warner Books, 1995

Jaffe, Azriela: *Honey I Want to Start My Own Business*. NY: Harper Collins, 1997

Northrup, Christiane: *Womens' Bodies, Women's Wisdom*. NY: Bantam, 1998

Ryan, M..J.: *Fabric of the Future: Women Visionaries Illuminate the Path of Tomorrow*. Berkeley, CA: Conari Press, 1998

Stone, Elizabeth, in *The Quotable Woman*. Philadelphia: Running Press, 1991

Williamson, Mariann : *A Woman's Worth*. NY: Random House, 1993

COACHING THE INTENTIONAL LEARNER

Crisanne Kadamus-Blackie, M. Ed.
Janet Etzel, M.S.
William Stone, Ed.D.
William Wells, M.Ed.

When it comes to learning, we believe that every human being has a responsibility to be the architect of how they intentionally or purposely choose to keep the learning spark alive. Learning about ourselves, what the world around us has to offer, and how the two work together, should be our goal. You may be thinking that you know yourself and the world around you. Whether you are reading this chapter for yourself or to coach someone else, we challenge you to open your eyes to the possibilities that exist around you and within you.

Throughout this chapter we will give you our observations on learning and the method that has worked for each of us and for our clients. We call the method our "Four Task Model." It is a guide, offering a strategy for igniting the learning spark that exists within. The four tasks are Strength-Building, Scanner-Tuning, Synthesis and the Search for Synergy. The words may or may not be familiar to you, but we believe you have already experienced them. We hope that by reading this book, and especially this chapter, you will take a more intentional look at your life and how you learn. Each of the following sections explains one of the four tasks. We discuss each task individually, but all work together simultaneously.

At any given moment, one of them may be more pressing and in need of your focused attention, but you will move from one to the other in the blink of an eye. Imagine that you are looking into a bowl of alphabet soup. As you stir the soup with your spoon, different letters bob to the surface. You know other letters are there, they just aren't in your direct view, but with another swish of your spoon they appear. Each letter in that bowl of soup is just as important as another one in satisfying your appetite.

Client Case Studies of the Four Task Model

Strength Building

Our first client, Jenny, was focusing on the first task of Strength Building. Jenny came to us after being laid off. She had worked for the same company since she graduated from high school, 12 years ago. Unclear as to her career direction, Jenny knew that she needed to go to college in order to make herself more marketable. After working through her career goals with her coach, she was able to identify her learning needs and was ready to set her educational goals. Jenny felt that she was not a strong student in high school and admitted that she really didn't like school at all. The question that came to her coach's mind was "how can Jenny be ready to go off to college without a strong educational background?" Jenny's coach knew that she had the ability to be successful. She had proven herself successful in her previous occupation and had participated in a number of corporate training programs. But did Jenny believe she could be successful? Not at this point. So, how do we coach her to believe in herself?

Clearly, Jenny needed to build her strength before she walked onto a college campus. Through coaching, Jenny looked at her past experiences, and began to identify when and how she had been successful. One way to help Jenny was through the development of a timeline. We encouraged her to develop a timeline that represents their learning experiences. Some clients draw a straight line, others draw a circle and still others draw arches. The form does not matter, it is the content that we want to work with. Jenny chose to draw a straight line and to include such activities as learning to drive, graduation from high school and training by her former employer. Her experience also included becoming a Maine Guide, a very rigorous and difficult process. When asked about becoming a Maine Guide, Jenny passed it off as "no big deal." She explained that she always loved the outdoors, would prefer to hike and fish over being in school.

This was a breakthrough. Jenny identified a learning experience that was a personal success, and one that she enjoyed. Coaching helped her to see how the skills she used to become a Maine Guide are many of the same skills needed to be a success in a college classroom.

Her coach encouraged Jenny to explore her Maine Guide experience and to answer such questions as: what motivated you to learn this new information; what did you achieve or accomplish through this learning experience; and how was what you learned a benefit to you and others? Jenny's answers to these questions helped her to develop a framework for her learning plan and a success strategy. She found that she learns best in a hands-on program. Therefore, she will look for opportunities to participate in experiential learning programs. She also identified that she has educational gaps such as algebra, needed for a college level program.

At this point, we encouraged Jenny to explore taking courses in an adult education program. Studying with other adults, would give her the opportunity to be back in a classroom and the support she needs to be successful in the college preparation course.

We have found it helpful to ask our clients to write or talk about successful and unsuccessful learning experiences. For it is through the successful experiences that we build strength, and through unsuccessful experiences we begin to understand what needs to be in place for the experience to be successful. Both pieces of information help our clients to strengthen their understanding of themselves. Like Jenny, our clients come to believe that with the right pieces in place, they can be successful learners.

Scanner Tuning

Scott came to us unhappy in his current job of many years. He was one of the top sales staff for his company but he never enjoyed selling. In his late thirties, he felt that he was ready to make a change. At first, it was difficult to identify the learning issues that Scott will face. However, remember that learning is constantly occurring and does not need to take place in a formal education setting.

Scott had changed jobs before, and had the support of his wife and family. He had the strength necessary to move forward but he was confused, and as he had always been in sales, he was unclear as to what his options were. In Scanner Tuning, we coached Scott to determine what matters to him and he went through a process of focusing on internal and external factors.

Scott and his coach decided to begin with an internal scan. It is through this examination that our clients come to realize their values, interests and skills. Once these are examined, a new awareness evolves, allowing them to spot new opportunities. Scott discovered that his core set of values included independence, prestige, expertise and knowledge. After exploring these further with his coach, it became clear that Scott loved being the expert; he didn't like having a lot of supervision and he loved learning new things. When his coach asked why his current job did not fulfill these values, Scott explained that he disliked being required to make a set number of sales per week. He did not feel valued as part of the team, and felt that his innovative ideas were dismissed by his supervisor.

Next, Scott wanted to explore his interests. He took an inventory that identified some broad areas of interests. His coach asked him to look beyond what his currently knew. Scott was encouraged to talk to professionals outside of his field of expertise, to read publications that he hadn't been exposed to before, and to be open to every opportunity to gain new knowledge and insight.

In a week Scott met with his coach again. He reported that he had identified some new areas of interest, including real estate, financial planning and construction. He also told his coach that, while watching TV and scanning through the channels, he came across an infomercial on real estate investing. He began to listen with great interest and came up with a list of questions and additional resources that he could explore. Plus, he was able to identify, based on the type of people who were interviewed, others who had similar interests.

Scott's learning spark was ignited. Within a week he had networked with several people who referred him to real estate investors. He read two books on the subject, went to internet sites and began to find the answers to his questions. Scott was amazed at how motivated and excited he had become. He confided in his coach that he had not felt this excited in years and could not believe that an infomercial was the catalyst. His coach assured him that it was not the infomercial, but his willingness to step outside of his comfort zone to begin to explore new ideas. What Scott experienced is what we call the external scan; looking to outside resources for new information and identifying new questions that need to be answered.

Although Scott did not come to us looking for a learning experience, that was exactly what he achieved. His learning was self-directed and self-motivated. He was ready to keep moving forward and began to put a plan in place for a new career.

Synthesis

During Synthesis, we helped another client, Josh, to integrate information into a conditional learning plan. He was a high school senior getting ready to apply to college. Josh had a lot going for him. He was ranked second in his class, played two sports, and was involved in several community service programs. He wanted to get into one of the top physical therapy programs in the country. At first, this seemed to be a pretty straight forward process. However, Josh was concerned about leaving his small town in Maine and attending college in a large city. While in high school Josh was a leader, but he was afraid he would be lost once he got on a large college campus. He had seen friends go out of state, only to return the next year.

Several issues surfaced when Josh and his coach met. Recalling the first two tasks, we noted that Josh had work to do in Strength-Building and Scanner Tuning. We will focus here on Synthesis issues. Often through the planning part of Synthesis, a client's confidence and strength are built and the client is able to determine "what matters" to him or her. The tasks are concurrent, so beginning in Synthesis is appropriate. We knew that Josh would shift back and forth between all the tasks before he was finished.

Josh had gathered a tremendous amount of information about physical therapy and about the colleges that offered the program. One of his community service activities involved volunteering at a hospital where he had gotten to know some physical therapists. Josh was off to a great start. His coach spent-time helping Josh determine his level of commitment to studying physical therapy. What would happen, his coach asked, if he found out that he didn't like physical therapy? What would happen if he didn't get accepted at one of the top colleges? Was this truly his decision or did he feel pressure from parents, teachers and peers? After assessing his own commitment, Josh was sure that he wanted to study physical therapy. His coach suggested that part of his plan should include sitting in on physical therapy classes at a college and talking with the physical therapy students. This gave Josh additional information upon which to base his decision.

Josh also needed to learn more about where physical therapists worked. He had only been exposed to the physical therapists at the hospital. His coach then asked him "who can help you find this information?" and "what other resources do you need to explore?" Josh found that he could not answer these questions. He needed to spend more time in Scanner Tuning so that he could go beyond the obvious.

Josh gathered additional information on the top colleges. Based upon this information, he would be able to narrow down the number of colleges he wanted to visit. He would arrange to visit the colleges, make all the travel plans himself, sit in on a class and if possible request that he could stay overnight in one of the residence halls. He also decided, that he would ask the admissions office on each campus if there were any students from Maine attending the college. He felt that it would be important to talk to these students in order to learn about their experiences.

Josh's coach prepared him for the possibility that the new knowledge he gathered during his campus visits might not match his expectations. It was important for Josh to understand that from the new information he was gathering, new questions would arise and possibly new directions for himself.

After Josh completed his exploration, he was ready to develop a plan to take him through the application process. Josh was not only very successful with his plan, but through the process he also learned a great deal about himself.

Synergy

Carol was having difficulty communicating her ideas at work. She liked her job but felt that she had more to offer. She wanted to develop a self-directed learning plan for her department. Carol came to us because she needed help in marketing herself and her plan. Carol needed Synergy. She needed to establish the personal connections and relationships necessary to build and market her plan. The first thing Carol's coach did was to encourage Carol to think of herself as her own small business. Her learning plan became her business plan. Carol, like Josh, at times needed to revisit the other tasks in order to be successful.

Part of the difficulty Carol was facing was marketing her ideas to her vice president, who had decision-making authority. Her coach asked Carol to identify, on a scale of 1-10, where her comfort level was in terms of meeting with her vice-president. She revealed that she was at about a 3 on the scale. Her coach then asked what needed to be in place for her comfort level to be at 5? You may have heard other coaches use this approach. We have found that it is necessary for clients to begin to identify the pieces that need to be in place so they can then begin to develop a plan.

Carol said that she was afraid that her vice president would ask her a question to which she did not know the answer. This terrified her and when it had happened in the past she become flustered and lost her confidence. Her coach helped Carol identify someone within her network to ask different questions than she herself would ask. Through utilizing her networks, Carol could get help in answering unexpected questions.

Carol's coach suggested that she needed to be able to state how her plan for self-directed learning was solving a problem at work. Once she identified the problem, Carol was able to identify what aspects of the proposed solution she would be able to control and which aspects she would be willing to take responsibility for. Carol was almost ready to move forward. Her coach asked her "In order to offer a solution for your company, what change needs to occur in your behavior?" It was through this question that Carol realized that she may need to acquire some additional skills and gain a greater understanding of the company's future plans.

Carol decided that she would learn more about how adults learn best, what companies were using self-directed learning and how successful it had been. Carol was ready to begin developing her own learning plan.

Putting It All Together

Our final example client pulls together all of the tasks in the model. Heather learned that her company was developing a web site. She discovered that if she became the webmaster, all web page modifications could be done more efficiently in house. Heather had a solid computer background (Strength Building) and has researched the potential training opportunities to become the webmaster (Scanner Tuning). While researching, she discovered that a local university offers a one-year webmaster certification program (Synthesis). She developed a learning plan that would market her to her company. This plan would include why a webmaster was important, and set Heather's educational goals. It also stated why the company should pay her tuition, and a date when she would be able to take over the webmaster responsibilities. Next she would present her case to the person who approves education plans within her company (Synergy). Heather was also encouraged by her coach to develop an additional plan that focused upon the admissions process to the program. This included documenting her background and training (Strength Building), completing the application (Synthesis) and presenting her portfolio to the admissions office (Synergy).

Concluding Thoughts

Once we began working with the four-task model, we found that it is applicable to all aspects of life. We believe that learning is constantly occurring, only the situation you choose to learn in changes. Through the identification of learning issues, our clients are able to become intentional about what they learn, their career goals and how they live their lives.

Many people choose to let someone else make decisions for them, and have lost their passion for learning. We believe that everyone has a learning spark. Our goal is to encourage others to find the spark within themselves and to help them ignite it. Once ignited, their life and view of the world will be changed forever.

To learn more about the Maine Educational Services Foundation, please visit our web page: http://www.mesfoundation.com. The authors may be contacted at 1-800-922-6352, or you may e-mail us directly from our web page.

COACHING SALES PROFESSIONALS

Phyllis Sisenwine

As an outside sales rep for over 20 years, I was approached by many sales people when they were in a slump or had just lost an account. I was always able to encourage them with my positive attitude and support. Having a positive attitude in sales is critical. When I was a sales rep, if I had a challenge with an account I always went on to my next prospect, rather than be down about it. I knew it wasn't about me; it was the situation. Salespeople are their own breed. Many are entrepreneurial types. This means they don't like structure and have many ideas at once. Sometimes it's difficult for them to stay focused. When I decided to leave the outside sales arena, it became obvious that sales coaching was my calling.

Sales people need someone to be accountable to, other than their sales manager. There are many consultants and home based businesses proprietors who do not have anyone with whom to share their plans and goals. The sales coach becomes a partner. We brainstorm, set goals and design plans. The client becomes accountable to the coach and then the magic begins. The client has someone to celebrate "wins" with — someone who can keep them focused.

As a sales coach I empower my clients. They all have talents and unique abilities that they may not see. I work on identifying their strengths. Do they love or hate networking? How about giving seminars? We identify possible centers of influence. I encourage them to develop relationships with other professionals. So my

CPA clients form alliances with attorneys, and the attorneys get together with stockbrokers. Here are two of my success stories:

Beth, a graphic designer is a very talented artist. Working alone out of her home office was a challenge. Since she hired me as her coach her business is growing. I helped her to focus on being a businesswoman, not just the creative artist. Now she is concentrating on learning what the client wants. If you don't give the client what they want they won't come back. By giving her objective, honest feedback she was able to see that she was being a "temperamental artist," and not the business person she needed to be. She shifted and is now more client-driven.

Stacie also has a home based business selling promotional products. She was having all orders shipped to her home so she could personally deliver them to her customers. It was taking hours out of her day to make these deliveries. Very often the client wasn't even there when she delivered the product. I pointed out to her that she was filling a need to be appreciated, and that her time was too valuable for that. By having the merchandise drop shipped she was still able to stop by at her convenience to see the client, but without the pressure of getting the product there that day. She now has several more hours weekly to network, prospect and make more sales calls. Her business has increased dramatically.

One of the biggest challenges for salespeople is their willingness to delegate. They are used to being in total control of their business and often want to do everything. I work with them to make a list of everything they either don't like to do or that they can easily delegate. Once they recognize the value of this exercise, they start to let go of some of their time consuming tasks. Then their business increases rapidly. A sales coach is there to support them through the difficulty of letting go some of the tasks that are not critical for them to handle.

I request that my clients write on a 3x5 card "Is this the best use of my time right now?" Looking at this several times during the day helps them stay on track. The great benefit of sales coaching is to assist the client in staying focused. It's too easy to get caught up in putting out fires. The day gets away from them and they haven't accomplished anything to get them closer to their goal. As their "partner/coach," I help them stay on track by breaking down a yearly vision into 90 day goals, then monthly and weekly goals. Let me emphasize that these are the client's goals and not the coach's. I might suggest stretching a little when the client expresses their initial goal, but it is clearly to be the client's vision. The coach supports, empowers and encourages the client. I am their cheerleader.

When clients hire a sales coach they usually want to earn more money or have more time in their life. They are sometimes surprised when one of the first things I ask them is if they have clutter in their home or office. In order to be effective in business one has to get rid of clutter. It drains you of energy. Are their papers neatly filed away? The salesperson is often not a "detail person." If they admit to a messy desk and being disorganized, that is where we begin. They commit to a plan for organizing their office. I often suggest hiring a professional organizer to assist them. It is worth the time and money to have systems put in place. The second choice is to get a "buddy." It's much more fun to organize and get rid of stuff with a friend helping you. I request a time commitment from them. Perhaps, 3 hours on a Saturday or a few hours each evening. They block it out in small chunks and it becomes a feasible plan They need to put it on their calendar, otherwise it is overwhelming.. When their files are organized and their office is neat, they pick a reward to celebrate. The reward makes it more fun. It is important for the salesperson to simplify many areas of his life. Closets get cleaned, trunks are emptied and clutter is gone. It's incredible how this affects the client's life. They never realized how draining the clutter was. They are now ready to go out and become the successful salesperson that they are.

When they have gotten rid of all the unread magazines and books that they'll never read, I suggest a great book called *Power Networking* by Sandy Vilas. Networking is an important part of success in sales. People buy from people they like. It's really relationship selling. This book takes the selling out of networking. It teaches how to attract business, rather than the promotional approach to selling. If you become attractive to prospects they will want to do business with you. I work with my clients to make friends with their prospects.

Ten Powerful Solutions For Business Success

1. Have An Action Plan

A plan is like a roadmap. Unless you have a plan there is no way to get from where you are to where you want to be. I ask my clients, "What is your vision for one year from today?" It might be more money, more customers or working fewer hours. Whatever it is, it's the client's goal. The coach's role is to support that vision and hopefully get them to stretch a little. A year's vision can then be broken down to a three month goal. I ask, "What can you do in the next three months to get closer to the goal you want to reach in one year?" If the one-year goal is an additional $10,000 in commission, then in three months they want to earn $2,500. Breaking it down to one month, they need to increase commissions to approximately $850. I ask, "What can you do in the next week to get closer to that goal?" The old joke, "How do you eat an elephant? One bite at a time," is a good reminder for the salesperson to stay focused on their goal. The sales coach supports the client to keep him or her focused.

2. Be Passionate About Your Career

The client must love what they do. To be successful in sales it's important to enjoy the field you have chosen. If it's not fun, success takes too much effort. I want my clients to really care about their customers. Authenticity breeds success. It's important for a salesperson to have a great introduction. I met Mary Barnett at a networking function. I asked her what she did and she said "I'm a graphic designer" I asked her if she was willing to change her message. She agreed, and when it was time for a group introduction she said "I'm Mary Barnett and I put power in your presentations!!" It was passionate and effective. Barbara Jones has an alarm service. After coaching her she now says, "I'm Barbara Jones and you can sleep at night because we don't!" A powerful introduction makes a big difference.

3. Become Irresistibly Attractive

What it means for salespeople to be irresistibly attractive is that people want to do business with them. Someone who is caring, helpful and not always thinking of his next commission check is attractive. People do business with people they like. Rather than the high pressure salesperson who is always promoting themselves, the ideal salesperson will attract customers just by being themselves. Having integrity and being ethical makes someone very attractive.

4. Identify the Ideal Client

Sometimes salespeople are so interested in making the sale that they will do business with anyone. Very often it's because they haven't identified their ideal client. Clients that are not ideal are a real drain. When the salesperson deals with the customer who is demanding and difficult and who doesn't respect the salesperson's boundaries, tremendous stress and anxiety result. I work with my clients to identify their ideal clients; those with whom they would like to do business.

5. Network, Network, Network

Once the ideal client is identified, you have to find out where he is. That's where networking comes in to the picture. Sometimes the salesperson is reluctant to network. He or she feels uncomfortable in a room full of strangers. My suggestion is to just make friends. As mentioned before, people do business with people they like. The power networker isn't selling, but is available to support and help people in his/her network. He/she becomes a resource for his/her prospects. It's important to determine where your prospects are. Is it the Chamber of Commerce? Is it a local Rotary Club? Successful salespeople are visible. I get a commitment from my client to network frequently in places where his/her prospects meet. Networking is more than just exchanging business cards. The successful salesperson builds relationships. Giving speeches or presentations also gives the salesperson great visibility. I assist my clients with topics, support and encouragement.

6. *Consistent Daily Prospecting*

Many salespeople get too busy putting out fires to be looking for new business. Unless they keep the funnel filled with prospects, they will soon find themselves with no new appointments. My clients often commit to a plan for making phone calls. I usually suggest a minimum of three days a week between 9 A.M. to 10 A.M. Sometimes they call me on voice-mail when they complete their calls. Unless they are accountable for their plan, making prospecting calls often doesn't get done. They sometimes see no appointments in their book and wonder why. Committing to their coach that they will make their calls is often the accountability a salesperson needs.

7. *Listen, Listen, Listen*

To be successful in sales today the salesperson must listen to his/her prospect. The salesperson is busy telling the prospect how wonderful their company is and all the great things they can do for them, but they don't hear what the prospect needs. The sales coach works with his/her client to practice listening skills. The prospect is thinking "What's in it for me?" The successful salesperson fills the needs of the customer. Without listening, they won't know what that need is.

8. Underpromise, Overdeliver

Many salespeople today promise the customer anything in order to get the order. They might promise same day delivery without checking to see if the item is in stock. If the item is backordered or the service can't be provided, the credibility gap begins. I work with my clients to underpromise. Tell the customer it will take two weeks for delivery and when it gets there in 10 days the salesperson looks like a hero.

9. Become An Expert

The sales coach works with his/her clients to become an expert in their field. I ask my clients to give ten reasons why someone should do business with them. It is a great exercise for the salesperson. When I ask, "Why should people buy from you?" it becomes a very positive experience for the salesperson. He/she is able to list their strong points and the benefits of their services. This serves as a great confidence builder. This step empowers salespeople. We look for their unique ability. He/she is good at what they do, and it is the coach's role to facilitate the client's strengths.

10. Use Positive Self-Talk

Salespeople can sometimes get discouraged. They face a lot of rejection and must keep talking to themselves in a positive way. With every new client, I recommend a book *What To Say When You Talk To Your Self* by Shad Helmstetter. This is a wonderful book on positive self-talk. It's non-productive when a salesperson says to himself, "I can't write proposals, or I'm not good at making presentations." Positive self-talk makes a big difference in their lives. By changing the "I" messages they give themselves their confidence increases dramatically. Your brain is like a computer. Whatever you tell it, it will believe. The salesperson needs to say to him/herself "I am good at what I do. People want to buy from me." Positive self-talk really works.

As a sales coach, these are the steps I work on with my clients. With the support of a coach they are empowered to reach the goals that they have set. The client must really want to achieve success. Working with a coach gives the salesperson the support and motivation to stay focused on their plan. The client is held accountable and has someone to talk to who is objective, and not in their business or family. The coach is there to share the "wins" and to be a cheerleader. Accountability and support is truly the "magic" in coaching salespeople.

Phyllis Sisenwine of Powerful Solutions is a professional sales and business coach. You can e-mail her at coaching@bellatlantic.net, or phone 215-321-8114.

Recommended Reading

Helmstetter, Shad: *What to Say When You Talk to Your Self.* (NY: Pocket, 1987).
Vilas, Sandy: *Power Networking.* (Austin, TX: Bard Press, 1991).

COACHING AND THE "AH-HA" MOMENT

Dr. Jane Flagello

Intentional Change Meets The "Ah-Ha" Moment

As a coach, the thing I listen for most is my clients use of two pronouns: "they" and "I." These two words tell me volumes about how the person I'm coaching perceives his world. It tells me how the person sees himself "fitting" in, and his perception of himself. Is he a partner or parent/child? Does he describe himself as in control or being controlled? Is he a victim and helpless, or a victor, an empowered one? Is he coping with his environment as it appears or creating an environment worth living in?

What I have realized through my coaching is that too many people sell themselves short. Their fears about failure and success grab them by the short hairs — and those fears don't let go, forcing people to fill up their days doing things they really don't want to be doing. What I want for you, as a coach, is to help you begin to explore yourself, to uncover your challenges and struggles, find clarity in your clutter, connect with your personal inner power. Through this process you can learn how to re-frame your world view in such a way that it creates a more powerful you.

A quick, easy exercise I often use when speaking to groups may bring this point home for you: Hold up your hand. Your fingers represent the various roles that you play. Your pinky may be you as parent, the ring finger may represent you as spouse, the thumb you as boss/employer and so on. If you have more than five roles, just put up your other hand for the additional fingers. Make sure, however, that your palms overlap.

Your palm represents you. It is the inner you — your "SELF" that I want to speak to in this chapter. If you hurt one of your fingers, say you break your pinky while roller blading one day, the rest of your roles can continue on. The pinky gets a splint and the rest of the roles continue as if nothing really happened. But let's say you bang your palm and hurt this very center of your hand. The entire hand will hurt. You won't be able to make a strong fist. You won't be able to hold items because the palm controls the fingers.

I personally experienced this metaphor the hard way. I hurt my palm, I don't remember how, but I do remember that my hand was not able to function well. And, so it is with people. People live their lives on many different levels. Often we ignore our inner level because that is where our personal truth lives. In this metaphor, hurting your palm represents not being true to your inner self and living your life as a lie, as a convenience to what someone else wants you to do. When we do not pay attention to and enable our real "selves;" when we live our lives based on other people's expectations; when we keep so busy that we don't have time to think and dream about what we really want to do. Our roles may go on, but not as strong or as well done as they might be, and there is a longing for a life lost. It is our center, our core, our "SELF" that is suffering; and most often it suffers in silence.

I find that this is when people come to coaching. My mission as a coach is to facilitate an adult's life journey. Coaching is about helping people learn how to live consciously. I support them while they learn and apply the lessons of life to their professional and personal lives. It is about living "at choice." The coaching relationship provides the safe space, the coach provides the unconditional love and support, and the clients bring their unique life issues.

This is a combination that really can't be stopped. It is a dynamic trio. Within every walk of life, there are people ready to make use of a coach to create the lives they really want to be living. Imagine the possibilities!

The "Ah-Ha" Moment

Intentional change results from "ah-ha" experiences. None of you are strangers to "ah-ha" moments. Most people have these many times during their lives. They are shifts in perception; a change in our world view. They are that moment when you see — really see — what is happening. They breed instant understanding and instant clarity.

Let me share a classic exercise that I use to help my undergraduates experience an "ah-ha" — a shift of perception,. You may be familiar with the old lady/young woman picture — the picture where both images appear in the same drawing. Depending on your line of sight, where your eyes engage the image, you will either see the young woman or an old lady, or both.

After the class has pointed out the images, I leave the drawing on the projector while I continue to talk about perception. After a few minutes, almost without fail, a student will shout out, "I get it!" The student has just had an "ah-ha." He has finally seen the dual images for himself. A shift in his perception was made. Earlier in class, when everyone else claimed to see both images, he just went along, not really seeing both. Then, when left to his own time frame and his own mental gymnastics, he got it! The "ah-ha" escapes from his lips before he can contain himself. It is a teacher's fondest moment!

When I coach, I find that it is in the very heat of the struggle that the "ah-ha" moment most often appears for my clients. The "ah-ha" moment can be best described as the moment when the fog lifts, the image crystallizes, thought turns into *knowing*. You *know* the answer from deep in your gut. There is no doubt or fear. You know. It just is.

A client of mine had gone through many different jobs. The person moved from a teaching career into sales and then into management. Each position gave rise to the next one. It was a nice progression and looked impressive on her resume. The client was successful, continuing to achieve higher levels of monetary reward for sales and management activities. Whenever the client was restless she just took on a new project.

When you follow your passion, the Universe conspires to help
*you achieve it. ...*Anonymous

A "God event" (one of life's little attention-getters) created the "ah-ha" moment that resulted in a shift of focus to one of taking charge — personal empowerment. The question was simple; what did she really want to do during her days on earth? The answer was not her current job. She wanted to control her own time, what she did every day. She needed to create her own company. This client also recognized that she needed a lot of variety in her routines. She realized that she needed larger projects to fulfill her creative nature. Working together, a plan was created, the time frame for completion was set, and action initiated. The actions came in stages and each built on the previous action and led to the next. The more she followed her own agenda, the more successful she was. A coach helped her align her focus, gave her unconditional support and encouragement, and suggested options when she thought her way was blocked.

In this story the "ah-ha" came when the client knew she did not want to give her soul to corporate America; to unseen men in far away offices controlling her earning power and her job assignments. Her livelihood balanced on the stock market. She had been damaged by a thoughtless and careless manager and she decided in a moment — an "ah-ha" moment — that her life was too important to be put into that type of situation ever again. She wanted to work with companies, but not have them own her outcomes. Sink or swim, this client wanted to be in the driver's seat of her life and was ready to take whatever action was needed to secure this seat.

The client above is me. The initial coach was also me — the inner me — and I was ready and willing to listen to my inner voice, and take action. I also had an external coach who provided the objectivity my journey needed, and who stuck with me through-

.. the journey. I will be forever grateful to his coaching at this time of my life.

The inner shift of mind that results from an "ah-ha" moment is instantaneous. This shift is also very powerful. Your world view expands and a surge of energy is released. You may try to avoid this knowing at the action level. You fill your days with busy work, your mind with insignificant clutter, reasons why you can't do what you know you must do. Alas, this type of knowing lingers and finds a way to disturb your days and interrupt your sleep. This is the lesson the Universe wants you to learn, this is an answer that has come from deep in your soul, this is a shift of consciousness that cannot be stopped. It will not be silenced, and ignoring it is done at one's own peril.

Over time I have learned that simplicity is the way to the "ah-ha" moment. I ask my clients really simple questions. When left to our own devices, many of us make things much more difficult than they are, or have to be. We add layers of stuff to the process. Over 90% of what we worry about never happens and yet we fill our minds with baggage and worries that weigh us done. Coaching creates a unique relationship between two people, one that can cut through the garbage, uncover the facts and realities of a situation, and then create a structure for the client to follow. I wait in the wings, in the silence. There is no hurry. It is in the silence that the "ah-ha" moment bubbles up.

Sample Questions

- What outcome(s) do you really want now?
- What are you willing to do to create this outcome?
- What are you not willing to do?
- Who can act as a resource for you now?
- What has to change about how you are arriving, being and acting in this situation in order to create the opportunity for the outcome you want?
- What relationships are at issue in this situation?

- How will you have to alter your perception of another person to create what you want for them and for you?

The answers are usually as simple as the questions. As a coach, my role is to assist my clients as they move inside their own delicate journey of self-discovery. Anchored in the safe harbor of the coaching alliance, the journey is encased in unconditional love and non-judgmental listening. My goal is to coach myself out of a job by giving my clients the tools and techniques they need to be successful on their own terms.

I invite my clients to use a simple process to uncover and expose the lesson that needs to be learned. The process starts with a discussion of the symptoms of the problem, then goes deeper during the coaching sessions to find the real source of the situation. This is not a therapy encounter, but this step is critical to magnify the key elements of the problem. The point of coaching is to not have the problem show up again, to assist the individual in moving forward with his or her life. In today's quick fix world we want fast answers, instant problem solving. These do not get to the heart of the matter and often cause the problem to reappear. It is in the deepening of the discussion that the client is able to uncover the answers. When the client knows what the outcome must be, he or she comes to the solution. Coaching then continues to devise the strategy and structure to create the solution and make the knowing real. Coaching also provides the unconditional support during the client's "work in progress" actions.

When the student is ready, the teacher will appear.
— ZEN PROVERB

This is the space where I coach, a space created for and with my clients to allow them to journey, and to find the answers they need, at precisely the moment they are ready for these answers to appear. It is here, in this space, that direction can be applied to your knowing, and intentional action begins to take root.

"Ah-ha" moments are power moments — real, authentic power

moments. These *knowing* moments finally germinate the seedlings of empowerment that lie dormant in all of us. Peter Block, in his book *Stewardship*, defines empowerment as "the act of standing on our own ground, discovering our own voice, making our own choices." Empowerment is about your ability to get in touch with your inner knowing; that place deep inside your core being that is the essence of natural power, natural creativity, idea generation, energy, commitment, and peace. It enables reflection upon your actions that then generate your ability to act with purpose and intention in a way that enables you to create what you really want in your life, both professionally and personally. Defined in this manner, empowerment is perhaps the ultimate "inside" job. Fears of retribution and defensive posturing disappear. You *know* that your actions are "right actions," that you are coming from a place of strength, self-confidence, a place deeper than ego.

The one truth of all my coaching, regardless of whether a client comes for business coaching or personal coaching, is that all coaching *is* personal coaching. Coaching is about relationships; the relationships we have with others and perhaps most importantly, the relationship we have with ourselves. Our relationships exist within us; with our perceptions of the other person and situation. Change the perception and the interaction of the relationship changes too.

> *Shift of mind — from seeing ourselves as separate from the world to connected to the world, from seeing problems as caused by someone or 'something' out there, to seeing how our own actions create the problems we experience.*
> — PETER SENGE, *THE FIFTH DISCIPLINE*

The problems and situations my clients bring to the coaching session are rarely new or unique. My business clients want to talk about people who report to them or people they report to. Personal clients want to talk about their spouses, lovers, children or co-workers and friends. Regardless, it always comes down to how people treat one another in relationships, and how to change, modify, improve, and enhance them. When push comes to shove, the client is always trying to get someone else to do something else, behave some other way, improve performance or attitude, play better with others, and be nice.

And herein lies both the problem *and* its solution. The critical understanding that must be internalized goes something like, "Do not do to other people what you do not want done to you." We can find this concept at the core of most of our major religions — "right conduct to others." Other people are not broken. They do not need fixing.

To source the problem or situation is to look inside! There is something that you need to learn about you, what you are doing, how you are being, how you are appearing to others. When you learn what that is, and change what you are doing and how you are showing up, the problem will go away. As you work on finding your own truth, and experience your "ah-ha" moment through knowing this truth, the problem will diminish.

In addition to working with clients from all walks of life, I've experienced this personally many times. And each time I am confronted with a situation and my first reaction is to blame something or someone else, I stop myself and ask simply, "What am I suppose to learn from this situation?" Then I can respond, not from ego, but from knowing. This is the key question that I work to instill in my clients' repertoire, "What am I suppose to learn from this situation?"

What I have found as a base line truth is that there is a higher order connection within the Universe. We are all connected via energy bonds and when we act from truth, that energy unites and becomes a more powerful force to help us achieve our goals and create positive outcomes for all. Why then, you may ask, is there so much strife and dissension in the world? Because more people are acting from ego rather than from truth and right action. There are lessons to be learned. Often people who need to learn them are simply not paying attention!

How do my clients and I know we are "at truth?" It's easy —

the solution triggers an "ah-ha;" the deep knowing I've already spoken about above. The strategy becomes crystal clear, the structure is easily built, and once set in motion, the problem begins to diminish. It ceases to be.

All this comes from a few simple questions and a client who is *ready, able* and *willing* to do what it will take to make the needed personal changes and move back to center — to peace. When we don't reach truth, the problem or situation reappears, usually sooner than later. It may be in a different body, with a different customer, employer, spouse, friend or lover, but when these variables are stripped away, the source of the problem is unerringly familiar! The lesson has not been learned, and the client must repeat the frustrations and pain of the lesson, hoping this time to get to truth, learn and move on.

Segué To Action

The truth-filled action that follows the "ah-ha" experience must happen. These newly found truths may stay in the shadows of your soul. Their resulting actions may not always be immediate, but these actions can simply not be stopped. Alas, often when a person does try to ignore this knowing, their actions move them to the extremes — anger, revenge, hate, jealousy, betrayal — all actions that appear to strike out at others, when in reality, the greatest harm is done inside the person utilizing these ego-centered, self-defeating tools.

Coaching provides people with a safe haven from which to explore new tools and techniques in order to build stronger relationships, communicate honestly and interact effectively with those in their world. The "ah-ha" moment comes when a person realizes at a fundamental place that, although there are different types of power available to him, the only lasting and authentic power is that power a person finds within. This is authentic power, used with intention and with purpose in the service of others. This is the power that comes from the triad of head, heart and soul fully expressed not to control others, but to create a space from which everyone can achieve greatness in their own way and it is the only sustainable power that exists. Through coaching, individuals begin to open up to themselves; to exploring their own inner conversation and authentic power potential, a dialogue too long silenced by fear.

Imagine the possibilities...

You might argue at this point that nothing is as easy as it first appears to be. And you would be right. Nothing about change is easy and that is what coaching is about — change. The change is moving from an ego-centered personal world view to a "self" centered world view. The ego and all of its accompanying energies; guilt, anger, judgment, shame, force, control, fear, impatience, desire, pride, cease to be the driving force of your actions. Your energy anchors change to right action: knowing, humility, calm, innocence, acceptance, patience, grace, modesty, tolerance. All of these energies show up when you align with a higher power or Universal power that then enables your true inner power.

Here are a few key principles that you must take to heart regardless of whether you are reading this chapter because you are considering becoming a coach, want to bring coaching into your company, or because you are ready to become a client. At a surface level many of the following statements may seem to be common sense, easy to do, no-brainers, if you please. It is in this simplicity that these points gain their strength. It is in the simplicity that coaching works its real magic. From here everything becomes possible!

Life Is About Growth.

You are not here to work, you are here to grow. Each of us is here to become all that we are capable of being. The journey that is your life is an expression of your contributions, and it is through these contributions that you grow. Work is the vehicle through which you serve and make your contribution, whether that work is in the home, in the community or in a company. The underlying truth is that life is about giving. The more you give the more you get. Giving is the beginning action, always.

Whenever you wonder why people seem so disenchanted with their lot in life, why people sound so cynical, why their focus seems short-term and self-centered, look further to see whether these people are givers or takers. My guess is that they will be takers. Takers are not growing. They are ignoring a basic principle of life. The negative energy released by their "taking" lifestyle is extracting a high price, namely happiness. This cost — lack of happiness — does not discriminate. It does not care where you are a celebrity or the local plumber, rich or poor. It only knows that you, as a taker, are draining the Universe rather than enriching it. And the Universe has a sense of humor so it sends you a message.

Life Gives Lessons.

The Universe's sense of humor gets played out in lessons. Ever the ultimate teacher, the Universe gives exams. It places a lesson in your path. The sooner you learn the current lesson in your path, the sooner you move on to the next lesson. Everything happening in your life right now is happening in order for you to learn the current lesson. Although this may seem like a harsh statement if your lessons are causing you grief and struggle, it is an important one to understand.

Remember the question I asked earlier in this chapter: "What am I suppose to learn from this?" Here is its use point. What life principle are you suppose to be learning from the circumstances you are facing right now? Is it patience, humility, service, compassion? What?

If and when you fill up your every moment with busy work, odds and ends, chores, clutter, and people so that you have no time left to think about this question, the situation will continue to show up. It won't magically go away, no matter how hard you pray, or how much you drink, or smoke, or eat, or any other mind-deadening vice you care to name. No amount of crowd pleasing theater will end the lesson until you face it, ask the question, and change your behavior to be in line with the learning the Universe wants you to get.

Change Is A Personal Process.

No one can change another person, although many who know this concept continue to try. Any change is personal change. As a result of any change I make within me, my outside world changes, because my perceptions of it changes. The same goes for you.

Often you may fear changing because it will move you out of your comfort zone. You may have to face letting go of some people you thought of as friends, but were really draining your energy, keeping you down because that was where they could control you. You think you'll be lonely, alone, and won't be able to connect.

Coaching creates a safe space for people to explore new opportunities for personal change. This is one of the key distinctions between coaching and therapy. For someone to make this type of change, to move out of a comfort zone, past issues must be resolved first. Any needed therapy must have already taken place. Coaching is a step after therapy, or a process for healthy, fully functioning adults who do not need therapy, but who would benefit tremendously from having a coach to support them during a change process.

Empowerment Is An Inside Job.

It's the "E" word — empowerment. Empowerment is not about some employer allowing you to make decisions. It is not the "be all and end all" of the nineties business world. The word has taken a bad rap, been maligned and misused. Empowerment only comes when you are authentic to who you really are. The more your actions align with the you that you really want to be, the more authentic you become. This gives you a feeling of strength, confidence, power and an empowered person is born.

No one can empower another person. No one can empower you.

Other people can only create an environment where you will feel safe and secure. From this inner feeling of safety and security, the real you will begin to emerge. At first it will be like dipping your toe into the pool to see how cold the water is before you jump in. You will begin to make your own small choices about the life you want, the contribution you want to make. You will change this, and tweak that about your*SELF*. As you measure the outer world's response to your initial forays into being the real you, and find who is supportive and who is combative, you learn how to evaluate their reactions to you against how you feel about your*SELF*. You grow stronger and stronger as the authentic person inside you comes out. It is your own personal debutante ball, your real *SELF* coming out party.

These are the truths of life, and in truth there is power. It is your decision what to do with these simple truths. Perhaps you have been fighting them, struggling to get what you think you are entitled to have and what you deserve. Life is not about struggle; it is about challenge, commitment, growth and love. This is not some soppy, warm- fuzzy, touchy-feely, new age advice. It is the way of the ages, the wisdom of the sages, older then time. Perhaps it is time we all listened. Coaching shows us the way to listen and the "ah-ha" moment shows us we have been heard.

Dr. Jane R. Flagello, president and owner of Direction Dynamics, Inc. coaches business and private clients in empowerment and finding their own inner power. Jane's mission as a coach is to facilitate an adult's life journey, to enable workplaces where people are free to contribute their greatness, and to assist people in creating the high quality lives they really want to be living. She can be reached at 630-637-3318 or e-mail drjane@xnet.com

Recommended Reading

Block, Peter: *Stewardship.* (San Francisco, CA: Berrett-Koehler, 1996)

COACHING FOR NEW CENTURY LEADERS

C. Richard Pohl, Ed.D.

My Brand Of Coaching

My coaching niche is working with and partnering with a company's CEO, to do what it takes to integrate the "*people system*" with the "*technical system*" of the organization. I refer to this unique style by extending the healthy challenge, LeadYourShip©! I prefer to work with my clients both on their site and on board a sailing vessel. The actual experience of sailing can be anything from an adventurous orientation at the beginning of coaching, to a periodic, in-depth study of executive synergy throughout our working relationship.

The *technical system* consists of all activities of the company which deliver the product or services to the customer. It is "what" we do. The technical system always is "business specific" to the kinds of work performed. Unfortunately, in an older business paradigm, the technical system dehumanized life in the company. The ruthless emphasis on "getting the job done" degraded and demoralized the workforce.

The new paradigm, on the other hand, recognizes the existence of a *people system* in every organization. It is the "how" we do what we do in business. This system is universal, rather than being "business specific." People are treated as living organisms, both to participate fully as individuals, and within the boundaries of their own larger environments. This interactive people system is still being missed by many companies.

I coach the CEO through the process of replacing the old model which supports working independently, with that of mutual participation in developing the company. As it is required aboard the sailing vessel to ensure safety and comfort, company leaders learn how to make decisive decisions, which include an appropriate amount of consensus building. This involves me with the senior leadership core of an organization. Training the CEO to establish a humane executive core group of coaches comprises the majority of my practice. Coaching is the leader's natural role, but it is rare to find someone who possesses the knowledge and skills of coaching and mentoring.

Early in my career as a professional business and life coach it was hard to obtain clients at the CEO/Core Group level, and I was willing to work with down-line managers. I hoped that strengthening the people skills of middle management would bubble upward — not so. I, inadvertently, became like the "warm-up" act that gets the audience ready before the major attraction takes the stage. CEOs wanted to pay someone else to "get the troops ready." They did not want to be bothered with the details.

I realized that I was merely staying in business by opting for contracts CEOs were willing to let me have. Because the CEO and senior executives considered themselves "exempt," they could not supervise people into the deeper levels of mentoring and coaching. Phrases such as, "I want my people to be able to.......", were delivered as a mandate from a massive blind-spot. CEOs were unaware that it is the behaviors they personally practice which become the pivot or core operating philosophy of their organization. In the big picture, no CEO or senior executive can "take it from here" unless that person has "developed it so far." Because they designed it by default, CEOs were each left behind in their fantasies. They could have used a paraphrase of some sagely advice: "You cannot do unto others what you have not permitted someone to do unto you."

Each time, the middle management with whom I worked became more frustrated. Now, they could facilitate many of the challenges which had stymied them earlier. Their heightened awareness also brought home to them the absence of solid support from the executives to whom they reported directly. Their bosses, being clueless about the establishment of loyalty at the core of each reporting relationship, continued undermining their decisions and rendered them helpless. The upshot; I was regularly reminded of the phrase from the medical field, "The surgery was a success, but the patient died." I had done some excellent work. But, no matter how good it was, it was set on a collision course with failure because I was not firm with the CEOs about how all life must live creatively, "within" it's larger contexts.

Today, my work is compelled from the conviction that all possibilities for personal human betterment exist in a larger context. The popular logic in the phrase, "You can do anything you want to do, so long as it doesn't hurt anybody," assumes the impossible — that it is possible to live a disconnected life. Life, no matter what is the faulty logic to the contrary, is forever defined by its connections and relationships with something bigger than self. Anyone can declare, "I'm the captain of my ship!" so long as it is remembered that the ship is subject to the mercy of some of the most powerful forces on earth. The sailing ship permits only what a sailing ship is designed to do. Only within that context, are specific choices possible.

Being an avid sailor, I am quite aware the major contrast between a "power launch" mentality and a "sailing mentality." By no means is this illustration intended to label specific boaters. Operating a power boat requires a certain mind-set and skills. Sailing requires a different mind-set and skills.

Throttling up the power boat assumes that the forces of Nature exist to be overpowered with one's own will. The bold power boat fantasy believes that people should over-ride and power through all extraneous influences, which are like waves in your way. On the other hand, life aboard a sailing vessel denotes a very different story. The sailing mentality is one which requires all aboard to do what it is possible to do, first given the crew's present resources and skills to take responsible risks, and second, in the continuously uncertain larger environment.

Mechanistic thinking cannot dominate much longer. There is too much evidence to the contrary. Yet, "living organism thinking" is almost impossible to see with the mind's eye which is trained to see the world as a machine. How do organisms behave? How do we know how to behave? Imagining how a living organism works and relates to the big picture is a foreign concept to the mechanistic world view.

The old paradigm thinking says everything and everyone is to take care of itself. This creates a massive blind spot which blocks the differences between a machine, made by humankind, and an organism, created by God. "Being alive," according to the old paradigm, is merely a different kind of machine function, covered by plant material or flesh. The sad result is that there is no common idea of how a living organism works. In this way of thinking, knowledge of flesh-and-blood interactions simply is not acknowledged.

To generate a powerful mental picture for of the new paradigm, I employ the analogy, metaphor and experience of cruise sailing. It is important for the reader to understand that the act of sailing by itself is not the objective. Sailing a vessel with grace and elegance is an "isomorphic metaphor," or an exacting parallel for applying the principles of the new paradigm in a company. The need for a mental model which is able to simulate organizational life in the big picture grows with the passing weeks. As the sailing genre has the "ring of truth" for me, I'll offer the following case studies for this powerful sailing metaphor — a simulation of a real-life, real-world experience, under the big sky, in surround-sound.

Disconnected Dad

One of my early coaching clients inherited the family business, a franchise of a national product. He enrolled his immediate family in my sailing outing designed to deepen the relationship between parents and teenagers. Dad was an "out of the box" thinker. He had read all the books, and firmly declared his passion for "new science" and "living systems." For eight weeks, his family and I spent one evening a week together aboard my sail boat. The first evening began with a short ritual I hold with every group, each time we sail. It is about "leaving your ego on the dock," which I borrowed from practicing the martial art, Aikido. The Aikido player removes socks and shoes prior to bowing and walking onto the practice mat, with the intention of "leaving the ego off the mat." The ego, or immaturity, can stand in the way of learning life's most important lessons.

Prior to the group's arrival, I wash down the boat and swab the decks. As each member of the group prepares to board the boat, the drill is to "wipe off your shoes" on the wet mop to leave the grime and his/her ego on the dock. This symbolically invokes the "impossible to screw up" rule for the evening. There is no right or wrong — only opportunities for learning. We take the mop with us, should there be a later need. Dad always joined the ceremony and occasionally, under sail, would produce the mop for every one to refresh their shoes. A light dinner aboard was enjoyed on the way to the chosen sailing area. The sails are hoisted and we set sail into the theme for the evening's outing, followed by individual and group reflection on the sail simulation experience.

During the fifth session, each of the four family members was to take a turn at the helm while blindfolded. Each family member now understood the basics of sailing and they were working pretty well together. This was the evening for exploring how the family might give encouraging support to whomever was "at the helm," steering the course of the boat. Each person would spend 15 minutes sailing the boat blindfolded, after which we would heave-to (stop the boat with the sails up) and reflect on what happened and how to increase support for each other. Being at the helm produces the same full weight of responsibility felt when believing something is "up to me." Since I emphasize both physical and psychological safety, each participant knows that I am always there beside the helmsman to give suggestions, guidance and occasionally to step in and get us out of a tight spot.

Now, it was Dad's turn. He was the last at the helm. Off we sailed in the middle of the lake. Dad had offered mild, joking support to the others ahead of him. Behind the blindfold, Dad was lost. No matter what Mom or each of the kids suggested, Dad would over-steer, first one way, then another. They tried joking, which didn't work either. I looked behind us to see that we were leaving a wake like you would imagine if the skipper was intoxicated or "three sheets into the wind." Dad's hands on the wheel never stopped moving. He could not listen and respond to what he heard. He could not let the members of his family support him. He could not translate what was happening to the boat or to himself. Something inside him appeared terrified of being out of control. He could not trust his family or the process. Within ten minutes, he ripped off his blindfold with frustration ranting, "I don't know why I'm even paying for this damn outing. I really needed your help and all I got was joking around. I can't count on any of you and, as far as I'm concerned, we don't need to come back for any more of this!"

The "storm" blew over and we finished all eight sessions. Both kids often spoke about the importance of this time together. Dad turned out to be the hero who provided a great family event. My professional coaching services were soon requested for the executives and managers of his company. Organizational themes were "simulated" aboard the sailing vessel. Each session was filled with "just like" references between what was occurring among the sailing crew and how things worked back at the office. They "got it."

Dad asked me to help him locate a sailing vessel to purchase, began sailing on his own, and even featured me as a guest speaker for a business owner retreat to demonstrate these sailing similarities. Sadly, he would not accompany any of his own executive groups and graciously refused to participate at the helm with his friends aboard. This "outside the box" thinker who read the right books and attended the latest, expensive seminars, froze when faced with the challenge, LeadYourShip©.

It would be easy to point to the ego for getting in this man's way. We could say that, although he embarrassed himself in front of his family, he could not afford for his own executives and friends to see him that way. I, however, discovered something different which I have continued to witness to this day. Prior to participating in a sailing program with me, my CEO friend had no clear mental picture to help him function in a situation where he had no control. His modus operandi was to get upset and everybody will take notice. Unfortunately, he only knew how to be at the center of things. Now, sitting at the helm, he attempted to be successful in a different world, a world which requires the full participation of the crew. He was able to think the thoughts of New Quantum Science, but when it came time to lead into uncertainty, he did not have what it takes.

I might have coached the junior executives for this CEO for years, enjoying my consulting fees, but, ethically, I felt it wrong to be a paid stand-in for abdication. Human bonding and teamwork in the real world is a by-product of successful, one-on-one interactions. In natural human interaction, no one can hire something done which is designed by creation to be a personal responsibility.

Many non-sailing executives truly are "out of their element," as they attempt to "get the feel" of the sailing yacht. They are intelligent, able to make instantaneous decisions and exude confidence, until they "take the helm." I've lost track of the times I have witnessed a leader behave similarly to the blindfolded, disconnected dad. It was as if accessing their full range of intelligence, as opposed to merely thinking, came up as a blank screen. In the first few minutes at the helm, under sail, they found their reserve of linear logic, which usually appeared to keep them on top of most things, was depleted. Searching for a visceral intelligence to respond accurately to their surroundings was a frustrating exercise in futility.

I have sought every way possible to omit the few paragraphs ahead, but find that deleting them also evaporates the focal point of need. In the new paradigm, it is precisely at this point of frustration, that we hear the muffled screams for help.

It is said that the best learning happens when one is "out of their comfort zone." That being true aboard the sailing yacht, I believe I must have witnessed many geniuses in the making. Properly coached to work within their full set of surroundings, each leader becomes fascinated with a world of perpetual individual and group challenge. Hours seem to fly by, with the wind. Analogies begin to flow. Members of the executive core group remark, "That's just like........back home!" I have never seen "the lights come on" like this in conferences, seminars or classrooms.

I do go to a lot of trouble to transform the sailing vessel to an "organization simulator" on the water. Lagniappe (lan'yop), meaning to give something extra, is a core value with me. In fact, Lagniappe is the name of my boat. More than just my style, I am convinced that it is going to this kind of trouble which is required to facilitate individuals through the unfolding, complex paradigm shift.

dysNexia©

The new science of living systems reveals that the general misery that business leaders, and people in general, experience as increasing stress is directly rooted in the flawed, inhumane, mechanistic ways of thinking. Boiling everything down to its lowest common denominator also boils people down to a one-dimensional life, instead of one which is fully engaged with its larger surroundings. The old paradigm turns people into doing-one-thing-at-a-time junkies. As a result, there is a focus on a single theme, the pursuit of mere individual happiness, and intentionally disconnecting from what keeps life alive on the planet — deep relationships.

What mature living beings seek to know is the larger scheme of things, and how to fit into it. The old paradigm, however, has eliminated the importance of the larger scheme of things; it falsely teaches those who follow it that the epitome of the grand scheme is the individual. No doubt, this feels marvelous, but the hidden result is that everyone becomes a victim of a culturi-wide learning disability in the process. I call it a learning disability because only an active community can empower individual freedom. Yet, most people are unable to figure out where and how they "fit" into the larger scheme of things. As a bit of an aside, the question can be asked, "Is the enormous amount of rage which plagues modern life stem from the masses which have "no-place" to fit into society, except for whatever job efforts are possible for making money?" The experience of feeling cast adrift in an uncertain sea to "sink or swim" is a lonely, maddening prospect.

Since this pervasive learning disability was unknown, it had no name. Ten years ago, I coined the term, dysNexia©, from the word, nexus, which means a centered, integrated wholeness. dysNexia© is the dysfunction of disconnecting from self, others, organizations and the world-at-large. With only an occasional exception aboard the sailing vessel, new sailors obsess on finding the right clues to help them sail the boat. Remember the executives' first time at the helm mentioned earlier? A dysNexic© behaves exactly as he or she has been indoctrinated by the old paradigm. The disconnected skipper, believing "Everything's up to me and how well I do," either steers the course of a dizzy drunk, or like an athlete on steroids defyies the wind to heel over the boat beyond his strength to control. Neither work. The sails keep flogging and the boat starts and stops, or the sails catch a puff of wind which quickly tilts the craft, as if it might turn over. This all happens because each fledgling skipper, understandably, was attempting to sail the boat as a single action without considering the wind, weather or currents. One can almost hear the monotone reaction of a robot: "This-does-not-compute."

An illustration: the dysNexic© attends classroom instruction on basic sailing and hears that a sailboat cannot sail directly into the wind. The bow of the boat needs to point away from the head wind, at least at a 45 degree angle for the sails to fill with enough wind to power the boat forward. "I can do that," thinks the dysNexic©. "If I just keep her at 45 degrees, I'll have this licked in no time." Many sailboats have wind direction indicators on top of the mast which always point into the wind. So, our intrepid skipper reasons that you steer the boat by keeping your eyes on the top of the mast, visually gauging by the wind direction indicator whether the boat is pointing away from the wind at 45 degrees. The top of the mast is usually a minimum of 20 feet above the water. The "wheels are turning" in his "thinker." He's trying to get this one right thing "right." He's oblivious to everything else because he can't hold the sailboat still long enough get it pointed exactly to 45 degrees off the wind. Sound familiar to any other situation you've experienced?

Continuing this illustration, there are the pieces of yarn on the sails to indicate the wind flow across the sails. Also, there is a distant destination on the shore ahead. Now, add watching the direction of the waves and visually locating dark spots on the water, alerting the crew to approaching wind gusts. There are too many individual, right things to do.

By now, the reader gets the point. Because the skipper believes that sailing, like everything else, should be boiled down to one thing (old paradigm logic), the skipper and crew are miserable. Though included in the classroom instruction, the sailor did not remember to feel the wind on his or her own face and head, to feel the tipping of the boat or lack of it, to understand what the boat is telling you, or to hold a straight course and ask other members of the crew to tighten and loosen the sails to manage the tilting (heeling) of the boat.

My heart goes out to all at the ship's helm who can NOT stop locking on to single cause/effect answers. They do not know that they do not know; that the only course is to become increasingly aware of the multitude of things in their surroundings, and go with it. These folks are getting a strong taste of the new paradigm which urges people to respond from their intuitive hunches, based on an increased sensitivity and an awareness of how things work in their larger surroundings.

Understandably, the 20th Century is right to boast of great technology, but few in our culture understand how individuals thrive and interact within a larger, integrated whole. Therefore, I believe it is reasonable to declare that dysNexic© is the inbred learning disability of our own making. We are disconnected to one degree or another from ourselves, others, and our surroundings.

For twenty years, attempts to transition from the old to the new paradigm have been that of presenting enough new, but logical, evidence to convincingly over-ride the old ways. This doesn't work. Why? The current language system belongs to the dominant, old paradigm. Linear, descriptive language always requires breaking questions down to either/or alternatives.

The old paradigm, in fact, has a built-in insulation from the new paradigm. Already, I know that your mind may be drifting into other thoughts. Something inside is saying, "come on, get to the point!" I'm sad to report that this internal urge, demanding that we "get to the point" is one of the core symptoms of dysNexia©. "Get to the point before I get bored!" is an unintentional tactic, linked directly to the core of dysNexia©. I hope it makes sense to the reader that "getting to the point" is about boiling off the larger context, stripping away the supporting elements, attempting to make something stand alone when it's impossible.

I have found that the sailing ship is easily transformed into a "paradigm transition vehicle" to teach the art of living. Everybody knows that sailing vessels are traffic stoppers. Why is that? Those in coastal areas hear "traffic alerts" because there's an automobile accident caused by someone gawking at a sailing vessel. It is as if those sails, filled with invisible wind, beckon us to some mysterious homecoming, long over due. I am convinced that is true, but it's more than being drawn to the sea. It's about reconnecting with a distant memory of creation's universal design.

"Sail-simulating" generates a superlative practice field for re-connecting in-house leaders with each other, their organizations and a larger climate that has a mind of its own. Sailing together is the perfect living metaphor for accurately experiencing the connections which exist in every organization. The sailing vessel is a dynamic laboratory for co-researching how to personally integrate wholeness into an organization through functioning together in the vital contexts of survival. Setting sail together supplies the proper instrument for probing solid ways to connect and communicate. Facilitated correctly, cruise sailing captures (for those who will keep the ego out of the way) a clear mental picture to reference regularly as an authoritative connection with the real world.

Modern humankind does not have collective access to a mental picture to help them connect with the real world. We are a dysNexic©, disconnected culture. Businesses in the future will be successful to the degree that leaders understand and facilitate the integration of flesh-and-blood within their larger containing environments. This will be the model for good business.

Accurate Mental Pictures

How do people make sense of things? By seeing internal mental pictures. Most people do not see words or sentences on a chalkboard in their mind's when they explore an idea. They see the best mental picture they have available in their mind's eye. As I mentioned, these mental pictures are derived from earlier experiences or their imagination. When in a new situation, people naturally do what Neuro Linguistics Programming (NLP) deems a mental "trans-derivational search." "What mental pictures do I have in my mind which are derived from similar experiences?" A picture or "just like reference" appears in the minds eye as "the answer" and the person takes action based on that mental picture. Actions afterward are based on the mental picture.

Unfortunately, since most of modern humankind has lost touch with the natural spark which ignites the integration of body, mind and spirit. Westerners are ingenious when it comes to mentally taking things apart and separating them from each other. I have found that, usually their mind is devoid of mental pictures which integrate. This is because of the "let's divide it up" mentality which makes Westerners dysNexic©. Instead of seeing "patterns that connect," they tend to look only for things which make life easier for them to bear. They often consider themselves as "me against the world." Alone. There is no better analogy for the lived experience of the CEO of any organization. This personal loneliness, I have found, is directly related to the absence of a dynamic mental picture which integrates the processes of the organization. The CEO feels "set apart" from the rest and, as well, views each department as being separate from the rest. They believe, some how, if there would be a way to add up everyone's effort, effectiveness and excellence, they would have something to lead. But, there is no mental picture available to them.

I'm convinced that the crucial mental picture awaits aboard the ocean-going sailing vessel. Why on a sailboat? Why can't you just use your mind and imagine what it's like? Our present culture does not honor personal experiences of the kind which are crucial to forming such mental pictures. Therefore, if leaders are to "get the picture," it is up to us to supply them with personal, contextual experiences which develop their ability to see with a new mind's-eye.

We must realize that one of the hallmarks of dysNexia© is the obsession with thinking apart from the simultaneous awareness of sensing and feeling. Only recently has it been realized that the famous watch-word of Rene Descartes, "I think, therefore I am," is far from being the lofty wisdom for which it was touted. Actually, the singular focus on analytical thinking may have "dumbed down" the over-all intelligence of people. Analytic thinking supplies no internal mental pictures to reference, as someone attempts to navigate uncharted regions. Remember the wilderness of taking exams? Memorizing answers runs counter to the way people make sense of things.

Daily, we're in scores of conversations. We all look up with our eyes when searching for those mental pictures. All the time, I see people look back at me with their eyes glazed over. They don't "get it." They cannot locate a mental picture, based upon directly parallel experiences. Because of being indoctrinated to always "break everything down," they are lost. They assume, by analyzing their situation (taking it apart) that the answer will magically appear.

They are attempting to "think it through." This cannot work because they must now operate from impressions or hunches related to real life experience of being a fully functioning individual, while simultaneously, participating as a full member of something much larger than self-service.

When people sail with me, I am honored to witness the opening of the eyes of their soul. They are discovering those vital, missing connections through personal experience, rather than merely attempting to get their analytical minds around a concept. They embrace the full experience what it's like to function in the four simultaneous worlds outlined earlier. The obsession with knowing the right answers ahead of time is discarded in favor of learning to reach conclusions together through practice.

Almost everyone who sets sail with me has never been on a sailboat. But, within an hour, I can have the members of each crew doing a pretty good job of basic sailing. Then, I invite them to do whatever they believe it takes to make things work better together, to keep the boat on a compass course. Everyone is excited with this new sailing toy and goes to work to "make it happen."

As mentioned earlier, I watch the person steering at the helm attempting to respond to every shift of wind and wave. Now, the main sail handler, with eyes to the sky, is seriously attending to task of getting the canvas trimmed just right. Attention is equally directed to handling the front sail, called the jib. Though everybody is achieving an excellent individual performance, the boat doesn't stay on course or doesn't go anywhere. The helms person complains that sails need to be readjusted. The sail handlers readadjust the sails. Then, the sails are trimmed either too tight or want to blow, accidentally, over to the other side of the boat. They work harder. Most of the time, it just gets worse.

What the sail handlers were too busy to notice is that each time they made an adjustment, the helms person made another steering adjustment, which canceled out what they were trying to accomplish. Everyone was so bent on getting it right, or "thinking it through" by themselves, that it doesn't occur to them to talk to each other, to reflect on what worked and what didn't. This becomes an opportunity for a living lesson. Now, I have the opportunity to assist the crew in making the necessary changes in their behaviors to find the sailing "groove."

I don't do seminars for groups of individual CEOs. No matter how well I could present or simulate the information, the insights would not be integrated. Integration is impossible without the entire crew aboard. Without the actual crew, the experience cannot move beyond the game of "Thinker Toys." My work, during a serious sailing retreat, is usually with fewer than ten people. My focus is with the CEO's inner, executive core. Without exception, I have learned that the behaviors among a group of people who work together are similar wherever they are together on the planet. Most likely, the individual behaviors of trying to "get it right" and "think it through" by one's self are the same both aboard the sailing yacht and in the executive office. Each crew's performance is directly parallel with the way they do it back home.

Observing the actual relationships in an executive group invites a coaching opportunity in real time. These executives, guided through a positive change of behavior while sailing, mentally film a video tape to take home with them. This adventure allows them to take home an experience of how each member is (1) a competent person, (2) integrates his or her self with the crew, and (3) works within an organization limited by a specific design, (4) while attempting to read the signs and signals of a climate which is unforgiving. The mental picture they take home is of their group functioning together, and functioning well.

Simulated Sailing Drills

Under sail, we perform repetitive drills which simulate office situations. Each drill is followed by reflection on further refinement and application in the business setting. All simulations are designed to encourage each executive to intentionally integrate self, crew, organization design and climate. One simulation initiative brings home

how every member of the executive team is influencing the organization (boat) and the rest of the crew. Since there are three main "work
stations" aboard a modern sailing vessel, we sail-simulate in teams of
three. One team takes over and the other teams observe. Before the
next team takes over, the first team orients them to their duties, and so
on. Each team learns that any one member's actions can completely
alter the progress of the boat. The helmsperson finds out how the
need to make the boat point in his or her own desired direction makes
the crew work harder. Every slight movement of the steering wheel
causes the boat to turn ever so slightly. If the skipper keeps heading
the boat more into the wind, before long the sails are flopping because the boat must be pointed at least 45 degrees away from the
wind to sail at all.

Sometimes the skipper may keep turning the bow of the boat
slightly away from the wind. Now, because the sail handlers are
attempting to keep the sails tight, the boat merely drifts down
wind. Sailing down wind requires easing the sails out so the wind
can begin to push the boat ahead of it. When the weather conditions are mild enough, I usually permit the crew to experience an
"accidental jibe." In heavy wind, this is a "no-no." When there is
no potential for harming members of the crew or the boat, the
experience creates a surprise effect. Imagine a yacht sailing down
wind or with the wind. When the wind is pushing the boat, the
main sail has been let out as far as possible to one side to catch all
the wind possible. As the skipper continues pointing the bow of
the boat away from the wind, as before, there will soon be a moment
when the wind mysteriously jumps to the other side of the sails.

Everyone becomes bug-eyed and all mouths fly wide open, as
the big main sail directly above them takes on a life of its own.
Now the wind has caught the other side of the sail and tries to
slam it all the way over to the other far side of the boat. It is the
dreaded "accidental jibe." Talk about believing how great things
are going with the "wind in your sails" and the next instant, you're
going nowhere! Remember, this initiative is done in fairly light
winds and there is no danger of turning the boat over or anyone

being hurt. There's more. The wind, now blowing on the opposite side of the sail, immediately leans (heels) the boat over to the other way. Adding to the surprise of the crew, the front sail on the boat does not fly over to the other side like the main sail did. It's being held, back-winded, by the rope which was controlling it on the other side of the boat. One second, everything was "all down wind." The next thing you hear is some form of, "What the....."

Experienced sailors will recognize what I have just described can also be a form of "heaving to," while sailing down-wind. In light air, good sailors intentionally rely on this very maneuver, to bring their boat to a stop for lunch or rest, without lowering the sails. This is an almost magic maneuver which permits the boat to take care of itself, so long as the water is deep enough. CEOs need to know at what level their own company can "take care of itself."

Preparing For A Pradigm Shift

From the time participants step aboard until the retreat ends, the executive group must live in the dynamic mix of self, peers, limited organization design and uncontrollable climate. Why make so much of sail-simulation? First, no one alive has been through a paradigm shift. At its core is a change in our view of the world. *A paradigm is the collective understanding of how the world works.* All of us have been intentionally reared to believe that we have the ability to stand apart from creation, just as a mechanic stands apart from a machine. I am convinced that the chains of dysNexia© can be counted on to hold this old paradigm in place with a death grip. It is my experience, that it takes nothing less than personally engaging the powers of the planet to penetrate the enormous blind spot, i.e., "You can't argue with Mother Nature."

I've spent years attempting to communicate the meaning of living systems to audiences and acquaintances. I believe the answer lies in letting Mother Nature "do the talking." Let it be her wise council which directs our individual lives, our relationships with our peers, and our organizations.

The reader should understand that a sailing retreat is not expected to be magic or a panacea. Retreats are designed and delivered as an "awareness opening" activity for executive core groups who wish to embrace the new paradigm from personal experience, rather than from a virtual imagination. Frequently, an executive group prefers to work with me or another coach for a period of time prior to going sailing together. So, rather than an orientation in this case, sail-simulating is truly an integrating practice retreat.

Psychological Safety: Man-Overboard Drill

How many people do you know who feel secure in their jobs? How many of those people will tell you that they feel certain that the company which employs them keeps their best interests at heart in all business decisions? The truth is that those who own or run businesses still fail to represent both people, and profit to their stockholders, with the same level of commitment. Because the old paradigm insisted on emphasizing interchangeable parts, people are treated as expendable resources. Psychological safety is a glaring embarrassment. Yet, as it is dramatically taught aboard the sailing yacht, it is the direct responsibility of the organization to make everyone aware of how to keep themselves, and others, safe from extinction, both physically and psychologically.

Before the yacht leaves the dock on each day of an executive retreat, we cover a man-overboard drill. One or two members of the crew volunteer to be a "spotter." In the event that anyone falls overboard, everyone is encouraged to yell, "Man overboard!" Another crew is to throw an identified seat cushion in the direction of the swimmer, who already is wearing a life-jacket. The spotter is instructed to point directly at the person in the water not to divert his eyes away, even for a second. As the boat turns and maneuvers, this job requires the spotter to move about the boat pointing, until there is direct contact with our fallen comrade. Should this actually occur, either I, or a professional skipper hired for 50' boats or larger, have taken the helm to quickly get the boat back to the crew member who's in the water. Other crew members are to keep tossing seat cushions in the water to leave a "debris trail" back to the victim. One of several methods of quickly getting the boat back to the accident scene brings the yacht slowly along side and up-wind of the swimmer. The fallen member is taken aboard.

I've never needed to conduct an actual man-overboard procedure. Yet, I practice the sailing drill at least once a month. Good skippers always take the time to accomplish the spoken drill with the crew because no one is dispensable. Executives come face-to-face with an elaborate contingency plan, which, most likely will not be needed. The lesson is clear. If we give this much attention to something which, for all intents and purposes, will not occur, what does that say about the psychological safety that must be considered in the day-to-day operation of each member of the crew?

Throughout the day, I urge the executives to reflect on my behavior — "what" I did as the boat skipper and "how" I did it. Rarely am I at the helm of the sailing vessel once we're outside the boat harbor. I know "the feel" of what's happening everywhere on board. I affirm each person on duty at the three work stations (helm, main & jib sails). I urge crew members to become more aware of their cohorts needs to get away from having each merely do their own thing. Each new initiative is carefully introduced, with as much explanation as possible before actually simulating the endeavor.

At the end of the day, when returning to the dock, each member is included as a part of the successful docking procedure. By the third day of a sailing retreat, very few of the earlier assignments are necessary, because the sailors have already taken the initiative. Through the numerous reflection periods, executives both watch and participate in identifying learning parallels between the sailing experience and operating their organization. Psychological safety now is more than a promise. It can become something to model.

Building Individual Trustworthiness

There are so many things in modern society that are backwards to reality. Trust, as it is misperceived today, is expected to exist at the onset of a working and/or love relationship. When something goes wrong, as it will because people are human, the victim blames, "I thought I could trust you!" That's backwards. Real trust is a by-product, rather than a given one "should" be able to count on.

Trust develops as both sides of a relationship behave trustworthily — they consistently come through for each other. Coming through for the other person is about proving your words with your behavior. It doesn't matter how sincere your words are, if they not backed up with identical behavior. No amount of urging, "Trust me," works. No amount of the excuse, "I'm working on it," is acceptable. It's simple — mutual trustworthiness creates trust. A little formula helps me jog my memory: t + t = T. Trustworthiness (t) plus trustworthiness (t) equals Trust (T). To paraphrase a TV commercial: "You build trust the old fashioned way — you earn it."

A couple of years ago, I was working with a group of executive nurses aboard my boat, *Lagniappe*. Present were the owners of the home health agency, their accountant, the director of marketing and a nurse manager. The nurse manager, Pat, had never been aboard a sailing vessel. Pat announced that the only reason she was present was that she didn't want to let her team down. Once aboard, she would only sit down after her life jacket was snugly around her. She knew that smaller sail boats turn over and she could not swim. It did not matter that she was now aboard a small ocean-going yacht. Pat was deathly quiet behind her sunglasses. She slowly moved her head through a long, sweeping scan of the cockpit, locating and memorizing every hand-hold possible. I reassured her that I would take every opportunity to work on dissolving her trepidation. After the crew-overboard briefing, we got under way, motoring through the harbor and beyond the breakwater. Each person on board took turns steering the vessel and doing slow, 360 degree turns under power. Next, the sails were up and engine was silent.

Outside the breakwater, I gradually turn the boat over to the guests. As I take the boat through each basic sailing maneuver, I pass off part of the responsibility to willing members of the crew. Within the first hour, I have non-sailors completely operating the boat. It is my practice to alert everyone about what to expect as we move from one maneuver to another. As each initiative unfolds into experience, I again talk everyone through the situation. I give them as much time as I can to get ready for the upcoming change. The owner of the home care agency continuously affirmed everyone's efforts and was genuinely happy for each thing they accomplished together. Most of that evening, we practiced tacking through the wind, followed by holding the boat on a steady course. We were sailing "in the groove." I guided everyone to relax more into their seats when they were sitting on the down-side as we skimmed over the water.

Pat was the last person to handle the line which controls the main sail. The way the rigging is set up on *Lagniappe*, the main sail handler can stand in the middle of the boat where the heeling is the least noticeable. She was still quiet, but I could tell that she was doing as well as anyone else. Tacking back and forth, we were making good headway. All of a sudden, right in the middle of an excellent tack, Pat spoke up: "Girls, I've got this figured out! You've got to pop those sails when we go through. It keeps your speed up — Did you see that? We did it! Let's make that baby happen again!" Pat worked the sails and drove again that evening. She was among the ones on deck to hand off a dock line when we returned. When she was leaving for the evening, I had to remind her to take off her life jacket and leave it with me. She had forgotten she was wearing it.

During one of our later reflection periods, I asked Pat to explain what had happened. Her answer was spoken without thinking: "I saw that everything happened the way you said it would. I didn't know if I'd like it some times, but I knew what to expect every time. I remembered that you promised to step in if anything got dangerous. The rest of the group was really getting into what we were accomplishing together. She was animated. I told myself, "Girl, this is ridiculous. You could be having a great time. He's telling us everything that's going to happen. We're able to get ready for everything. Everybody else is having fun. So, let's get with it!"

Before the evening was over, Pat was telling us how she planned to be a part of developing mutual trustworthiness with her field staff, between the executive group on board, and with her kids at home. She was very aware of the boat (organization) making it's way through an uncontrollable climate. She realized that she was influencing everyone on board the boat, whether it was done intentionally or passively. She was aware of herself and found a way to move through a challenge, instead of disconnect from it. Pat proved herself and came through. Pat could trust because she could see that she was a part of a trustworthy situation. Experiencing trustworthiness, she felt free to become trustworthy.

Prepare To Tack!

"Prepare to tack. Ready about? Helm's alee." These commands, heard aboard the sailing ship prior to a definite course change, serve to focus and integrate the energy of all crew members. "Prepare to tack" announces that navigation conditions are such that the organization, with everyone aboard, are about to undergo a disruption together. Unless there is immanent danger, the "prepare" command is spoken early enough to permit every crew member a short time to get up-to-speed, alert and ready to embrace the pending chaos with confidence. Confidence is a quality—when things are as prepared as possible to do what is necessary, so the unexpected will receive appropriate attention.

When as much time as possible has elapsed, the skipper calls out, "Ready about?", anticipating a resounding chorus, "Ready!" Talk about buy-in. No matter how many times this exercise occurs during a sailing event, this exuberant rally is the collective announcement that your elegant vessel is about to dance. Poised on the peak of an opportunity, all hands await only the last command, "Helm's alee!"

I'm a salty enough sailor that I like to sound off with, "Hard alee!" It means the same thing — on boats steered with a tiller, it is pushed (alee) all the way down wind. The boat heads up into and through the wind to reposition the sails and boat on a 90 degree turn. Both on board and from a distance, when it all works, there is no better description of magnificence. You cannot take your eyes off of what is happening. When such a tack is complete, you are still riveted in amazement.

Something nearly miraculous happened in the midst of it all. The best of technology was harnessed in a deep moment of relationship between souls who are counting on each other. It's hard to make a sailboat "come about" and do what sailboats are designed to do. Every year, thousands attracted to the beauty of sail purchase boats that will be back on the market when the sailing season is over. Many more will sit on trailers and in boat yards because "something is wrong" with them. I have lost count of the times someone has said to me, "I don't want to work this hard." Once again, the voice of the old paradigm. Not, "Coach us so we can learn to do what it takes to make this happen again!" Only, "It would be nice to do that, but I don't want to work that hard for it." Come to think about it, I've also heard my share of CEOs say the same thing about intentionally blending the *people system* with the *technical system* of their company.

Here we are at the dawn of a millennium that no one before us has ever experienced. It promises to be a time like no other to look forward to. Perhaps it's important for us to ask, "Did everyone hear—Prepare to Tack!" This call to alert came to us almost 100 years ago through Einstein and others. Paraphrasing, "We've discovered that everything is far more complex than anyone had ever imagined! What we've been led to believe for hundreds of years is barely the beginning, instead of the grand climax. Like adolescents, we've behaved like we've arrived, but in reality, we've only arrived to be on our own for the first time." The space between "Prepare to tack" and "Ready about?" is reaching it's crescendo. The paradigm is about to shift for all of us, whether we are ready or not. Many times, when I've asked "Ready about?" I've heard someone say, "Wait! Wait!" Most of those times I could give them a little longer. I'm well aware of others when all I could do is yell out, "Hang on! Here we go!" Another few feet and we'd been on the rocks having a really bad day.

What a delightful point in history for professional coaches. People are compelled to expand their response-ability even when it means to simplify. But, these are not simple times. Times are complex, chaotic, and threaten to end up sailing us on our ear—if we continue insisting upon straining backward into the old paradigm. It is the coach's voice which can loosen the anxiety which translates itself into suffocating controlling and further disconnection. Coaches can be there to encourage their clients to lean into the chaos, with a new knowledge that the possibility of order and creativity exists only on the other side.

Ports Of Call

LeadYourShip© retreats for core executive teams can be conducted anywhere on the globe where sailing yachts are chartered. Currently, 2 to 3 day retreats are conducted in settings on each coast of the U.S. LeadYourShip© retreats achieve the best results when integrated into a coaching relationship. LeadYourShip© supplies the integrative practice during the sailing retreat and is ready to link the company with a professional coach to ensure the learning transfer.

C. Richard Pohl may be reached by phone at (405) 722-4129; fax, (405) 722-3895, or E-mail: dick@LeadYourShip.com. Visit the LeadYourShip© web site, http://www.LeadYourShip.com

CORPORATE COACHING

Judi Craig, Ph.D. & Bill Thomas

A General Manager in the entertainment industry was told by his superiors that he needed to develop leadership and team building skills. He had a poor professional presence. If he was to continue his employment with the company, he had to change. A corporate coach was brought in to work both with the GM and members of his team, utilizing role plays and communication-building techniques. The GM and his coach also worked on improving his professional presence, using more powerful, less tentative language. The coach helped him in upgrading his wardrobe for a more "corporate look." After six months of coaching, the executive had a highly successful opening of an entertainment center. Three months after coaching concluded, he was promoted to Senior General Manager of several entertainment centers, and was selected as General Manager of the Year by his corporation....

An architectural and engineering firm called for help after the loss of many of their electrical engineers. The coach interviewed company employees, finding that the engineers had left not because of improved opportunity, but because of discontent over tremendous changes in the structure of management. The environment within the company was not conducive to growth for anyone, and the electrical engineers happened to have a number of other attractive options open to them in the community. The coach brought the corporate officers together to rethink and create a new vision and mission for their company as well as for team-building activities. Working from the top down, the coach was instrumental in bringing about realignment with the corporate values within the entire company. This translated into increased employee satisfaction and, consequently, improved employee performance....

These scenarios represent typical reasons why we are hired as corporate coaches. We are success-partners and collaborators who are professionally trained to guide companies, and the people in them, to be more successful. Coaching works because corporate coaches are specialists in human interaction and development; the "people" part of business.

As is true in all coaching, we don't come to you with the answers, but we do ask tough questions. Whether you're a CEO, an executive, a manager, a supervisor, a department or a team within an organization, we make you think. We help you (and the corporation) discover how to bridge the gap between where you are and the vision of where you want to be. We're about supporting you, helping you hone your skills and talents, encouraging you to find direction, moving you into action and increasing your personal accountability.

As corporate coaches, we create a more collaborative model of communication and motivation that today's business environment demands. As hundreds of articles in the national media (i.e, *New York Times, Wall Street Journal, USA Today, Harvard Business Review, Money, Newsweek, Investor's Business Daily*) will attest, coaching develops the highest potential in people within the organization, creates a productive environment and motivates employees toward ever higher performance standards.

The Corporate Entre'

We prefer to enter a corporation at the highest level possible, usually initiating a conversation with the CEO, General Manager or

Director of Operations. We do this for two reasons: First, we want to be with a decision maker; second, we know that the people at the top of the organization must be enthusiastic about coaching if we are to get acceptance for any work we do with other employees. Sometimes we are directed to the Human Resource or Training Departments and are happy to initiate a conversation with them as well. However, we want to meet with the decision maker as quickly as possible, if that is not the person who initially meets with us.

Our best referrals come from other satisfied clients and from business people we meet through networking in various organizations such as Chambers of Commerce, Rotary Clubs, Leads Clubs, Business Organizations, etc., who sponsor us or invite us into a company. We also send out marketing packets to CEOs and business owners, following up with a phone call to answer their questions and to invite them to set an appointment to explore coaching opportunities in their organization. Additionally, our personal coaching clients refer us to people they know within organizations and businesses. We frequently receive calls from companies whose employees have attended a presentation or seminar, or who have read an article we've written (or has been written about us) in the local media. Never doubt that wherever one goes, there are potential clients!

Proposals

Every proposal is customized to the needs of the client corporation; we do not send blind proposals. We prefer to meet with the decision maker who will be hiring us to find out the needs of the organization and how coaching can help. Possible approaches as well as the range of fees are discussed. Once we have a clear idea of what a company is asking for, as well as their budgetary constraints, we submit a proposal. This includes a listing what we think would be the most appropriate course of action, along with the necessary investment. By then, there are no surprises either to us or to the company. We also enclose a statement of Ethical Practices defined by the International Coaching Federation with every Coaching Agreement or proposal.

We find it ethically imperative that confidentiality issues be specifically defined up-front in working within a corporation. Our Coaching Agreement spells out three options regarding confidentiality for the person hiring us and the persons being coached:

1. Everything the client (or team) says is totally confidential and not shared with anyone else in the company (unless the client or team members choose to share it).
2. The coach will provide written feedback to the client's (or team's) manager or boss, but only after the client (or team) has examined the report and approves of what is written. The coach, along with the client, will meet together with the client's (or team's) manager or boss to provide feedback about the progress of coaching.

The third option often provides "coachable moments" both for the client as well as the person who hires us. These are moments in a conversation when an individual is open to taking in new information that will bring about a shift in knowledge and/or behavior. When the person being coached as well as the supervisor is present, we have an environment where each can be coached. Sometimes we are asked to coach someone in a company whose job is on the line and coaching is being used as a "make or break" measure. If this is the case, we insist that the person be told in advance that his or her job will depend on the outcome of coaching.

Coaching Executives

We often are hired to work with top performing executives to give them the edge in their own executive development. Other executives are selected for coaching because of "blind spots" that keep them from achieving maximum performance: problems getting organized and meeting deadlines, poor interpersonal skills, attitude problems, an inability to delegate, weak communication and leadership skills. These executives may have outstanding strengths in many areas but need further developing. We have also coached CEOs or owners with succession planning.

A human resources department head was referred for coaching by his CEO for an "attitude problem." He was perceived as cold, aloof and abrupt by both his direct reports as well as his fellow department heads. He saw himself differently. Specific interventions by the coach included having him go to lunch once or twice a week with another department head, spend five to ten minutes daily in the break room socializing, and take some time almost every day "managing by walking around" his department. The coach focused on his finding ways to take better care of himself by "working smarter instead of harder," and by including some activity each week that he found personally satisfying and fun. At the conclusion of coaching, he was perceived much more positively by his staff and his colleagues. Also, he reported that his wife was delighted that he was spending more quality time with his family and that he seemed generally more relaxed.

Companies are learning that firing executives who don't meet expectations is costly and traumatic. Expensive severance packages need to be created. More often than not, headhunters have to be commissioned to look for replacements who, in turn, need to be relocated and familiarized with unfamiliar surroundings. Most importantly, the "new kid on the block" has to earn the respect and acceptance of management and peers as well as the people who work for him/her. While sometimes firing the executive may be the only solution, more often it is not. By working one-on-one with the executive for a period of typically six to eight months, we can assess their strengths and weaknesses, help them set goals and develop a plan of action to reach them.

So what do we actually do to fully develop an executive? A department head in the computer industry was referred by her human resources director due to the filing of several sexual discrimination complaints by two men in her department. Assessment of her general managerial approach and communications style revealed that the problem with the two men was likely related to communication style differences, rather than gender discrimination. Shadow coaching (watching her interact with members of her department in individual meetings) also revealed problems within the entire department regarding accountability. She did not feel comfortable with confrontation; she would put up with missed deadlines for awhile, then explode at the offender. Through coaching, the entire department was taught a process for clarifying communication about desired outcomes including the "what by when" needed for accountability.

Typically we begin with an assessment phase, having the executive fill out various personality or behavioral instruments. To see how the executive is perceived by others, we often use a "360 Degree Feedback" process where the individual is anonymously rated on a number of management and interpersonal dimensions by peers, direct reports and superiors. We also use the Personal Coaching Styles Inventory (PCSI), a quick self-assessment of a person's communication style, as well an assessment of emotional intelligence. We may supplement these with a variety of other coaching self-assessments.

"Shadow coaching" typically occurs as part of the assessment phase. We will spend a half-day or day as a silent observer, watching the executive give a presentation, lead a meeting, meet with his direct reports, participate in a team, etc. We then give him or her feedback about our observations. After the executive is given the results of our assessments, we ask him/her to develop and commit to an action plan. We then coach the individual on a weekly basis to support him/her in reaching desired goals.

Since executive coaching is about who the executive is, as well as about what he or she does, we typically will scrutinize (with permission) the individual's professional foundation. This includes personal standards, boundaries, level of integrity, organizational skills, needs, values, and professional presence. We will ask a person to list everything he/she finds stressful (home and work environments, relationships) and then find healthy, effective ways to eliminate those items. The executive is asked to build up reserves; not only in finances, but in time, health and energy. He/she is asked to learn extreme self-care, taking time to nurture him/herself, celebrating the "little" accomplishments, and having more fun. Integration of work with time for a family and personal life is highly encouraged so that life balance becomes a reality, rather than a wish.

Having a coach also fills the "loneliness at the top" void experienced by so many executives. After all, where can a CEO or a senior management executive turn to for confidential partnership without judgment? Friends and families may be supportive, but hardly objective. Consultants make recommendations in their areas of expertise, but typically they don't do personal follow-up on a regular basis to assist the executive in obtaining the desired results. The coach provides a solution to this common dilemma.

Experiences In Coaching Teams And Groups

A director in the real estate industry had read about coaching and wanted a group of managers to learn coaching skills that would facilitate their working with other managers who reported to them. The group participated in a two-day training, learning a structured process for collaborative discussion as well as specific coaching skills. They were given a communication style assessment, learned to recognize four different styles, and then practiced their own style with others. They were divided into groups of three to practice what they had learned, and to coach one another over a six-week period. After a half-day wrap-up to reinforce their learning and refine their skills, the group felt ready to use their new coaching skills within the organization.

Frequently, we are asked to coach departments or groups within a corporation. In some cases, we begin with the coaching skills two-day training described above. In others, we will interview a group's members individually, learning their concerns and suggestions for improvement. We may gather "360 Degree Feedback" from the group along with an assessment of each person's communication style. Or, we will coach a group regarding communication, performance issues, or problems with those they supervise.

A general manager in the transportation industry developed a five-year plan for her board of directors that included the creation of a coaching initiative within the company as well as a change in management style. She wanted them to develop a collaborative, team approach. We began with individual coaching with her and several department heads, along with coaching skills training for both the senior management team and supervisors. This led to specific work with one department that had tremendous morale problems. To resolve the schism within the department that had been sabotaging the team's performance, we scheduled departmental group meetings, 360 Degree Feedback for all members, team building skills and individual coaching with the department head and several of the supervisors.

When coaching teams, we usually begin with an assessment of each member's communication style, using the PCSI. We find that helping them to identify their own, and others', coaching styles greatly facilitates understanding one another. Not only do they relate to the strengths and potential liabilities of each style, but also they often see that what they believed were "personality differences" between members are more likely to be differences in style. Next, we ask the team to identify their purpose and clarify any confusion about their mission. We also coach the team to establish ground rules for respectful communication (maintain confidentiality, everyone gets to speak without interruption, etc.) and discuss how the inevitable conflicts that will arise can be constructively handled (one person tries to dominate the discussion, a member talks negatively about another member outside the group, etc.). At this point, we may recommend a team retreat and/or enlist other professionals in providing a ropes course or other kinds of special activity to foster team development.

After laying this foundation, we work with the team in a variety of ways. We may coach the team ourselves or assist the team leader by facilitating the team process. Or, we may coach the team leader apart from the team. We also give interactive mini-presentations on a topic we think will assist the team's development.

Sales Success Coaching

Working with a top real estate agent who wanted coaching on sales and marketing, we used the "Attraction Model of Selling," focusing on individuals growing themselves in order to grow their businesses. Both the agent as well as the company made major shifts, emphasizing "who" they were in their business rather than strictly on the "what" of their business. Personal performance groups were formed so members could assist their peers in building their professional foundations, as well as providing ongoing feedback to one another. Company performance rose overall; the agent not only maintained her number one status, but nearly doubled her sales and income.

The "Attraction Model" was developed by Thomas Leonard and the coaches of Coach University. It encourages sales success by having the sales person learn to be a role model for integrity and high standards, maintain solid boundaries, focus goals, and develop personal organization and life balance. The salesperson learns to under-promise and over-deliver (a great way to make sure you always make your deadlines), to give up tolerating negative aspects of life that can be changed, and how to over-respond rather than react. Key concepts are taught on how to "attract" clients, opportunities and the relationships one desires. In today's world of competition, having a good product or service is not enough. We coach sales persons to add value to maintain customer loyalty. As with other teams, we also teach them how to understand their own and others' communication styles as an excellent tool to improve personal rapport.

Retreat Facilitation

We are often asked to facilitate and/or participate in company retreats. As coaches, we help groups develop their five year plan by a process called co-visioning. We also lead presentations on a variety of topics: stress management, listening skills, customer service, communication styles, coaching skills, team development, the "Attraction Model" and goal setting. We keep our presentations interactive and experiential. When we facilitate a retreat, we work with the group in developing an action plan during the retreat. We know how all those great ideas and notes can wind up on a shelf afterwards collecting the dust of benign neglect.

A Common Coaching Theme: Recognize Others

Whether we are working with individuals or groups within a corporation, we often hear employees express a common feeling that their individual efforts are unappreciated. We teach that people at all levels of the organization need to be recognized for their efforts and achievements. Even those executives, managers and supervisors who are quite good at acknowledging the people who report to them, typically don't acknowledge those lateral to or above them in the corporate structure. The higher up the ladder one is, the less likely he/she is to receive this kind of positive feedback.

While acknowledgement can come in the form of plaques, certificates, buttons, movie tickets, employee of the month awards and other tangible items, the most cost effective and highly successful acknowledgment is often a simple verbal remark. "You really do an excellent job in organizing a lot of information," "Have I told you how glad I am that you're working here?" "You are someone who can always be counted on to give 100%," "I can't tell you how much you contribute to making this department successful." How easy to say, and how often left unsaid.

Benefits Of Coaching To A Corporation

Coaching has become a "must have" in the corporate world, and opportunities are abundant. Corporate Coach University International's Coaching Clinic has identified the following paradigm shifts that commonly occur as coaching moves through an organization:

- From managing for results, to developing the strengths of the employee.
- From controlling the employee's actions, to empowering individuals to take better actions.
- From "You report to me," to "Tell me how I can help."
- From manager as boss/parent, to self-directed work groups.
- From manager saying, "It's your job," to the individual saying "It's my responsibility."
- From using competition to motivate, to creating alignment around a bigger picture.
- From solving all the problems, to helping others prevent and solve problems.
- From "management by crisis," to management/team collaboration and planning.
- From not having a life outside of work, to having a balanced life with work in perspective.
- From maintaining status quo/trends, to leading toward continuous improvement.

The benefits? Employee performance and morale improve. Companies find better ways to recruit and retain talent. Employees move from compliance, to commitment, responsibility and self-management. Executives resolve the barriers that may have stood in the way of the career advancement. People work more efficiently and effectively. Customer relations and marketing improve. Lines of communication are kept open. People feel valued and appreciated. Accountability thrives.

The end result? Every corporation's dream: a positive impact on the company's bottom line.

A Personal Note

We have found it very exciting to be involved in the rapidly expanding field of corporate coaching and enjoy mentoring other coaches who want to work in the corporate arena. As you can see from the vignettes in this chapter, working with even a few of an organization's leaders can shift the focus of the corporate mission to empower the work force — affecting hundreds of people. This, in turn, creates a ripple effect to those employees' families and to thousands of customers. Consequently, several hundred thousand lives may be touched.

The model for corporate coaching is useful in any industry because the focus of coaching is not just about what people do, but on who they are and who they may become. We are delighted to be a part of this very workable approach to creating a more fulfilling and productive corporate culture.

Dr. Judi Craig and Bill Thomas are both graduates of Coach University International and certified by the International Coaching Federation as Master Certified Coaches. They have their own companies, The Coaching Connection and The Thomas Coaching Institute, for personal coaching clients, as well as co-owning Coach Squared, Inc. for corporate coaching. Web site: http://www.coachsquared.com. Phone: 210-496-6833.

Recommended Reading

Belasco, James A. and Stayer, Ralph C. *Flight of the Buffalo*. (NY: Warner Books, 1994.)

Blanchard, Ken and Bowles, Sheldon. *Gung Ho*. (NY: William Morrow, Inc., 1998.)

Cooper, Robert K. and Sawaf, Ayman. *Executive EQ*. (NY: The

Berkely Publishing Group, 1998.)

Daft, Richard & Lengel, Robert. *Fusion Leadership*. (San Francisco, CA: Berrett-Koehler Publishers, 1998.)

O'Brien, Maureen. *Who's Got the Ball?* (San Francisco, CA: Jossey-Bass Publishers, 1995.)

O'Neil, John. *Leadership Aikido*. (NY: Random House, Inc, 1997)

"The Personal Coaching Styles Inventory" is available from Coach Works International, Dallas, TX, http://www.coachworks. com.

Corporate Coach University International can be accessed at: http://www.ccui.com

A PERSONAL JOURNEY INTO COACHING PEOPLE WITH ATTENTION DEFICIT DISORDER

Linda Anderson

What is a coach and what exactly do we do? There's something of the teacher, the manager, the organizer, the therapist, the minister, the administrator and the healer in each of us. By simply being there for our clients, we validate their existence and their efforts. We help them discover possibilities and new ways of looking at things. We applaud their efforts. Although, as coaches, we may have some of the same tools in our coaching repertoire, it is each individual coach's career and life experience which distinguishes and flavors our coaching style and abilities.

It's doubtful whether many of us presently working as coaches went through our school years thinking, "Gosh, when I get through college or grad school, I'm going to be a coach. No. Not a sport's coach. A coach." What happened, instead, is that most of us discovered coaching after having first pursued other careers. Once we became aware of the fact that there was such a profession as coaching, we began to seek out coaches and opportunities to learn from them. Although we had different life experiences, we shared certain similarities. We learned along the way that we liked helping others solve problems, face challenges, and reach for their goals. We also discovered that we had certain skills and gifts in helping facilitate change in others. We knew that there would always be more to learn about how to do this better. In pursuing a career as a coach we knew that we enjoyed the job itself, the art of coaching. As an extra dividend, we learned that we enjoyed our client's success, as well.

Here is the story of my own stumbling forward into coaching. In 1970, I graduated from a small liberal arts college with a double major in literature and political science. In retrospect, some of the more formative opportunities which I experienced during those college years didn't have much to do with either of those subjects. In highlighting two of those experiences, I can illustrate how they brought skills into my coaching today:

I was introduced to Carl Rogers and his book, *On Becoming A Person*, in a psychology course. Rogers' ability to convey the simple art of listening and its therapeutic and organizing effect on the human being made its mark in my consciousness. In addition to studying Rogers, the professor of this class organized us into a "T-group," or sensitivity group. Over the course of the semester, I experienced what it felt like to be listened to and had the opportunity to practice the skills needed to reciprocate. The gift of being listened to, of listening, and the skills involved in communication, I continue to value, study, and bring into my coaching today.

As the result of my participation in another class, a visiting sociology professor from the University of Chicago offered me an opportunity to work as a community organizer. Under his guidance I helped him to organize a working class neighborhood to take charge of their community. This was the tumultuous 60's, a time for demanding one's rights and liberties. Under his encouragement, I also organized an employment agency in the same neighborhood. Motivating, organizing, gathering resources, learning how to delegate and when to stand aside, were skills both observed and practiced during those years. I also learned that empowering others was something I enjoyed.

From college, I went on to Northwestern University, graduating in 1972 with a master's in English literature. In my last year at Northwestern I completed education courses and did student teaching at a high school, portrayed on the cover of Life magazine as a model high school. In this environment, I learned that I enjoyed teaching, loved the creative interaction with students, and feared the underlying bureaucracy still imposed upon us. Instead of teaching high school English, I worked for the next ten years in underprivileged ethnically diverse neighborhoods in Chicago, Philadelphia and Bucks County, Pennsylvania. I began as a teacher, moving on to curriculum coordinator and, for several years as a coordinating director of day care and early childhood education centers.

I was both encouraged and given tremendous opportunities to study how young children learn, how learning environments are created, and how all of us, children and adults, alike, learn best. Before being hired to do so, I would coordinate training opportunities for staff members and myself. I learned, during these years, that I loved putting together resources. I looked for what was needed. I liked the synergy of putting people and ideas together and watching the results. Today, I encourage my coaching clients to look for the wealth of ideas and support that is out there for the asking. I often hear clients wondering whether they might call a specific person and ask for their advice, ideas or help. Or I will hear a client who could really use the support of their co-worker, mate, or their children, in resolving something. My familiar phrase of encouragement is: "You could ask nothing, and nothing will likely happen. Or, you could ask for something, and something just might happen."

There were yet other life experiences in this meandering journey. During my years of administrating, I had the opportunity to work closely with Dr. Barry Ginsberg, author of *Relationship Enhancement Family Therapy*. After working with Barry, I trained teachers in the use of play therapy skills in his "Sensitivity To Children" program. In addition to practicing listening skills, trainees learned how to set limits, set workable boundaries, and to make requests that facilitated choice and change. These are skills needed by many coaching clients who are learning how to better navigate in the world of relationships.

Unlikely as it may seem, a hobby further shaped my coaching skills. I took cabinet making classes at a vocational technical school and repeated the course for several terms to work on various projects. I had always wondered, what joins things together, so neatly? How does one end up with a cabinet or bed that fits together snugly, starting with a tree?

In cabinet-making, I learned how to use tools. I learned about the nature of various woods. I learned that a seemingly obscure and difficult task can be broken down into steps or groups of steps, then put together. I learned how to use a story stick to plan the making of a cabinet. A plan or map is a useful guide on any journey. Today, I help my clients take on new, but challenging tasks, with the same assurance from their coach, that each goal is accomplished by breaking it into "do-able" steps. I also learned to ask for help when stuck, and as my teacher would say, "There's more than one way to skin a cat," meaning there's often more than one solution to a problem.

When I left my position as an administrator one week before having my first child, my life completely changed direction. I consulted in the field of education, had a second child and, soon after, found my attention split in a variety of directions. I worked on an invention to patent with a friend, and tried a number of entrepreneurial ventures. I did substitute teaching and worked part-time in organizing fund-raising endeavors for two private schools. Most of all, I wrote, working on several stories. What I didn't know was that I was doing field work in preparation for what was yet to come. I was trying to manage some of the very same opportunities and challenges that my future clients would face day in and day out.

This abundance of activity and opportunity continued until one life-changing day, I woke up to realize that my life was spilling over into too many possibilities. It was spilling into an uncaring universe, like a precious liquid dripping between opened fingers, as I tried to hold onto it. On that one day, when the heavens opened up, I was divinely hit with the awareness that if I narrowed my activities to one or two projects, and put everything else on the back burner, I would be a lot happier. Being successful at one thing would bring me greater happiness than being partially successful at a truckload-full of incompletions. I understood that creativity, containment, focus, and the need for all three in my life, were integral to success. These principles were now applied to my daily living.

I then found myself throwing out actual stuff surrounding me, i.e., papers, files, clothes, inherited knick knacks collecting dust on shelves. I went through cupboard, closet, and drawer, letting go of whatever I wasn't using, whatever felt like excess. And so I began to sort, let go and contain. All of those left-brained highly organized skills, which I came by naturally, supported me in this clearing. They helped contain the more right-brained, creative, free-flowing, associative part of my life. Both were essential to my well-being. Creativity and structure became very important for me. Knowing how good it felt to experience the balance of both would become another principle in my approach to coaching.

After this period of "letting go," an event occurred that would send me in the direction that I still move. It was as if I had cleared the pathway, creating the space for change to occur. I had a conversation with a woman, Jacqueline Fox. In this conversation we shared our life experiences. Jacqueline, whose training was in organizational development, had worked in this country and abroad as an consultant. At the present, she was working part-time in this field, and had also begun a business called Simply Organized. She helped individuals in corporations, small businesses, and in their homes get organized. She also coached them by phone. Jacqueline asked me to work with her.

In 1972, professional organizing was on the cusp of being recognized by the public as a new career opportunity providing a service much needed by others. Coaching was also about to come into the public consciousness. Jacqueline had a foot planted in both worlds. I had no idea where the journey ahead would lead, yet I knew that this was exactly what I should be doing. It was a deep intuitive knowing. I also knew that it was a window offering me a frame through which to view a future of possibilities. It was a vehicle allowing me to do, in time, all the other things I enjoyed.

I began to read the concepts shared by Stephen Covey, Charles R. Hobbs, and many others. The organizing perspectives of these two individuals were carefully balanced against the equally enjoyable ideas encountered in Barbara Sher's book, *Wishcraft—How To Get What You Really Want*. Once again, I found myself utilizing tools to manage time, task and priorities, while at the same time valuing the need to envision, flow freely, and create. In helping my clients and myself live life to the fullest, an essential premise is understanding the need in the universe and in one's life, for both creativity and containment. The learning curve sloped sharply upward for the next several years, as I read and researched books in the field of organizing. I was introduced to the National Association of Professional Organizers (NAPO) in 1993. From other organizers and authors, I would learn yet more.

Through my clients and other professionals I learned about Attention Deficit Disorder (ADD.) As I worked with my clients, I learned what challenged them the most, what worked and what didn't. I became a keen observer of these wonderful people who invited me into their often chaotic, but frequently creative and interesting lives. Clients dared to share with me their "dis"-order, their chaos. They expressed relief that I was there to witness, without judgment, their confusion and inability to maintain order. Frequently I heard the words, "Not even my therapist knows about this." Among them were doctors, lawyers, authors, professors, business owners, entrepreneurs, "home managers," and ...oh, yes, a go-go dancer. What made it so hard for them to get and stay organized? Collectively and individually, they had experienced a lifetime of challenges and failures regarding: time, which never seemed manageable; distraction; short term memory problems; and a lack of focus.

A few short months after working with these clients, I was introduced to Sue Sussman, who was about to enter the world of ADD coaching. Sue, with a lifetime of personal knowledge about ADD, and a masters in education, was embarking on her coaching business. She continues to coach, has put together an ADD coach training program, the American Coach Association (americacoach.com), and an ADD coach training workbook.

I had begun to ask questions regarding ADD: "How does the brain, chemistry and genetics contribute to chaos, incompletion, lost time, and disorder, yet, at the same time contribute to immense creativity and intelligence?" Today, I know that Pulitzer prize winners, V.P.'s of major corporations, and members of top law firms, to name a few, may be secretly crippled by an inability to file papers and stay focused. They have the will to do it. They may have developed terrific compensatory behaviors and, if lucky, have the help of terrific assistants or mates. They may be highly successful in their jobs, yet other areas of their lives can be seriously compromised by their ADD. And no matter how successful, there often remains guilt and a sense of inadequacy.

By August of 1994, I knew the name of my new business, *Getting Clear*, and I called myself a professional organizer/coach. Initially, I worked with clients primarily on-site. I helped them organize papers, offices, desks, kitchens, closets and basements. I helped them organize their jobs, look for new careers, manage work and family responsibilities, develop new businesses, and get clear about what they really wanted to do most. Organization was integral to success. I began to present seminars at conferences for the National Attention Deficit Disorder Association and the International Children and Adults with Attention Deficit Disorder. The tools and techniques which I shared were constantly honed by the creativity, wit, and wisdom of my clients. I began to attract clients from across the United States, because of the presentations and referrals and my growing expertise in working with ADD clients.

At this point, I decided to take teleclasses with Coach University. Through Coach U. I had the opportunity to listen to other coaches modeling their own skills and style with clients. I learned about client types, such as the entrepreneur, artist , manager or CEO, and some of their specific challenges. I felt validated in my approach to coaching, learning that coaches indeed dealt with a whole life being shared with them.

Another fortuitous life-changing relationship developed out of the Coach U experience. I discovered a class facilitator, whom I respected and enjoyed, Madelyn Griffith Haney. Madelyn herself has ADD and was developing an ADD coach training program. Today, the organization which Madelyn founded, the Optimal Functioning Institute, provides ADD Coach Training (ACT), in an 11-month teleconference course. At Madelyn's invitation, I took part in the ACT program in 1997 and have added to OFI offerings by designing and leading Organizational Skills training modules for coach and organizer. I made the shift from professional organizer/coach to coach specializing in ADD and organization. From that time to the present, I coached my clients by telephone. I now refer clients to professional organizers who have skills in working with the "organizationally-challenged."

The clients who are seeking my services today want to finish the book, complete the Ph.D., change jobs or survive the one their in, open a business, etc. They share similar challenges, however. They want to learn how to stay organized and on track. They want to learn how to successfully blend work and family time, how to communicate their needs and requests in both those environments, and how to relax and have fun. They want to get clear about what they do best, what they can say "no" to, and how to connect to professionals for help with managing their ADD. They want to take better care of themselves.

ADD coaches need all of the skills that coaches use today in helping their clients succeed at their goals, but they need much more. They need training in and familiarity with the symptoms, traits and treatments of ADD. They need to understand the co-morbidities, which are behaviors, physical conditions, and addictions, which can mask or co-present with ADD. ADD coaches need to ask important questions about their client's background. They need to know what the challenges and strengths were in their client's schooling and work history. A knowledge of learning modalities is also important, if the ADD coach is going to help the client understand how they learn best, how they process information and make effective changes.

Certainly there is a great deal of structure in what I provide as an ADD coach. I frequently think of myself as an skeletal framework, providing my client with the space to be their creative best. It is also my goal to impart this framework to my clients; to share the tools, systems and resources for creating their own life structures. There is another image of what we do as coaches. I call it body doubling. I once worked with a retired corporate executive, who discovered late in life that ADD was a part of his whole history. He had survived by his intelligence, creativity, energy and by the organization and wits of his administrative assistants. Now, in his office at home, managing three other businesses, as organized as he looked, he still felt all in pieces. But, he had discovered that sometimes, if someone simply sat in the chair near him, he could get a job done that was otherwise impossible to get started. He could focus. As he explained this phenomenon to me, I knew exactly what he was talking about. I had experienced it before with other clients. He was using a body double.

As ADD coaches we certainly need to know about the subject of ADD, but bottom line, we share with all other coaches one very basic guiding principle. It is applies to any and all of our clients, whether they are at the beginning or end of their coaching journey. It is expressed in the following question, which I may ask my client, at any point in time, "How are you taking care of yourself, today?" If we keep that one idea clear, it becomes a guidepost for both of us.

Linda Anderson began her business, Getting Clear, in 1993. She is a business and personal coach with expertise in professional organizing. She specializes in Attention Deficit Disorder (ADD) adult coach-

ing. You may visit her website at www. gettingclear.com or contact her at 215-230-7315 or e-mail Linda@gettingclear.com.

Recommended Reading on Organizing:

Buzan, Tony: *The Mind Map Book.* (NY: Penguin, 1994).

Covey, Stephen: *First Things First.* (NY: Simon & Schuster, 1994).

Covey, Stephen: *The 7 Habits of Highly Effective People.* (NY: Simon & Schuster, 1990).

DePress, Max: *Leadership Is An Art.* (NY: Dell, 1989).

Felton, Sandra: *Messie No More.* (Grand Rapids, MI: Fleming H. Revell, 1993).

Hemphill, Barbara *Taming The Paper Tiger.* (NY: Dodd, Mead and Company, 1988).

Lehmkuhl, Dorothy and Lamping, Delores Cotter: *Organizing for The Creative Person.* (NY: Crown Trade, 1993).

Silver, Susan: *Organized To Be The Best.* (Los Angeles, CA: Adams Hall Publishing, 1995)

Taylor, Harold: *Say Yes To Your Dreams.* (Ontario: Harold L. Taylor, 1998)

Recommended Reading on Attention Deficit Disorder:

Hallowell, E. & Ratey, J.: *Driven to Distraction.* (New York: Pantheon Books, 1994)

Hartmann, T.: *Attention Deficit Disorder: A Different Perception.* (Lancaster, PA: Underwood-Miller, 1993)

Kelly, K & Ramundo, P.: *You Mean I'm Not Lazy, Stupid Or Crazy?* (Cincinnati, OH: Tyrell and Jeremy Press, 1993)

Nadeau, K.: *Attention Deficit Disorder in Adults.* (New York: Brunner/ Mazel, 1995)

Solden, S.: *Women With Attention Deficit Disorder.* (CA: Underwood Books 1995)

COACHING FAMILY BUSINESSES

Terry Schaefer

My life path has been a wonderful journey on both a spiritual exploration and a quest for developing what comes naturally for me. I was born and raised in Cincinnati, Ohio, the first son, third child of an affluent couple. My parents had limited parenting skills so I raised myself, with the guidance of several important and influential people that took me under their wings. Through the developmental phase of my life, I observed families with a great deal of financial wealth. I realized that money was not the key to their happiness. I was always interested in how families functioned, how they communicated, and the daily interactions of family members.

I attended an undergraduate business school to learn business and management skills, hoping that someday I would be able to run my own company. Upon graduation, I started working in the corporate world, with a company that gave me on the job training in my areas of interest; marketing, operations and management. Over the next 16 years, I moved from sales to operations to corporate strategic planning. By the time I was 35 I had my own company. And I was depressingly unhappy.

I started psychotherapy in the mid-1980's when I was having problems that were causing some personal tension. My therapy opened up other possibilities in the world that I had never been exposed to, and I was eager to explore what was new to me. At the advice of my therapist, I shifted my career orientation toward the helping professions. I completed three advanced graduate educational degrees, in drug & alcohol counseling, family and child dynamics, and organization development. During this period of re-training, I gained a real appreciation for the aging process. I took positions with different federal and state agencies that directed me to work with the elderly, both individually and within their families. As I look back, my path was laid out in front of me. All I needed to do was to walk down it. I started to enjoy what I was experiencing.

Over time, I saw a pattern in my life. I had corporate experience, an entrepreneurial spirit, my heart for helping others, an interest in working in family systems, a gift of inquisitiveness, and my own personal experiences of evolution and growth. I wanted to incorporate these aspects into a life and career path that was as much a part of me as my red hair. In late 1996, I read an article on the coaching profession and I recognized that in my work I was using a coaching model of problem solving — a task oriented approach involving accountability and strategic planning. I pursued further education in the coaching field, and have found that coaching is the vehicle by which I can integrate all that I've learned with what is important to me.

I work with people dealing with transition and aging issues. There is a structure from which I work. I find it very beneficial to begin working with my client to define and developed their value system, and to discover what is joyful to him/her, and what are his/her natural talents. We can then create a life he/she wants to live. Within a month, these key elements of a person emerge like spring flowers planted as bulbs in the fall. From there, my clients take the lead on where they want to go next, and I help them stay focused on what is important to them. With a strong personal foundation, one can build anything they want, since the essences of their life is clear.

Understanding Systems

My formal education introduced systems theory to me and how it fits every day life. Simply explained, each person has many different and diverse systems influencing how he/she thinks, feels, behaves, learns, etc. This individual system is part of a larger or smaller system in the bigger universe. For example, a man and a woman are individual systems. As a couple, they are two systems joined together to form a "couple" system. Both individual systems have other systems (family, education, work, etc.) that effect how they act in relationship to the other systems in their life. Each individual brings with them familial issues and traditions (rituals, myths, comparisons, sibling rivalry, succession planning, what to do in the third quarter of life, children responsibility, etc.) which are handed down from generation to generation, being blended with other systemic rituals along the way.

Families are compiled of several systems interacting simultaneous with each other, sometimes smoothly, sometimes not so smoothly. As one looks at family business systems, there are several different and complex systems interacting on a regular basis, trying to work harmoniously so they do not clash. The most prominent systems are individuals, family, and business. These systems intertwine within each other, and have actuating over-lapping parts. This can be confusing when looking at different systems' responsibility and accountability. Using coaching to help specify the working elements of their functionality, brings to the surface factors that cause conflict and tension.

So where do you start? There is no steadfast rule or process. The coach needs to listen and use his/her intuition to provide the client with exercises to bring priorities to the surface. I like to start by assessing the individual's belief and value systems, and look at what challenges are facing them. A good approach with a family system is to examine and chart how the family members view themselves in contrast to one another. Using an assessment instrument can assist the family in seeing their fundamental differences.

The Blues: A Family Business Case Study

To preserve confidentiality, the Blue family case study is a fiction-alized combination of families I've worked with. The case study provides examples of the issues often found in coaching a family business. Mrs. Blue contacted me. Mr. Blue had had a heart attack and his physician had recommended a lighter work load. She was worried that under the present situation, Mr. Blue's health would deteriorate to a point where their 45-year-old manufacturing company would be in jeopardy.

Mr. Blue had started his firm in his twenties, upon returning from the Korean conflict. He had no formal education. Early on, Mrs. Blue worked in the business helping with administration and bookkeeping. The first several years were lean, though. Mr. and Mrs. Blue are determined people, and hard work was part of their western European ancestry.

In the sixties, the Blue's children were born. Joseph Jr., Emily, Katharine, Mathew, Timothy and Dorothy were born within eighteen to twenty months of each other. Mrs. Blue took responsibility for the family, and Mr. Blue took on the responsibility of the business. In late 1969, the Blue Manufacturing Company started producing an essential part for most American-made automobiles. The business took off. Over the next 20 years, the company became an innovator of specialized parts.

When I met Mr. Blue, I sensed a proud man who loved a good challenge. He built his business to provide for his family. I also sensed he was attempting to prove a point, one that was not clear until my later involvement with the family. A talented man, Mr. Blue can visualize something and create it without a blueprint. He knows how to resolve a problem to his benefit. Mrs. Blue is a gentle woman who found real pleasure in her children. She ran a tight household, watched the family finances, and participated in each of her children's lives. She has a creative side that keeps her busy with gardening and decorating. She is quiet, and when she says something, she has thought through it completely.

Joe Blue was born in 1960, four weeks premature. He was transferred to a big city hospital upon his birth. He was slow in maturing, though he excelled in music. He was a good student, semi-athletic, wrote articles for his school and college newspaper, and pursued a liberal arts education. Upon graduation, he returned home and started working in the family business on the assembly line. He moved into sales, then into marketing, and has become the head of that department. He married Susan Green in 1984. Susan comes from a farm family, with rock solid values. She is graceful and playful, able to relate to many diverse people, and is creatively talented. They have three children.

Emily, born in 1961, was a quiet child. She is creative, very smart, able to improvise and became rebellious in her college years. Emily was intrigued with the theatre, and expressed herself through acting. After college, she returned home for six months before heading to New York to attempt a career in acting. She attended acting school, did some modeling, and was picked as a "fresh face" for the modeling magazines. She rode the fast lane for a while. She became bored with it, and performed in several small movies. One caught the attention of some big Hollywood producers and took her career to where it is today. She is not married, though would like to settle down. She is contemplating adopting a child, against her parents' wishes.

Katharine, born in 1963, excelled as the tomboy of the family, always in a tree, or in the manufacturing plant walking on the iron beams. In her mid-teens, she was chosen as class president, which lead her to discover her natural talents in leading others. She was an average student, though a hard worker. In college she started a small delivery company that she has built into the largest courier service in her city. She is married to Derek Brown, Esq. Derek has followed in his family's footstep, his great grandfather was a state supreme court judge. That is his aspiration as well, though he likes his bourbon. They have one child.

Born in 1965, Mathew is best with anything that concerns numbers. Ever since he was a small child, he had the gift to do complex calculations in his head. He is bright and knows how to decipher situations to the smallest detail. He was athletic and played football and baseball on varsity teams in both high school and college. Upon graduation from college, Mathew entered the Peace Corps and worked in South America for two years. Upon his return in 1991, he bought a sailboat and set out to cruise the world, which he did for three years. He returned, worked in the family business for several years before starting an internet web design company from a back room in the family business. He is not married, lives in his hometown, and he sails his boat often.

Timothy was born in 1967, and learned early that the squeaky wheel gets grease. He was an average student. His passion was working with engines, the bigger the better. At age 12, he built his own go-cart using two chain saw motors. He would push the envelop on anything he put his mind to, and his family was no exception. At 14, he took the family station wagon and ended up in a high-speed crash. Timothy lived, but his two passengers did not. He was suspended from one school after another. Military school was the only option the family had for high school. The day he graduated from military school in 1986, he excused himself from his celebratory dinner to go to the bathroom, and that was the last time any one of the Blue family members saw him. He left a note on his chair saying he was never going to be with his family again. But in 1990, he called his parents, and in the past several years he has started to communicate with his siblings through e-mail.

Dorothy is the last child, born in 1968. She is patient, soft spoken, bright, and likes being creative. She excelled in the sciences in high school, graduated from college with a degree in mechanical engineering, and worked for a top engineering company on projects in Southeast Asia. She returned to the United States to get a MBA from a top business school. Upon graduation, she joined a top consulting firm. She is dating a physician, and when I met her, she was contemplating returning home. She said she wants to raise a family.

I look at a family as a huge jig-saw puzzle. My approach is to interview each member of the family, get them to talk about family and business issues, look for slivers of information that might help me build the jig-saw puzzle picture. Once I get familiar with each member of the family, I get a picture of what the family is all about. When I met Mr. and Mrs. Blue, I requested information on their children, and I received information on five children, not six. I learned about Timothy through both Dorothy and Mathew. Why was Timothy left out? It took me a long time to locate him. Once we connected, I found the most sensitive and charming person of the whole family. Timothy is bright, articulate, and very successful as a designer of high performance racing cars. He is another self-made Blue family member, and very content as his life has evolved. I also learned that he was interested in re-entering the family, though he did not know how. He told me that he'd learned a great deal about himself outside of the family, and what he learned at military school was to be himself. Even as an adolescent, Timothy knew he had to separate from the family. He explained to me that his anger was so strong the night of his graduation that he knew it was time to branch out on his own. So he took the step. I asked him how he wanted to re-enter the family, and we developed his strategy into a workable plan. I did not include his information on the initial assessment of the family, but I did find out some interesting family history.

I requested that each family member take an assessment test, so that we could get everyone to see if there were differences in each others' perceptions. We started with Mr. and Mrs. Blue's answers, which were bunched in the one side of the chart. As each of the children's answers were charted, one could see that there were several differences in the perceptions of the Blue children and their parents.

Mr. Blue was shocked at the differences among family members, and wanted it to be corrected immediately. I wondered what the hurry was — it had taken over 40 years for this to form, and it is going to take a while to re-shape it to everyone's satisfaction.

Mrs. Blue calmed her husband, and I reassured Mr. Blue that the family had some rewarding work to do. Mr. Blue's autocratic style was becoming apparent, though I was there to mend fences and build rapport, not to slice and dice. I also noticed that when Mr. Blue spoke, no one else was allowed to discuss what was on their mind. By providing some thought provoking and supportive question, I believed we could get the family to open up and start to talk to each other differently.

From the assessment, we worked to develop a family mission, vision and purpose statement to get all the family members to work toward defining what is important for the family's future. Paying attention to individual needs will provide a wealth of information on how the other systems (family, business, ownership, etc.) have developed.

We started to do some exploration exercises that the family developed with some guidance from me. I would ask a specific question like "what does the family do well?" to build an understanding of the family's strengths. As we recorded the answers to questions, patterns appeared that produced more focused questions. It is like tossing more wood on a hot fire — it keeps the energy going. I saw the family as a group, start to change, to see the need to be responsible and accountable for what happened. Mr. Blue started to see the benefits of having open discussion with his children, and learned a great deal about their lives.

I often suggest that the family establish a "council of family members" to define, develop and deliver a family constitution. A family council is an opportunity for all the family members to voice their opinions, whether they work in the business or not. It serves as a vehicle to encourage a dialogue between family members, and where the future direction of the family and business can be discussed. An overview of the family, the business, the ownership, the asset base, etc., can be presented. Regular council meetings can provide an opportunity to family members to learn more about business, and establish guidelines for carrying the legacy smoothly into the next generation.

The Family Council Process

I was about to suggest establishing a family council to the Blues when Dorothy brought it up. Dorothy gave her own background with helping companies develop the goals for their future. I also noted that Dorothy had her father's attention, which the other children did not possess. Mr. Blue respected her education, which he knew he lacked. This was a big issue for him to admit, since it went back to his youth. As he admitted his feelings of inadequacy, his children started to see why he was such a task master, and why he pushed them so hard to achieve.

I recommended a family council be developed on a family retreat. A retreat provides opportunity for personal dialogue to develop, families to look back over important milestones, record a legacy of the family, and work to develop a family council. I sensed in this family that gatherings were important at holidays, though the festivities of the holidays did not generate time for the family to discuss important issues. The Blue's decided that a family re-treat would be a great idea. It would be held outside of town, in a place where they were not known. They picked a weekend, and I helped them develop an agenda. This was going to be a great ad-venture for them — in more ways than one.

During this time, I was watching how the other children were interacting with one another and within the family. Joe Jr. was quiet, did not move, did not say a thing. What was causing the eldest child, the only child working in the business, to withdraw? I also wanted to ask the family why they were not discussing the absence of Timothy.

During this time, I also was working with Timothy on creat-ing a re-entry strategy. It was his idea to re-enter at the family retreat. We ran all types of scenarios, and "what ifs." He was deter-mined to re-enter on his own terms. I gave Timothy the agenda, and told him where we were meeting. I had a room reserved for him to use. It was my intention to get the retreat started at dinner on Friday night by asking all the family members to build a picture memorial of their family experiences, and give a short talk about what their picture meant to them. The family went in age order. When Timothy's name came up, he walked in from the back of the room. Shocked was not the word to explain the atmosphere in the room. Mr. Blue did not even recognize him. Mrs. Blue must have cried for a half-hour, hugging her son. Timothy was her favorite, I discovered. She thought he was dead.

Timothy spoke for two hours, giving his story, telling why he left on his graduation night, and what he'd learned in the time away from the family. His was prepared, calm, and ready to discuss why he left the family. He was also apologetic for any pain that he caused. He admitted his faults, and wanted to go on. He also recognized that he was different from his family, and that they did not have to accept him back.

As I listened to all the children's stories about their lives, I recognized that Mr. Blue did not know his children really well. I could see in his eyes that something was missing, and he was really taken aback that his children were now grown adults. As the retreat evolved, each of the children revealed what the business meant to them, and what they wanted for themselves and their families. As their aspirations where revealed, it became evident that the family was coming together.

The family council process helps the family focus on the grounding factors that help the family business succeed. It has many functions, some which are listed here:

- Set standards and rules for working in the business.
- Provide a "private" place where the family can resolve conflicts without non-family management involved.
- Generate enthusiasm and support for further projects.
- Serve as a policy-making board for issues like family employment and compensation, business values, philanthropy, etc.
- Establish stewardship responsibilities.
- Interface issues between family and business matters.

- Establish a smooth transition from one generation to the next.
- Develop a mission, vision and purpose statement.

During the retreat, we also spent time discussing another system, the business, and how it was doing. Though the financial health of the company was sound, each of the children started to recognize that this business was a reflection of their father. Even Mr. Blue admitted the business was "his baby" and with the help of the children, we started to develop a dialogue on the future of the business. It was my intention to coach the family so that they would start to search for their own answers. At the end of the retreat, much progress had been made on opening the discussion between family members.

By developing this vehicle for dialogue, the coach acts as the facilitator to give each system a voice. Once you are in the middle of all the elements interacting together, change may be fast and furious. New ideas provide momentum to help the family see their future. The coach can identify inconsistencies and incongruencies in the system's behaviors.

Once the retreat was over, it was my concern that the momentum be continued. The Blue family was happy with what had happened. I had a full time job helping facilitate the changes in the family and helping them develop a future for the business. I also saw that some individual coaching work needed to be done, so I contracted to set up a bi-monthly family conference call on my telephone bridge. I would work individually with family members on special interests, coaching the individual to help them define and develop what they want for themselves. I worked with Mr. Blue first, since I expected that some depression might set in. This is not unusual in older men. The business was another child, and he needed to nurture it along on its own natural path. Within three months, Mr. Blue saw what he wanted to do, and started to develop a succession plan based on what he valued. I saw a transformed man, and renewed youthful energy showed in his face.

I worked with Joe Jr., which was a bit harder. Eventually, he started to trust that he had the power to direct his life. He recognized that he was missing out on his life. His real love was in teaching the classics. Joe and his wife, Susan, worked together on developing a life plan for themselves. He assessed his talents and what gave him personal satisfaction. Once he became clear on what he wanted for himself, opportunities opened to him in the education community. He now felt like he could move away from under the shadow of the Blue family tree.

The alliance of the other Blue children became very strong. Weekly, they found time to talk to each other as a group, and took what they had learned from their experiences to form a plan to take over the family business, to streamline it to move into the 21st century. The only one that did not participate was Joe, who was pursuing his educational interests. The Blues had become a functional family.

How do you know whether you are working with a functional family? There are many indicators that can help you recognize healthy behavior. It also will give you a picture of the family's integrity. Some of the qualities of a highly functional family are:

1) Open and clear communications.
2) Appreciation of the interface between family and business.
3) Open to develop a future for the family and business.
4) Flexibility — ability to and respect for change.
5) Shared core values and beliefs — honoring others opinions.
6) Honoring each generation's developmental stage, and learning from one another.

As the Blue children put together a future for the Blue family business, I could watch the transformation of a tightly knit, closed family into an open, expressive, family that respects each member. On the weekly family coaching calls, we were able to define who would take which roles in the business and in the family itself. Each child took a role that was important to him/her, that best fit their interests and talents. They all learned how to discuss difficult issues without descending into emotional debate. Even Mr. and Mrs. Blue showed renewed energy for their relationship, as well as their relationships with each of their children.

Mr. Blue started to take a real interest in his children's lives, and moved from being a parent to being a family partner. He was able to listen to new ideas without making negative comments. He was a natural learner, and started to blossom in learning new skills in his late sixties. He also started taking better care of himself; watching his diet and getting more exercise. His vacation schedule became more important, he interacted regularly with his grandchildren and he liked being more of the elder statesman of both the family and company. His role in the family flourished, and he moved aside as the Chairman of the Board of the business, though he was still active on the steering committee.

As a coach, I like to use my own internal indicators to tell me what is happening. There is a strong "use of self" in this field. Trust your intuitions. Listen with all your senses for what is not being said. Ask hard questions, and don't be afraid of the answers. A family system is emotionally based. Be a calming influence. Make sure that you stay balanced yourself. I recommended that you care for yourself consistently while working with family business. Be prepared to be drawn into the family's problems. Confront problems directly and authentically. Remember that as a coach, you are to help the system define itself. Stay away from the technical details. Remember, you are a model for them to learn. Set appropriate boundaries, by asking for what you want, with open and clear communications. By requesting appropriate action, you are modeling healthy behavior consistent with your plan to help the family business.

I find in working with families that the better they can articulate their aspirations, the better they work with their other advisors in charting their course. Having a coach work with the family first lets the family define what is best for them. From the information and clarity the family develops by working with a coach the accountant, lawyer, or financial advisor can design an estate or business plan that fulfills the desires of the entire family.

My purpose as a coach is to help the family articulate the integrity of the family business system throughout its developmental process and overall evolution, to understand the values of each of the separate systems and how they influence each other. By clarification of the responsibility of each of the systems, the coach helps each member learn *who* they are, and not just *what* they do. Through this learning process, respect for each system becomes apparent, and the systems understand what is important to sustain the future for all.

By incorporating my specific expertise in transitional aging issues with the family business system, I provide a service where the system gets to self-actualize and evolve. As a coach working with transitional aging issues, I want to develop different services to help others find what works in their life. You are invited to visit my website where new and exciting programs involving coaching systems are introduced.

Coach Terry Schaefer can be contacted at 410-255-6660 or email: Terry@TerrySchaefer.com. You are invited to visit his website at http:// www.TerrySchaefer.com.

RELATIONSHIP COACHING

Damian Nash and Elizabeth Carrington,
with dialog by Mark Nash.

Introduction

Let's drop in on a typical couple in the evening, after dinner. He's at his desk, working on paperwork, she's on the couch reading.

He: *Did you see this?*

She: *What?*

He: *See, you don't even look at these bank statements do you?*

She: *Yeah I do. I just hadn't gotten to it yet.*

He: *When were you planning on getting to it?*

She: *I'll get to it. What's your point?*

He: *You bounced another check. $80 for shoes?*

She: *Let me see that. Well, there was money in the account when I wrote the check.*

He: *Apparently not enough. Like you really need another pair of shoes, anyway.*

She: *Yes. Like you needed a $300 pocket organizer.*

He: *Well, somebody needs to be organized. At least that's practical. And I don't already have twenty of them.*

She: *Yeah, but you had a $17 planner you never used.*

He: *The point is you bounced a check and cost me $20. I work my ass off for that money and you're just throwing it away. But I guess you don't really care as long as you get your shoes.*

She: *Hey, I'm not the one who ran up $3000 on the VISA just to reupholster that damn Corvette which you'll never drive anyway 'cause you can't get it out of the garage cause there's so much of your crap blocking it in.*

He: *OK. Look, tell you what I'll do. I'll earn the money. I'll keep track of the money. You spend the money. And bounce the checks. That sound fair?*

She: *Go to hell.*

Sound familiar? A conversation begins, takes a wrong turn based on a tone of voice, a look or an assumption, and then quickly descends into relationship hell. Most couples at one point or another exhibit the same lack of grace. This interchange is a composite of many real-life situations we have seen. If the source of the disconnection isn't addressed and handled, irreparable damage can take place. If these two truly love each other, are committed to each other, and believe that a better way is possible for them, then they may soon seek help. A common place to turn is to a relationship coach.

In this interchange there are several opportunities to change the direction of the conversation, which each partner might realize in retrospect. Yet the reality of the moment was a downward spiral into oblivion, characterized by a lack of awareness of each person ("What am I saying?") and a lack of empowerment to change the course ("What do I really want to be saying instead?").

Ending up in the "wrong conversation" happens when defensiveness sets in, often unconsciously, and a wounded ego overtakes the heart. Typically one person feels threatened or vulnerable and then heads down a dead-end tunnel that leads away from the one partner they love. They stand at an intersection where most of the road signs point "Away from Love" or "To Disconnection." Suddenly, both people become more interested in being right, in vindicating their wounded feelings, than being in relationship. This shift happens, subtly or obviously, in almost every relationship. The idea is not to stop it, but to learn how to climb out of it quickly. What coaching makes available is awareness, new choices, and the restoration of true connection. Coaching makes it easier for people to read the road signs and quickly find the path back to each other.

When our clients learn how easy it is to wind up in the wrong conversation, they get motivated to "self-referee" future discussions. Looking back at the dialog between this couple, we see that his opening remark was laden with resentment, blame and anger. She picked up on that and immediately answered in a cautious and defensive way. Later she returned his attack, and a mud-slinging match ensued, without hope of any reconnection or caring partnership in sight.

However, if both had felt empowered to take charge of the direction of the conversation, either one could have "blown the whistle," called a time-out and requested a different way of relating. Fully empowered, he might also have chosen an entirely different conversation opener, like, "I want to work something out with you, can I have your attention for a few minutes?" or, "I'm feeling frustrated with something right now, and need your partnership to work it out." He would have realized, before speaking, that she was probably upset about bouncing a check also. Therefore, he could have chosen to work with her toward a better solution for the future. Instead, he heaped blame on her for an unchangeable mistake from the past, (probably built up over time from other bounced checks) and made an unfortunate situation worse by his misguided attempt to alleviate his own frustration by shaming her. Knowing that the issue was one laden with history, he could have opened it with compassion and genuine openness to her. Instead he marched out into a minefield wearing big shoes.

The point is that, with self-awareness on his part, the conversation could have been an entirely different one. If both people in the relationship practiced a higher level of self-awareness, and lovingly supported each other to maintain that awareness, the check bouncing would inevitably stop.

We'll take a look at how else they might have handled their

situation. First, however, let's see what might happen for this couple if they choose to enter coaching.

Relationship Coaching

There are a thousand good starting points for relationship coaching, and ways to set up a professional alliance that will support a couple in learning new skills.

People come to us because they sense that more is possible for their relationships, and they are ready to explore new ways of relating that feel better for both of them. After an initial meeting, where they each have an opportunity to talk about what they want to accomplish or change, we give them some tools, including our Love 101 Assessment and ask them to take a close, honest look at their relationship. Given that the assessment tools cover key areas of the relationship, we discover fertile areas for discussion right off the bat.

In the case of the couple discussing the bounced check, developing some additional relationship skills would be useful to them. It is important, in cases like this, to start with what is working well between them, acknowledge that, and help them remember why they fell in love with each other in the first place. In the coaching process couples are asked direct and powerful questions in order to loosen the logjam of frustrated feelings that block the of love between them, like, "Explain to me what drew you to her?" or "What makes you want to stay with this guy?"

These kinds of questions restore the motivation to move forward in other, more difficult areas of the relationship. We've found it essential to remember to challenge them to create a vision of what each category would look like if things were working well. In this case, the question leading to that vision would be something like: "How would you have preferred to interact about shoes and money?"

A question like that allows for a "freeze frame" analysis of a situation that happens quickly in the ongoing movie of people's lives. It asks both people to become conscious about something that might otherwise remain unconscious between them. When they've developed an answer, it gives them more power to control the outcome of future scenarios. Let's take a look at what might happen the next time shoes and money comes up, say, as they're walking down a street near some stores. We recommend you skip the comments in the dialog the first time through, then re-read it including the comments, which are in italics.

He: *... and then at the end of the speech, just before his big closing argument, this guy in the front row stands up and...*

She: *Hey, look at those.*

He: *What? Oh, another pair of shoes?*

She: *I don't have any like these. And I need something to go with that new green dress.*

He: *You're telling me that of the 15, wait...20...of the 30s pairs of shoes you own, you don't have a single pair that will go with a green dress.*

She: *Not in that style. Not with heels like those.*

This is a critical point in the conversation. She chose to answer him factually. The topic is triggering some emotions for him. Is he going to go into his knee-jerk habit of complaining about money? Or will he act consciously and choose a higher path for the conversation that might lead to a better connection between them? Fortunately, he made a commitment to his coach that the next time the shoe/money issue came up, he would choose a conscious, loving way to respond. And he knows his coach is going to ask about it, the next time they meet. So here's what he says:

He :   *(Gently teasing) Ah, of course. Heels like those. Well, there you go.*

She :   *You can't tell the difference.*

He :   *Well, no, actually I can't. Should I?*

She :   *Well, if you were a sensitive 90's kind of guy...*

She's trying to return his teasing, and you can hear that there is still some strain behind her words. He chooses not to take her comment in a negative way.

He: *Right.*
She: *Listen, if you don't want me to get the shoes...*

She's remembering the larger issue, and starting to look for a path that honors him too.

He: *No, if you feel like you need them...I mean, I don't want to tell you what you should or shouldn't buy.*
She: *But...?*

Here's an important turning point in the conversation. She just invited him to speak truthfully to her. Now the larger context of their coaching comes into play in the decision of the moment:

He: *It does seem like you have a lot of shoes and I'm feeling like our money's tight these days. So I guess it's not really about the shoes for me. I guess it's my fear around money that is resisting the shoes.*
She: *Well, resistance is futile. But I get it. And I don't need the shoes. I like them, but not enough for us to get worked up over them.*
He: *Thanks.*

You see in this role play that some major shifts have happened in the way they are relating. In the earlier example they had been arguing to hurt, coming from a win-lose frame of mind, and holding on to past anger. In this instance, he chose to listen to her first, rather than react, and they spoke respectfully in a way that allowed them to reconnect with each other and take a step forward in resolving the larger issue between them. In this example the coach was invisibly present as the "referee" in the situation, a role which is ultimately transferred to each partner.

During each coaching session the coach holds up a magnifying glass to interactions that individuals bring up, supporting them to look closely and discover what might have been overlooked. Throughout the process, we look for and emphasize positive things each person is doing, ask each one how the changes feel, and challenge them both to keep carrying their learning forward into "real life."

Every session ends with an invitation to action for the following week. It may sound something like: "This week will you work out a signal that let's the other person know your buttons are being pushed, and you're headed for another argument?" "Do you promise to use that signal as soon as you realize your buttons are being pushed?" and, "How will you respond to your partner when you get the signal?"

If the couple makes progress during the week, we celebrate it with them, and choose another relationship area to look at the following week. If they don't make progress or honor their commitments to the coach, it is a signal that they may need other professional assistance, such as a therapist, mediator, or an accountant.

After they have worked in several categories they will have improved the ways that they relate. Harmony and balance will be restored, and they will feel renewed passion for each other and for their relationship. Then the real fun of relationship coaching begins!

How could the shoe/money conversation become even more fun? We might use a question like, "What is the most enjoyable way you could imagine relating to each other around shoes and money?" This question stretches their imagination. No longer are they working on restoring trust and functionality. Instead, they're working to co-design a relationship that is extraordinary, that goes to the highest limits of their expectations and beyond.

Once they are fully engaged in this conversation with each

other, and are both highly conscious about the higher values they want to honor when shoes/money comes up again, each of them can come from a totally empowered place when the topic comes up again. Let's listen again to a conversation in front of a shoe store:

She: *Nice shoes.*
He: *You like those shoes?*
She: *I like the shoes.*
He: *You want the shoes?*
She: *The shoes would be nice.*
He: *So, what is it about the shoes?*
She: *Those shoes?*
He: *Well, shoes in general.*
She: *You know how you feel when you've just had the car cleaned?*
He: *Yeah?*
She: *It's the same thing with the shoes. I feel a little down, I spend a little money, and I get new feet. That gives me a whole new perspective a kind of temporary relief when I need it.*
He: *Got it. Well, I don't want you to feel down. You want to get the shoes?*
She: *Can we afford the shoes?*
He: *Depends. (Smiling) How do you feel about eating for the rest of the week?*
She: *Don't like the shoes that much!*

Notice a difference? Let's analyze what just happened. This area, which used to be a sore spot between them, has now become filled with lightness and fun. At no point in this conversation was the loving bond between them broken, or even challenged. Instead of reacting to past frustrations, he chose to use the opportunity to learn more about her ("What is it about shoes?"). In turn, she chose to respond by comparing her experience to his in a way that conveyed to him that she understood and related to him. She also was able to communicate her deeper motivations for wanting to buy shoes — a level of conversation which was completely un-available to them in the first dialog in this chapter.

Learning about her, he was able to appreciate and feel his love for her in that moment, and he was therefore able to address her deeper concerns (she was "feeling down"). His gesture of magna-nimity allowed her to address his deeper concerns (finances) which in turn gave him the extra boost to be playful in his next response. Their conscious commitment to making an "awesome" interaction together created a sparkling kind of energy between them. By each listening to each other, and by honoring the other person as more important than their attachments to things (shoes) or control (money), they created a positive flow of love between them that made the moment fun and joyous for both of them. All that in a short and snappy conversation!

Looking at a broader perspective, we as coaches might chal-lenge the couple to create an "Argument Free Zone" in their lives, and to live in such a proactive way that they will put potential conflicts a mile off, and find the fun and joyful path around trouble. The coach can request that they completely shift their way of think-ing, so that disagreement no longer represents a situation where they need to be "right" to feel good about themselves. Instead, they see disagreements as an opportunity to learn from the differ-ent perspective of a person they love and admire.

Does this sound totally unrealistic? For many couples it does, especially if the requests are made too early in the coaching pro-cess. However, just as in every other aspect of modern life, the main thing that limits people is their perception of what's pos-sible. If the coach gently and persistently stretches the imagina-tion, the clients will steadily move into ever more satisfying ways of relating to each other. And, of course, the effects spill over into every other arena of their lives.

In the remainder of this chapter we're going to join another couple's conversations in two key areas of relationship (Self-Care and Magic). Then we'll describe our view of relationships and how to break out of old patterns. After that, we'll explore the profound opportunity that relationships present for personal growth and evolution. Finally, we'll offer our perspective on where relationship coaching is heading in the future.

Self-Care In Relationships

Another key area that has a powerful effect on relationships is "self-care," or how well each person looks after their own responsibilities, needs and desires. In all types of personal coaching the theme of "extreme self-care" often becomes an important one. When the individual pays close attention to his/her own needs, and practices providing for her own happiness in greater detail, his/her ability to be in an exceptional relationship grows with it. As we learn to treat ourselves better, we can offer more to those with whom we are in relationship. Self-care is a prerequisite for mutual care.

Therefore, a large part of the coaching relationship explores the way the client treats him or her self. Working with an individual, the coach works for the well-being and happiness of the client. Working with a couple, the coach encourages the well-being of the relationship, and the happiness of each person in it.

This next couple is just coming home from a party:

He: *Well I'm glad that's over. I hate those department parties.*
She: *You didn't say anything about how my dress looked.*
He: *What do you want me to say? Looks fine.*
She: *Well, I know you wanted to impress your boss.*
He: *I didn't say that.*
She: *Well, why have I been on this diet, then?*
He: *Look, you're the one who's always complaining about your hips.*
She: *You're my husband. I want you to be proud of me.*
He: *I am proud of you. You're doing great. Maybe five more pounds and you'll be a knockout.*

Painful, isn't it? She's caught up in looking good for the sake of her husband, and for impressing his boss. He has some opinions about her level of self-care that can't be concealed behind encouraging language.

Coaching self-care in relationships offers a fast elevator to a new level of learning. Rather than dwelling on "why it isn't working," the coach goes quickly to "What does it mean to each of you to take incredibly good care of yourself?" The answer to that question yields a set of goals that can be easily translated into daily habits, and which can be worked into the structure of each client's life. As each person focuses on his or her own responsibility for self-care, the dynamic begins to change. Here's a snapshot of what the relationship might look like when both people are being fully responsible for meeting their own needs:

She:	*'Bye hon. See you in an hour. I'm going for a run.*
He:	*In the rain?*
She:	*Yeah....*
He:	*It's pouring out. Stay home. Cuddle. Be with me.*
She:	*I'll feel like a slug all day if I don't go.*
He:	*I'd really like it if you stayed here. With me. I'll make it worth your while...*
She:	*That'll be my motivation. Coming back to you, feeling great.*
He:	*(Joking) You're gonna come back feeling like a drowned rat!*
She:	*But my inner rat will be oh, so happy.*

Isn't this a happier scene? She's standing up for her desire to be and feel healthy, in spite of his attempts to persuade her to stay home. Clearly, she's not doing this for him, or his boss, or anyone else but herself. He's standing up for his desire to be physically affectionate with her, and persists. Their two desires aren't in perfect synch with each other, but they are all fully expressed. It's easy to see the next scene in this encounter turn into one where she comes home to a cup of hot tea and a big towel, and he gets all the affection he wanted as soon as she's ready for it.

Once both people have made the shift where they accept full responsibility for themselves, they get a renewed sense of independence and self-esteem. And the foundation for awesome relationships are healthy, responsible people.

There is still a higher level for couples, reachable through coaching, where two fully functional, independent people choose to consciously support each other in their development process. Let's take a look at what that might look like in the physical health category. He comes home while she is working:

He: *Hey, guess what!*
She: *What?*
He: *I just signed up for a massage.*
She: *All right! What made you change your mind?*
He: *Well, you always come home so relaxed and loose. And I thought maybe I could use a little distance between my ears and my shoulders (grinning).*
She: *You'll love it.*
He: *Thing is ... Paula only had room at three on Thursday.*
She: *That's ok, Hon, I'll get off early and pick up the kids.*
He: *You sure?*
She: *Absolutely. It'll be worth it. Having you come home relaxed and happy will be great for both of us.*

She knows what kind of a difference a massage will make for him, understands how it fits into his growing awareness of self-care, and makes an effortless accommodation to support him in his process. Can you imagine how much sweeter life feels for this couple that used to focus on how she impressed the boss and those five extra pounds? Genuine consideration and accommodation become a delight when each partner understands and trusts the other's process of self-improvement. Gifts given to each other (like picking up the kids) feel like investments in the relationship when that trust is in place, rather than withdrawals from what energy one person has available.

Magic

In general, the people we work with already have wonderful qualities present in their relationships — some are obscured by issues such as money management or a lack of prowess in handling disagreements — but behind all that there is some degree of "magic." Cultivating that magic is the arena we play in when a couple has realized a level of harmony in their relationships that gives them a foundation to look for what else is out there.

Magic is the most fun place to coach a couple. The eleven points in that category give some of the secret ingredients that can elevate the experiences of ordinary couples to new heights, providing a way of being together that is continually fresh and invigorating, even enchanted. As other areas of the relationship grow, more and more magic also begins to appear spontaneously. Here is another example of a conversation between committed partners:

He: *Where do you want to eat?*
She: *I don't know, where do you want to eat?*
He: *Wherever you want is fine.*
She: *I don't care.*
He: *What are you in the mood for?*
She: *I don't know. Whatever.*
He: *Well, I really don't care. You choose.*
She: *I don't know.*
He: *Well, just pick a place. I'll eat anywhere.*
She: *Let's go to Sweetwater's.*
He: *I don't want to go there. We always eat there.*
She: *Well, where do you want to go?*
He: *I don't care. Wherever.*

Can you feel the pulse of magic in this situation? No? Many couples experience boredom, predictability, ambivalence and apathy on a regular basis. Other couples worry that if they let go of the "drama" in their relationships, boredom will settle in. However, beyond drama and beyond boredom lie vast and wonderful opportunities for relating.

In the coaching process, both people learn to be more truly guided by their hearts, have more faith in their intuition, and become more aware of what they are learning from their experience. As this happens they may feel a new and profound level of peacefulness, and have glimpses of the limitlessness of life's opportunities. Life becomes more *Graceful*. When two people are both "in the flow" like that, "coincidences" start to become more common and an element of surprise is born. For example, she is returning home:

She: *Hi Hon, how was your day?*

He: *Fine. Except I think I tweaked my neck. Could you work on it a bit?*

She: *I'll do you one better. I just traded Betsy yoga lessons for massage. She's on her way over right now to give me my first one. It's all yours.*

He: *(pause) I would kiss your feet ... except I can't bend down that far.*

She: *That's okay. And after your massage I'm taking you out for seafood. I've been craving lobster all day.*

He: *Sorry, hon, we can't leave .*

She: *Why not?*

He: *Well, there ought to be someone home when the lobsters I just ordered get delivered.*

She: *(Pause) You are a god.*

He: *So I'm told...*

Is it possible to be in a relationship where such serendipity and synchronicity are common? Where life is a continual adventure? Certainly! Though they are still rare, there are examples of such wonderful levels of connection between lovers in every city on the planet.

The experience of these couples is the best evidence that humans have unlimited, untapped potential for expansion and discovery in their significant relationships, and an important reason that relationship coaching will continue to grow. The "high end" of relationships is not a static, finite place; the better a relationship gets, the more possibilities emerge. And this way of being is ultimately accessible to anyone and everyone.

Coaching Relationships

Every relationship represents a journey inward, to a deeper and clearer understanding of who you are, and outward to the discovery and ultimate acceptance of the realities presented by another person. At its best, intimacy is an opportunity for giving, receiving and learning with mind, heart, and body. On the other side, intimate relationships can lead to suffering, pain, and disappointment.

For fear of such results, people often stop themselves from being fully available to their partners and therefore to their own growth. A coach stands by clients through the joyful and sometimes difficult processes of claiming full responsibility for the success of their most significant relationship and consciously choosing to create love.

Think about this: What do we do when we love something, like a sport, or an art form or an intellectual discipline? We read about it, we look for it, we find out who's who, and what is happening in the field, etc. All of those actions represent paying attention. Attention is the currency of love; when we love something, or someone, we give our attention to it.

When coaching an individual, we create a safe environment where the client is expected to pay close attention to his/herself, and to the voice of his/her own heart. Coaching, therefore, means inviting a client to practice loving his/herself, and to exercise that muscle frequently on her own. In other words, coaching is one-on-one training for people to love and accept themselves fully.

Self-love is not conceit or ego-based arrogance. It is a deep acceptance and appreciation of who the person is. It is validating oneself from the inside out, not waiting for validation and acceptance from other. It means tending to one's own needs in a highly responsible way, and by doing so, storing up internal reserves so that there is more available to others. In our experience, it is also the only solid foundation for building highly functional relationships with others.

Who needs relationship coaching? No one, really. Some couples may need therapy for deep seated, emotional issues, but that's very different from the purview of coaching. Coaching is based on the desire for something better, not the need for survival. It's about moving from acceptable to awesome, not from awful to acceptable. Who hires coaches then? People who are doing reasonably well, and have the sense that they want something even better than what they already have, and realize that the support of an objective, trained professional will get them what they want much more quickly.

Relationship coaching is about the future, and about making it the best it can be. It is not about diagnosing problems or faults, but about celebrating strengths and quickly getting whatever information, skills and awareness is missing.

The coaching relationship fully engages both individuals in the process and in the outcome. Since they have co-designed the vision and have said what it is that they most want, they are personally invested in the results. Whatever the intention of the couple is, the benefits of a coach are substantial, including heightened awareness, increased articulation, better skills, and personal empowerment in the context of one's relationship to another. As a three-legged table is more stable than a two-legged one, so a relationship evolves more easily with the support of a coach.

Breaking Out Of Old Patterns

The popular stigma that "something must be wrong with me in order for me to seek professional help" presents a challenge for coaches, who seek to catalyze the movement from good to awesome. Those who seek professional assistance for an acute "need" they are feeling are often far beyond the "coachable" phase in their relationship; they are "needing" some intensive therapy or perhaps a good attorney. It is important to realize that the best time to hire a coach is when everything is going fine in your life. A small, yet growing percentage of the population is currently completely receptive to that idea.

Second-time singles are often more open to relationship coaching (and ready for it) than their counterparts already in a relationship. They know what it's like to have loved and lost, and therefore have more incentive to learn the skills, tools, and lessons that they need in order to operate in a mutually satisfying relationship.

We've run across some common challenges in our relationship coaching. Prominent among them are the client's limiting beliefs ("It isn't possible to be in a relationship and be respected," "I can't be loved and appreciated by a man," "I have to give up my freedom to be in relationship with someone," "Relationships just don't get any better than this, so there's no point in rocking the boat," and the list goes on and the violins play…). Whenever one of these emerges, we identify it and request that the client consciously replaces it with a more empowering one ("I can be fully loved and respected for who I am," "I can be appreciated fully and I am lovable," "I can be in a relationship and be myself," "What we have is good, and we can also have awesome if we want it," etc.). When the client takes action based on these new beliefs, the results usually reinforce the new way of thinking. In other words, "acting as if" something were so tends to make it so.

People get into patterns of relationships in their lives, whether or not they realize it. How people interact in their romantic relationships is often how they interrelate with others, only more intensely. There is so much history that comes into the present when people enter into romantic relationships, and the intensity of this is offset only when the individuals are doing their own personal development work. They have a choice to be conscious of their own patterns and managing them, or to be unconscious of their patterns and controlled by them.

It is not easy for most people to stay fully conscious in a relationship all of the time. It's easy to slip back into conditioned reactions and traditional solutions. Through coaching, people are able to move toward fully conscious living. As coaches, we journey with our clients into areas where they were afraid to go before because of a lack of knowledge. In ever widening circles, clients expand from what they already knew to what they didn't know (but sensed they needed to learn), and then into what they couldn't even have imagined was possible.

Relationships As A Playground For Learning

One reason people are attracted into relationships is that, at a deeper level, they recognize in the other person something they desire more of for themselves. We seek relationships as a way to understand ourselves better, and as a context for our own growth and happiness. The more a person tends to his or her own growth and development, the greater the possibility for true happiness becomes. Those who work on themselves naturally bring a more responsible individual into their relationships.

Relationship coaching can be a powerful vehicle for the process of life-long learning. A relationship coach can ask questions which require the client to step back and see the bigger picture of their whole life, and what today's chapter represents to them. For example, "As a learning experience, how is this situation perfect for what you need to learn right now?" Or, "In what ways is your partner serving as a valuable teacher to you?"

As each person begins to honor their partner as a teacher, a profound shift takes place. Your relationship will bring you all you need to learn. You can suffer because of it or thrive, the choice is yours. You can learn quickly and easily based on fully open communication and careful attention to yourself and your partner. Or you can wait until new learning hits you over the head like a frying pan. The choice is yours.

Relationship coach Ed Shea says, "Couples fall in love, then they fall into hell. That's how you know you're with the right person."

Differences attract, and then they often lead to criticism. Ed says all criticism of other people is ultimately based on self-criticism. When a person learns to accept his or her partner fully for who they are, they let go of criticism for their partner and they also ultimately release themselves from the stranglehold of self-criticism. As we learn to accept others, we heal ourselves. So Ed asks his clients to find the little pieces of heaven in every situation. In so doing, they discover the reason they were attracted to each other in the first place—and what they were unconsciously hoping to learn.

As coaches, we train people in what we call "the habits of intentional love." In a nutshell, it involves two steps: 1) get fully in touch with who you are and what you need so that you can 2) educate and inform the other person how to interact with you in a way that brings out the best of who you are (not the worst). When both people do this, and consciously provide their partners with what their partner wants ("The Platinum Rule" of relationships), then the whole character of the relationship alters. Ultimately, when people view the relationship as the icing on the cake of life (and not the cake itself), the fireworks that two people saw when they first fell in love magically reappear. The burden is off the relationship to improve the person's life and each accepts the other fully for who they really are.

The Future Of Relationship Coaching

If we look at the trend in health consciousness over the past 20 years, we may see important parallels to the future of relationships. People have learned how diet, exercise and relaxation are important to their health, and consultants have emerged in all three fields. Although the old model (based on bacon, sedentary lifestyle and eventual angioplasty) is still alive and well, today we have other options for health. Now people face health choices that were not available before. People have more information, are educating themselves, and possess a genuine willingness and desire to be on a path of personal health.

The same trends seem to be emerging in relationships. Because exceptional relationships are emerging in our chaotic and quickly changing times, the road is being paved for others to follow. We have more information, more resources for learning, and more desire go beyond where we may have stopped in the past. Just as health care is moving to a wellness model, so will relationship care move to a coaching model. We live in exciting times!

Relationship coaching is a field that was born to solve a problem. Far more is possible in relationships than most people experience, and people are becoming aware of that discrepancy. In the complex arena of modern relationships, people perceive that a better way of relating is possible for themselves, but often lack the specific knowledge, role-models, resources, support and/or community to create the relationship they want. Others lack awareness that an improved quality of relating is possible, and continue to live their lives in quiet desperation. Either way, there is a great deal of dissatisfaction with primary relationships, and people feel stuck in undesirable ones or stuck outside of a relationship with limited prospects.

Excellent maps for healthy relationships are becoming more widely available through role models and books (see recommended reading list, below). Translating the information from the map to the road, however, is not a given. There is a big gap between understanding intellectually and realizing in one's day-to-day life. A coach guides the client as they navigate questions like: "Where am I going?", "Is there a safe detour?", and "How do I get from where I am to where I want to be?".

Relationship coaching is new, vibrant and sexy. As popular consciousness realizes that a new choice is available, that there is a great opportunity for proactive relationship health, the choice will be an obvious one for many people. They will want to evolve.

Elizabeth Carrington, PCC, can be reached at (415)331-1480 or e-mail: elizabeth@carringcoach.com. Damian Nash at (435) 259-1715 or e-mail: damian@lasal.net. The Intentional Love Newsletter is a free, weekly e-mail publication of Love University. Visit us at http://www.loveu.com.

Recommended Reading:

Deida, David: *The Way of the Superior Man.* (NY: Plexus, 1997).

Ellenberg, Daniel and Judith Bell: *Lovers for Life.* (Fairfield, CT: Aslan, 1995).

Gorski, Terrence: *Getting Love Right.* (NY: Fireside, 1993).

Gray, John: *Mars and Venus in Love.* (NY: Harper, 1999).

Gray, John: *Men are From Mars, Women are From Venus.* (NY: Harper Collins, 1992).

Hendricks, Gay and Kathlyn: *The Conscious Heart.* (NY: Bantam, 1997).

Hendricks, Gay and Kathlyn: *Conscious Loving.* (NY: Bantam, 1990).

Hendrix, Harville: *Getting the Love You Want: A Guide for Couples.* (NY: Harper Perennial, 1988).

Hendrix, Harville: *Keeping the Love You Find: A Guide for Singles.* (NY: Pocket Books, 1992).

Lerner, Harriet Goldhor: *The Dance of Intimacy.* (NY: Harper and Row, 1989).

Levine, Stephen and Andrea: *Embracing the Beloved.* (NY: Anchor Books, 1996).

Louden, Jennifer: *The Couple's Comfort Book.* (NY: Harper, 1994).

McCann, Eileen: *The Two Step: The Dance Toward Intimacy.* (NY: Grove/Atlantic, 1985).

COACHING FROM A SPIRITUAL PERSPECTIVE

Sharon Wilson

My Story

My coaching practice emerged as part of an incredible journey which began when I was born. As a child I questioned everything, and seemed to be very unsatisfied with the answers people stumbled over as I talked about seeing angels and hearing voices. My questions and observations made people uncomfortable. I started to learn that some questions are better left unasked and that some things that we see are better left unseen. That began the journey into denying who I truly am.

One day, shortly after I started kindergarten, I brought a friend home because I wanted to help him with his alphabet. I told my mother, "The other kids laughed at him. But I know he can do it. He just needs someone to believe he can." My mother recalls this incident with tears in her eyes. "I knew even then, that you were going to help people in some big way. You were just born that way."

My journey through childhood into adulthood was beset with personal tragedies and many growth opportunities. Often I looked to the heavens and screamed, "Is this it? This is what we get here?" I couldn't understand what the purpose was. All I saw around me was pain and tragedy, inequality and injustice. I saw others who seemed to have a charmed life. They seemed unaffected by the tragedies and personal problems that plagued me and my family.

When would it be my turn for some of the good? I often prayed, but never really expected to hear anything back. I see now that I never learned how to interpret the heavenly guidance that is always flowing to us. I would see much later in my life that guidance was all around me even then, I just didn't know what to look for.

I left for college to get away from my troubled home situation. At college I found a freedom I hadn't experienced before and my desire to escape all the questions and pain catapulted me into drugs, alcohol and a wild lifestyle. I yearned for a loving relationship to fill the holes I felt deep in my heart and to banish the feeling I was somehow not good enough to be loved. I spiraled deeper into depression and my grades fell. I struggled with what to get my degree in. I was so afraid of going back to my family's unhealthy environment that I would do anything to ensure me a job right out of school. I loved my writing classes, but a professor told me I couldn't make any money as a journalist and although it was my favorite class, I firmly decided I would not be a writer. A little part of me, even then, cried out for me to pay attention to my passion. My heart yearned for me to look at what gave me joy as a compass to a career that would feed my soul and my pocketbook. But my heart was filled with years of fears and beliefs that taught me to see lack and limitation in my life. You are lucky to even have a job, right? You work to pay the bills. I was taught that I should expect to barely make ends meet. I learned my lessons from those who themselves had grown up feeling fear and financial insecurity.

At the prompting of a roommate, I attended a marketing association meeting and was impressed with all of the energy of the people there. They were all so excited about the field, and told me the sky was the limit as far as money was concerned. That was all I needed to hear. I majored in marketing and set upon completing the requirements to graduate. A part of me felt good, as I had made a decision, but another part me knew I was only delaying living who I really was. The part that was making decisions from fear was much louder than the soft, gentle part of me that advised me to look in my heart for what I loved to do. I listened to the loudest part; the part that was mesmerized by the promise of wealth, glamour and power. I felt if I could get enough money, I would feel safe. It was a choice made from fear. And, so I set out in the world of work.

The summer I graduated from college my father committed suicide. He had been drinking heavily and taking anti-depressants; a deadly combination. He had experienced a devastating blow in his professional integrity. He had learned recently that his new wife, for whom he left six children and eighteen years of marriage, was having an affair with someone in his company. He lashed out at her lover in the workplace and was severely reprimanded. This professional insult moved him to think life was not worth living. When I think now about my father's perspective about his life, I see how his heart had failed him long before his physical death.

My parents had divorced just four years earlier. It was a marriage filled with infidelity and mistrust. I learned not to trust men. I suppressed my feelings of anger towards my father and blamed God for my situation. He was far removed from my life and I felt no love from Him. The words I heard at church were stale. I soon stopped going. I felt God had deserted me, and maybe never had been there for me. I felt I wasn't good enough to deserve God's help. If I was, wouldn't he have helped me by now? My motto became, "Expect the worst and hope like hell for the best."

I didn't feel there was anyone I could count on for what I thought I needed most, money and security. Since I had been unsuccessful in getting a rich man in college, I decided I really did have to work in marketing and sales. So I took a job hundreds of miles away from my family and my painful memories. The first week on my new job was awful! After just one day on the job working with another sales representative I came home and wrote in my diary, "This is not IT." I told myself it wasn't great, but I had experienced worse situations and survived. So I stayed in my job. I was promoted very quickly and began to believe this job was who I was. All the while a deep apathy about life was forming. I became distanced from the spiritual, mystical experiences of my childhood. God and religion were put on a permanent shelf in my life. Guilt, however, was kept alive in my heart. I had decided that God was mad at me for not going to church and when I die I was going to hell. For the present, I needed to make sure I could take care of myself. I was creating my own living hell here on this Earth.

I wandered from one destructive relationship to the next, searching for the love that would make me feel whole. Instead, I found a line of men as wounded and filled with self-hatred as I was. Together we made explosive combinations of neediness, power and pain. One night a boyfriend told me he couldn't come over because he had work to do. The sound of his voice immediately told me he was lying. I went to his apartment and found two cars parked in his reserved spots. I waited until morning, when I saw him walk his guest out and embrace her. I was devastated! I felt like I was coming apart at the seams. I knew my life had to change. God and His angels were guiding me as I picked up a phone book and called a counselor. It was the best decision I ever made. Through therapy I began to understand a lot about my anger, and I was able to express the anger and pain I had held in for so long. I began the journey of healing.

I began to sense that I was meant to do something bigger than what I was doing, but what? I felt guided to make a difference in people's lives. I knew deep down in place I couldn't explain that I was here to do something that would make a big impact on others' lives. I would be of service to those here. I longed with all my heart to get out of my job. But how? The universe always provides. Two weeks later I was without a job.

I had plunged off of a high cliff of plenty of resources into financial insecurity, barely making my expenses each month. The hole in me that came out of doing work without passion had resulted in a spending addiction that maxed out my credit cards. I worked with a consumer credit agency and decided that I would get out of this situation. My determination was clear. I would pay off these debts and within five years be making twice what I made at that first job. That was my vision and I would make it happen. When I look back now at the sheer will and determination of my goals, I see how much easier it could have been if I would have teamed up with Higher Sources. I have often wondered why it seems it takes so much pain for us as to wake up to our Spirituality — to the essence of who we really are under this façade. I know now that it doesn't have to be that way. We don't have to lose everything to find ourselves. We have free will. Marianne Williamson says, " Sometimes a nervous breakdown is a spiritual breakthrough." I would see how true that is...

A year later I was already thinking of leaving my new job. I'd become disillusioned with the non-profit world. I saw situations were money was not used wisely and I saw elements like competition, greed, jealousy, and fear of change, just as in the corporate world. I began to see situations where the victims of disasters were seen as fundraising opportunities to prey on the emotions of public. I became more and more dissatisfied, wondering, "Will I ever find a career that fulfills me and provides for me to live comfortably?" My old belief patterns replied, "This is what you get, so just shut up and go along with the rest of the world." Still, I wrestled with this question for years until I finally got the answer I was searching for. But not before I would be a breath away from losing everything I had — including my life.

I continued on the path of fear for a few more years until one day, when nothing made any sense to me anymore. Suddenly, the whole idea of living one more day doing work that prostituted my soul was intolerable. I had married Bob, who was not making much money at that time and had sunk us deep into debt. As a way to buy a home we decided that we would build a large home with an in-law suite and combine our household with my in-laws. I expressed my desire to my husband that we would live on one income, so I could be a stay-at-home mom. I yearned for that day, but saw no real way this would ever happen and it depressed me terribly. I found my husband had been hiding debts that totaled thousands of dollars. The whole budget we had developed was wrong! When I crunched the numbers I saw we would barely have enough to pay for our minimum expenses. I would have to not only keep working in my current job, I needed to make even more money. I was devastated!

That day, as I drove home from work, I remember seeing the beautiful blue sky and white billowy clouds and thinking to myself I wish I could just pouf off this Earth and into the clouds. As I drove, I thought that if I just moved the steering wheel a little bit to the left, I would collide head on with oncoming traffic. I wondered if a head-on collision would live up to the explanation I had heard people use in accidents, "She never saw it coming." At that moment I felt a tremendous charge in my head and I felt very light-headed. The feeling jolted me back to my driving. I decided I wouldn't swerve into the oncoming traffic. "That's a big accomplishment for today," I thought.

The next morning at work I totally fell apart. The pressure of supporting a small family with the sales dollars I generated was taking its toll on me. The pressure finally got to me and I found myself crying hysterically and saying, " I just can't do this anymore. I am so tired. I just have to go." I left early and went to see my therapist from several years earlier. She took one look at me and said, "What happened to you?" After talking a while, she told me I had to leave my job. It was necessary for my mental health. "I can't leave," I sobbed. "We just signed our mortgage papers. Our builder already has broken ground for the foundation in for our new house. There is no going back." She told me that this was not negotiable and that she was very concerned about my emotional well being. She told me something had to give, and if I continued on my current path that it would be my emotional health.

On the drive home from the therapist's office, I noticed how calm the night was. I rolled all my windows down to smell the air and to feel the fall's night coolness. I felt strangely disengaged from my life. I felt no emotion or pain, just numbness. I watched myself tell my husband what the therapist said and heard Bob say gruffly, "Do what you have to do."

"How?" I said. "How can we manage all of this now. How can I leave my job?"

"I don't know." he replied. "But if you have to leave, just quit."

"He knows I will never do that," I fumed silently. "He knows I will just grin and bear it like always. This is just too much. I am done with all of this."

At that moment, I felt the sensation of being in a dark room with walls that began moving towards me making it smaller. I felt like I was suffocating and I knew I couldn't continue like this. I fantasized leaving him and running home to my Mother. But that wouldn't provide the stability and security I needed. Besides, I had vowed I would never go back there to live. Never. I cursed my father for leaving me. If he were here I could go and live with him. I cursed God for creating me and making me live this wretched life.

I wasn't surprised by Bob's response. I had heard this type of answer in the past. There were subtle messages attached to his surface words that went like this: "Do whatever you have to do, Sharon. I won't be doing anything more to help solve this. My parents will bail me out, they always have. They never let me fall. I know you will never let us fall, either. You will do whatever you have to make it all work."

I felt alone and frightened after our conversation, and went to sleep thinking I just wanted out of all of it — the house, the job, the marriage, this Earth — all of it!

A Divine Encounter

Sometime after four o'clock the next morning I awakened with a deep sense of urgency. I felt a sense of communication through my mind and even deeper, through my heart. I was told in this way of communicating to go into the living room. At first I thought, "Am I dreaming this?" But the gentle urging was powerful and loving. I went into the living room and saw and felt beautiful warm light. In that light I was showed my fears as creations. They looked like

me! They told me why I had created them. I kept them alive by
feeding them fear, anger, resentment and disillusionment. When I
understood how they were created, I felt a sense of sadness. They
seemed stuck in this way of being, unless I chose to let them be
different.

I heard a gentle voice say, *"Sharon, it has come to our attention that
you are not fully in this experience of living. You have your foot in both
camps and that is bad form."*

They showed me that I was not living in full energy here on
Earth, yet I had not fully decided to leave this life. This was causing a
problem for me at a deeper level of my being.

The loving voice said, *"You need to decide to either stay here or
leave. What do you decide?"*

I felt confused and I replied, "You have got to be kidding. I am
in emotional hell here. I can't even decide what to have for break-
fast let alone decide if I should leave Earth. Can't you help me
know what to do?"

There seemed to be a pause, almost like a kind of conferring
was going on, and then the loving presence spoke, very carefully.
"We can only say that we would not advise you to leave this way." My
immediate thought was, "Maybe if I leave now I will come back as
a frog or something, and things would be even worse." There seemed
to be a sense of chuckling from the loving essence. I thought, "I
don't really want to leave. I just want peace."

I was overcome with a warm, tingling feeling that spread
throughout my body as the voice spoke again in my mind, *"You
have chosen! And all of Heaven rejoices! You will stay and many Teachers and Masters will come across your path and you will have the peace
you so desire on this Earth! You will have love and harmony in your
marriage, and prosperity in your work. You will do work that you love,
leading many to find their own way to love."*

I was shown things that made no sense to me at the time. I
saw myself talking in front of groups, writing books and working
with others. I said to the presence, "But how will I do any of this?
I don't have any training. Who would pay me to do anything like

this? How can I show others to peace when I am such a mess? Didn't you hear my therapist? I am having a nervous breakdown here."

The loving presence answered, *"You are not alone. All will be shown to you. You will see that trusting is the way. Your life will be the proving ground. For your own sanity, you will not remember this experience is its entirety. Rather you will remember the appropriate information, when your consciousness is able to accept it and the time is right. As you expand your consciousness and remember your truths, you will remember more."*

At that moment I felt a very powerful force, like a huge embrace. All of a sudden everything in my life — every seeming tragedy and personal devastation — made perfect sense. I saw why I had chosen my parents, my friends, the jobs, my husband. And I saw that there were no accidents. Everything was engineered by me, by my soul. I knew that, even as I was immersed in these truths, I was forgetting them.

I seemed to be moving back into the bedroom and back into bed. I looked at the clock. What had felt like days was only fifteen minutes. I felt sleepy, and at the same time I realized that even more information was being somehow given to me. It was an odd feeling. As this knowledge was being presented to me, I understood it in a higher way. I knew these were huge revelations for all of mankind and I struggled to hold onto them. They seemed to be evaporate, like sand slipping through my fingers. I fell into a deep sleep with the thought. *"All will be revealed as it is needed. You are very loved."*

I awoke the next morning a new person. I knew everything would work out. I just *knew* it! My heart was full of hope and love. I never returned to see my therapist, but called her telling her I was totally healed and would not be leaving Earth for awhile. I had work to do. I imagine she must have thought I was in deep denial. How could I be suicidal one day, yet stable and calm the next? It can only be explained as a miracle! God and the angels broke through to me, and I was both confused and excited about the experience. I was not led to tell anyone what happened right away. I knew the time would come when I would share it with many others. But for now, I had to get to work.

Manifestations And Miracles

I would like to be able tell you that after this powerful experience, I opened a coaching practice and began my work. But it took me two more years, and a final work experience that would be my last journey into greed, external power, and fear. I would engineer the most powerful lesson that would finally test every aspect of my personal resolve and integrity. The lesson would be complete and I would know I needed to begin to trust God to find my way and peace.

Within those two years Bob and I experienced many miracles; Bob had found a new career in systems engineering making twice his previous income, I dove into the study of spirituality, metaphysics and new thought. Just three months after my mystical experience, a powerful and loving teacher shown up in my life. Soon I was attending weekly meditation meetings in her home, learning how to un-learn the negativity and old belief patterns. In with a group of like-minded people, I was re-creating myself. We were all called to a beautiful curriculum using our own lives as a case study.

The most incredible miracle was after seven years of trying to conceive I was pregnant. Soon I became very ill with morning sickness. I thought the word "morning sickness" was ironic, as mine lasted all day and night! I was so sick that many times I could not drive. Telling my employer of my concerns, I was met with a supportive and loving attitude, I thought. I was told not to worry. The president of the company assured me that I was valued. One month later I would be out of a job. Fired because I was pregnant! I would finally get the opportunity to let God in my life in a real way.

The only time I had relief from morning sickness was when I

was praying, meditating, or in complete silence. I would spend a lot of time that way during my pregnancy. I began to mediate and to write any thoughts that came to me. I would ask the question, "What do I need to know today?" I would wait until I felt a sense of thoughts pouring in to me. I wrestled with my mind , which argued that this was just my imagination. But the words flowed quickly and eloquently, and spoke to me. I could not dismiss this incredible information. When I asked a question about releasing a fear of something, I thought, am I making all this up? Instantly my pen began writing so fast I could not read it as it wrote, *"Do you really think and write so fast? You can't even read the words because you are writing so fast. Do you really think your mind alone could come up with these words? They don't even sound like you. Know this is the power within you that connects all things. This power is love!"*

I felt waves of warmth up and down my body. At times the words given to me would fill me with tears of joy. I began asking about everything, and began seeing that the answers given to me were always right! Many times the answers counseled letting go of fear and simply trusting. I would ask for help, and I would get a tool, a visualization, a phrase or an action. One time I asked, "There are so many different things I can do, but I can't seem to focus. How can I pay the bills, get out of this current job, and release the fear of not having enough money?"

I was answered almost instantly. *"Your guides have answered. You have asked for a sales angel before and one has been provided to you. Go into each sales situation and ask, 'What is important to this person?' Look deep into their eyes and say silently, 'My brother, I offer you peace, love and wisdom. I have come to provide you a solution to your problems.' Then simply listen. You are a good talker, but you need to listen more. Keep asking in your mind and heart, 'What can I offer you that is important to you, and will bless this Holy Encounter?' Spread love. Hold love in your eyes for all you see, and all will be well with you! You want assurances money will never be a problem? Money will never be a problem if you believe in you and do your own work. You must believe in you. We are pleased at your progress. Don't let your mind tell you that you are stuck. You are not! You are ready to zoom. Trust us! Trust in us and see in the next week what will happen. When things seem gray and dark, light will shine through and make the darkness go away! Affirm your trust and say, I trust completely. God gives all always!'"*

I had begun working with a life work counselor, after I read an article about how to do what makes your heart sing. The article really resonated with me, and I contacted the author. I became immersed in a journey of self-introspection and exploration about what made my own heart sing. Soon after we began working together I found out I was pregnant, and soon after that I lost my job. I had been meditating and praying for an answer to my career woes and my coach and I agreed the universe had provided a way out of my unhealthy job situation. I shared my journal transmissions with my coach, and she appreciated the beauty and power of the messages. I seemed to be led to intuitive insights easily. We talked about my working with her. We agreed this would be a great fit, and I began training under her.

My soul leaped with joy as I began working with clients. I began realizing that I had found my calling! My own way of working that was slowly emerging was a more direct approach. I would let go of each session and ask to be a vehicle for love and light. I was guided through these transmissions to see a white light around each client, and to ask for guidance from the Divine. I would soon be feeling the familiar pouring in of ideas and thoughts. I was guided to offer similar visualizations to release the fears and doubts of my clients. The sessions were incredibly powerful, as I watched clients connect with an energy that we both could feel. I began to sense that something different was happening here than mere visualizations.

But the process I was being trained in left little room for these sacred tools. I found myself wanting to do more spiritual work with my clients, rather than following a pre-determined process of linear thinking. I realized that just as with my sales work, when I fully let go and just asked to be the messenger for God, everything flowed smoothly. When I didn't, I would be overwhelmed with performance anxiety and self-doubt.

When I was eight months pregnant, my coach called me to say that working with me brought up a lot of her own personal issues. She was taking a brief sabbatical. The plans for my continued training were on hold, as were our plans of becoming partners. I heard her words and was surprisingly calm. I wished her love and affirmed she should be free of any fears or doubts. Five minutes after we hung up the phone she called back, a tense tone in her voice. "Sharon," she said, "I am getting the impression that you feel you are ready to do this work for a living. I disagree — you have a lot to learn yet. You aren't ready to do this. You aren't done." This was coming from the one who had bolstered me up and saw in my natural abilities. Now she was telling me she wouldn't work with me and I wasn't ready to do this on my own either! I saw, as I had been directed through my writing, to see light pouring into my head, through my heart and to my coach, surrounding her. I asked in my mind, "God, what will you have me say to her? If I am left to my own words, I'll tell her to go to hell. Who made her judge and jury? What kind of a model is she for this work?"

I felt the warmth of the light as ideas poured in, and I heard myself say softly, "I agree that we are never done learning and growing. You are very loved. Please know that, and take very good care of yourself." I knew I would never work with her again, and I accepted that. My whole world was up in the air, but this time it was OK. The life I was growing inside me was giving birth to a new me. I could feel it and I knew it would all work out beautifully. I had the same feeling I had when the Heavenly Cavalry rushed to my side in the middle of the night, as I had stood on the precipice between life and death.

The very next day I wrote in my journal and through meditation processed the question, "What am I to do next? Show me the highest guidance. I give my life totally to God. What do I do now?" I closed my eyes and felt a powerful surge of feeling. I meant these words. I had tried to run my life on my own, and I had made a mess of it time and time again. I was now ready to prove God really was there for me. I thought of the "Footprints" poem I so loved.

Divine Guidance

I had been complaining to my Divine Helpers for some time. It seemed that the information I received was never specific. Often, it was about what I needed to do to see things in a new way, or to send love to someone. Many times my divine helpers offered an exercise, prayers and affirmations, as a solution to my problem. One time I asked, "Why don't you tell me what to do? Why all the circling around? Can't you just tell me something specific about what I am supposed to do? I want work that supports my spiritual awakening, and I don't want to be poor. How can I achieve both? Why won't you just tell me what to do?"

The answer came back very succinctly. *"Well, Sharon, we could tell you to do this or that, but you would immediately begin saying, that you can't do this because of that, or that won't work because of this. We work with you so that you will uncover for yourself that which is you."*

My divine guides were very specific that day. I got the answers I asked for, and they scared me to death. The transmission was clear. *"Our guidance is that this would be a good time to open a coaching practice. Name it "A Choice for Joy." Name your baby Joy. Dedicate your practice, sweet child, to the Holy Spirit."*

I was told that Spirit, or Holy Spirit, is defined in this approach as the divine energy, love, that connects us all. I was also told that the word divine could be re-worded if that suits an individual. I was told the Spirit doesn't care about semantics, only love.

I was guided to openly acknowledge past mystical experiences that prophesied this work to me, as well as other information I'd received. I was guided to share the struggles and triumphs of my life journey and what I have learned, to help others. I was told to trust, and all information I needed to operate my practice would be given to me. I would teach others, so they could do the work they loved. By releasing their fears and doubts, they would let the Spirit work through them, thus touching thousands and thousands of lives!

I sat stunned, looking at the words my pen had just written. I read them over and over. It was quite clear. Then my head started questioning this guidance. How are am I going to do this? We have a mortgage to pay. I have no credentials to do this work. Who will pay me? How will I get clients? How will I work after the baby is born? It will take at least a year before I'll make any money! Replace my income with this? Am I crazy?

I let it all come out, and began writing in Ego-Spirit dialogue. This is a process my Divine Teachers had given me for a time like this. I let my ego have it's say — all the fears, the doubts, the worries, the moaning and groaning. Then I let Spirit speak to Ego. Spirit was to the point. *"You came here to do this. You agreed to do this, and now you are fulfilling your contract. All will be provided through you, many will benefit. You have all the information within you. It was given to you that night of love, when you decided to stay on Earth and be a servant of the light."*

Tears streamed down my face as I realized the truth of these holy words. I knew that nothing would stand in my way! I was not alone! I would give this fully over to God and I would find my peace through surrendering. I felt butterflies in my stomach. I had a sense of anticipation, and received the now familiar pouring in of ideas and feeling inside my head.

A week later I was helping my beloved teacher, Ruth Lee, pack up her material things for a divinely-guided move to Florida. As we packed, Ruth held out a magazine to me and said, "Sharon, I have been trying to throw this out, but every time I go to throw it out your name keeps popping into my mind. Please take it now." It was a copy of the New Age Journal. I had read the magazine occasionally, but didn't have a subscription. I thanked her and took it home.

That night I was praying and I had the inner prompting, *"Get that New Age Journal."* I retrieved it, and as I had been shown I held the magazine in my hands and asked for the highest guidance to come through. I waited until I felt a tingling or energy in my hands and then prayed for the Holy Spirit to guide me to what I needed to read. I opened the magazine to an article titled, "Create the Life of Your Dreams: Be a Coach!" My heart leaped with excitement.

I knew it was a confirmation of the path that had been laid out for me. I read with eager interest about the organization that offered training in coaching. As I read about Coach University's program, I felt deeply connected. I read that of all of the coaching programs, Coach University has the strongest spiritual and metaphysical underpinnings. I wrote the question in my journal, "Is it the highest guidance for me to attend this program? It is a large investment of resources." I got back, *"Yes, We see this would be helpful. We will tell you that you will go there and be a great success but you will see you are going there for a reason that has almost nothing to do with Coach University."*

I would soon see how on target my Divine Guidance was. I could never have imagined or willed the grand path that would emerge as I walked in trust.

I told my husband the whole story and asked his advice. He had become a very loving and supportive partner, and I respected his perception. Bob has great guidance about other people and I trusted his views. He is a man of few words, and he said very simply, "Well it's about time you figured it out."

"What do you mean?" I asked him.

"You have been working like a dog for years, putting your heart and soul into companies that have no heart and soul. You've been giving away your most precious gift, yourself. Even when angels came down and told you to do this work, you still didn't listen. No, you spent more years letting others drain your creativity and passion. You have known all your life what you love to do. But you have been too afraid to believe in yourself, too afraid that the money wouldn't show up, never fully trusting God, not listening to all the prompting you keep getting. Well, I think you are finally getting it. This is great! Do whatever you need to do. I know this time you will finally find peace and joy in your work of making a difference in others' lives. Just do it!"

I sat dumbfounded as I listened to his words. He was so right! And again I felt the now familiar sense of peace and calm. My baby was due in a month, and I knew I was giving birth to a whole new life for Bob, our baby, and me. Joy was a serene and peaceful looking baby. Strangers commented about her deep, thoughtful blue eyes. Many people said there was something about her that created a sense of calmness. I knew all that time in meditation and prayer had produced another miracle.

The sickness that held on to the eighth month of pregnancy had vanished. When I asked in my journaling why this happened, I was told I had been purging all the negativity from my years of drug and alcohol abuse. I had rid myself of the toxic years of worry, anger, resentment, judgment and negative belief patterns toward myself and others. (I felt like I had purged enough for the whole human race.) My divine guides thought that was funny, and told me I was purging myself of the belief in being human. I was told, *"You are a spiritual being first. This is all that matters. Life on Earth needn't be so hard. If you realize this, you can purge your mind of the negative energy of the collective mind."*

They assured me it was a process, and I was working through it.

A month after Joy was born, people began showing up in my life to be coached. This was a result of inner directives I was given through Divine Guidance. I was told to create an inner temple in my mind, a place that felt lavish. Before I envisioned myself going through the gates, I was to throw away any worries, cares, and concerns into a fire pit. I watched them transformed into something beautiful, like butterflies. The place to dispose of them may change, I was told, but this was a very important step in the process. I was told my mind would see I had no problems, and I was fully giving myself over to God. I was told to call in any ascended

Masters that fit my belief system, and to call in angels. I was told to ask for guidance on the days events and other situations. I would get information in many ways, I was told, through thoughts and being "downloaded" information. Soon I would be able to go into the temple, and would get guidance there. I was advised that, in the beginning it would be good to write in my journal after my visit to the temple. The phenomenal results I experienced in my practice came from these efforts! There is no other explanation.

Through Divine Guidance I was learning to create an inner temple in my mind where I could go whenever I felt the need to commune with my Divine Helpers and receive practical information on any aspect of my life. This one tool has been powerful in my life. My previous work included business planning, marketing and sales. The business person in me would have immediately created a business plan to develop my practice. When I decided to follow the guidance to open a coaching practice, my guidance was to go into my inner temple each day and fully surrender all my worries, cares, and anxieties about any specific situation. I was told in that way my mind would see I had no problems I was responsible for solving. I would still do things toward the resolution, but I would do only what I was divinely guided to do.

One day I asked how I would get clients. Where would I look for them? The marketer in me said I needed to have a plan, but my own inner guidance said it was more important and more powerful to do spiritual marketing on the inner planes of reality. There I would call to me those students and clients who would be best served by our meeting. I found this really hard to understand so I asked more questions about it. I was told they would show me what they meant. So I was asked to think of something I would like to manifest, something I loved. I thought for a moment and said, 'OK, I love grapes, I would love to manifest some grapes. Before the thought was complete in my mind I saw platters and platters of grapes! I said to my angels, "This is incredible!" They replied, *"In the inner planes, thoughts manifest instantly. All you had to do was think of it. On your plane, it seems to take more time. Go now and fully understand the lesson today."*

I left my inner temple and came back to full awareness. Then I heard my father-in-law calling for me. When I went to see what he wanted, I was dumfounded. There in my kitchen was a huge grocery bag filled with grapes. Grapes of all kinds!

"What is this?" I stammered.

"Well," he said, "I was at the store and suddenly you popped into my mind when I saw this sign for a sale on grapes." He said the thought suddenly came to him that Sharon loves grapes and I should get her some! He said he felt a very strong sense to get me a variety of grapes. I smiled, as I fully understood my lesson.

Each day I was given more information on tools to work with clients. I was using them for me and my growing number of clients. I was told that at each session I should light a white candle and say some centering prayers affirming the session was led by the Spirit. I was given tools to attract clients by using thought energy. I kept asking and trusting, and did as I was directed. I was told to say, when asked what I do, "I help people unlearn negativity using spiritual, metaphysical and energy methods. I guide people to truly listen and trust their inner guidance to create a life of their dreams." Within three months I was coaching 30 paying clients. After just three months of attending classes at Coach University I began receiving phone calls from other coaches who had heard me talk about my coaching practice.

I spoke in my classes about tools I used with my clients, based on the meditation and journaling method I was given. I told about one client who, after just two months into our coaching relationship, received clear guidance about a new career. Another was told she would be pregnant soon, after trying for many months. She asked her Divine Guides if she should pursue fertility treatments, and was advised it was not necessary. A few months later she called me and said she received guidance she was pregnant. She fretted over the implication if this was not true. "It would mean that I can't trust anything I have gotten through this process, if I am not pregnant." I was guided to tell her not to worry, her guidance is not wrong. I was not surprised when she called and tearfully exclaimed, I'm pregnant! My guidance was right!

Coaching from Spirit

After my Coach University classes, other students would call me, asking if I could teach them what I do. Many said they had a coach themselves, but their coach wasn't able to help them with specific tools to coach in this way. I asked for guidance on this one day as I was receiving more and more calls from coaches. I got back, *"There is a process. It is called Coaching From Spirit."* I felt such a desire to help these coaches and I knew I could help them in a bigger way than just personal coaching with me. I asked, "Please say more." The pen wrote, *"Patience is a virtue!"* I would soon see that those words were prophetic for me and many others.

Four months after I started coaching, I attended a health and wellness exposition. Many speakers on wellness and spirituality were to be there. Two years earlier, I had attended the show and had synchronistically met someone who led me to my teacher Ruth Lee. As I looked at the program, I noticed a speaker I had seen advertised in previous years, Dr. Doreen Virtue (and yes, that really is her name). She was billed as a Manifestation Expert.

I had considered going to Dr. Virtue's workshop when I first saw the program, but a call changed all that. A friend called to tell me that if I wished to, I could share a vendors' booth with him and three other companies at a fraction of the cost of a whole booth. I asked my Divine Helpers and they agreed that this would be a great way to get the word out about my coaching practice. As vendors we had to agree to be at the booth the whole time, and I wouldn't be able to attend any of the workshops. I mentally filed the idea of going to a workshop with Dr. Virtue. Even then, the angels were working to get us together, and they would be successful!

The expo was really crowded, and I had been guided to make flyers about my practice. I spoke with many people and made several appointments for coaching sessions. As the expo was drawing to a close, I saw a beautiful cherub-faced woman stop at our table. I was wearing a large crystal heart and many people had commented they had felt attracted to my heart. The woman looked at me deliberately, and was smiling from ear to ear. She came up to me and said, "My name is Mary Lynn. I am supposed to meet you. I can tell by the look in your eyes and the heart you are wearing."

She told me that she had attended Doreen Virtue's workshop. Doreen had told her she would uncover her life's mission before she left the expo hall! She said she was guided to walk down our aisle and was stopped by my heart pendant. She told me that in a visualization that Doreen led, she had seen my crystal heart! I made an appointment for Mary Lynn for a coaching session.

I had been given, through Divine Guidance, the suggestion to have each client bring a book to our sessions. It should be a book that is spiritually oriented or that they felt drawn to use that day. Mary Lynn brought Doreen Virtue's book, *The Lightworker's Way*. We prayed before starting the session, asking only for Divine Guidance. Both of us felt an excitement as the session began. I asked Mary Lynn to hold the book and wait for a sense of energy in her hands or fingers. When she confirmed the feeling, we asked for the Holy Spirit to guide her to a passage that would be a direct message form her higher self.

The Lightworkers

Mary Lynn opened the book and as instructed, and slowly read a description of a lightworker. As she read the description. I felt a tremendous bolt of energy through the top of my head and my whole body. I had a remembrance of the Divine Encounter I had had when I was suicidal. Words came back to me, "*You will work with workers of the light. Help them to free themselves of ego concerns, of fears and doubts. Help them to fully commit to what they came here to do.*" I suddenly saw that my whole coaching practice was about coaching lightworkers.

My hands and whole body shook from the jolt of electricity that went through me. I felt like I was in the room, but also somehow circling above the room. The session with Mary Lynn took on an even more powerful feel as we both shared our experiences of feeling not connected fully to our bodies. I closed my eyes and saw bright sparkles of light flashing like light bulbs in my mind I heard a voice in my head say, *"Get that book!"*

Within three days I had a copy. It was Easter — a day of resurrection and celebration. It would be for me a day that marked the beginning of my work with Doreen Virtue and the angels — work I could never have planned to do in my rational and logical mind.

I finished the book in one day. On nearly every page I felt a sense of inner excitement. Tears rolled down my face as I heard about Doreen's own struggle to find peace. She realized that she was being called to fulfill a mission of love. She was to help others free themselves of fear, and fully embrace their inner power. I was spell-bound as I read about her angelic encounter, when an angel saved her life in a car jacking. She wrote of her angels confronting her, telling her she was throwing her life away. They told her in a loving way that she needed to get busy being a healer and writing spiritual books. I felt compassion as I read her accounts of all the pain she endured on her lightworker path. I knew she would understand all the things I had gone through, and she would relate to my own angelic experience that saved my life. I had no idea why I felt such excitement but as I finished the book I heard an inner prompting, *"Write to her. Tell her your story."*

My mind fought with that thought. "She's a best selling author. Why would she respond to me? She is going to think I'm a nut." I pushed my fears and doubts aside, and sat down at the computer. I closed my eyes and just asked for Spirit to type the letter. The e-mail was about three pages long when I saw myself hitting the send button. That was it — it was gone in a flash. As I re-read what I had sent, my mind told me that this was a big waste of time. Besides, what did I want from her if she did respond? I really didn't know why I was writing her, but I had become so accustomed to following these inner promptings I just did it. Most of the time I didn't ask why. Most of the time I just did whatever I was being nudged to do.

The Certified Spiritual Counselor

Later that day I received an e-mail back from Doreen, inviting me to come be part of her Certified Spiritual Counselor program. She said she was guided by God and the angels to teach others the tools and methods the angels had given her. She called them angel therapy techniques. In the CSC program, we would learn how to work with these techniques to help others heal themselves of pain, fear, and whatever was blocking them. All they needed to have was the willingness to heal their lives. She told me that each person has a sacred mission, a contract they agreed to fulfill. Many are so filled with anger, unforgiveness, resentment and bitterness, that they are not on the path to fulfilling their contract. They do, at a deep level want to fulfill it. They need first to begin to heal their minds and their own lives, and to take full responsibility for the power within them. You see, we all create our reality through our thoughts, our words and our feelings. Through the use of angel therapy techniques we could help people release the negative energy that was blocking them in their lives.

I learned that there was a CSC program being held in New York. I journaled and asked for guidance. I received back, *"You need to tell Mary Lynn about this. Get her there, even of you have to pay for her."*

Mary Lynn and I had only had a few sessions together, but I sent her the information. She replied that she felt a very strong pull to go, but would need some money. I told her not to worry, it will be provided. The next day she contacted me. Her tax check had arrived, with enough money to attend the program. We made arrangements, and decided to make the nine-hour drive to sessions over the next six months.

At the first meeting of the program I looked around and wondered, "What am I here for?" I thought that it was my job to get Mary Lynn there. I had done that, so now what am I here for? I looked up to see a beautiful woman standing at the front of the room. She exuded a radiant light all around her. I knew it was Doreen.

We all had been given copies of *The Lightworkers Way* for the program. Doreen was signing them as I walked over gingerly with my book in my hand. As I neared her, I began to feel a tremendous warmth and my eyes filled with tears. As I looked into her eyes, I felt a tremendous rush of love in my heart. I embraced her, saying, "Oh Doreen it is so good to see you." I sobbed into her soft silken dress and she held me gently. She said, "It is alright now Sweetie. You are home." We said no more to each other, and I returned to my seat feeling that same feeling in the pit of my stomach I had felt while I read her book. Doreen explains in her book that lightworkers agree before birth to help heal themselves and the Earth of the affects of fear. She believes that the Earth, with its material temptations, creates a form of amnesia in lightworkers. They then forget their divine and perfect identities and their ability to miraculously help the earth and all living creatures. When lightworkers forget their true identity and purpose they feel lost and afraid. Lightworkers are not special, just souls who have agreed to do certain work.

In *The Lightworker's Way* , Doreen lists the following questions for those asking if they might be lightworkers. Do you:

- Feel called to heal others?
- Want to resolve the world's social and environmental problems?
- Believe that spiritual methods can resolve any situation?
- Have (had) mystical experiences such as psychic premonitions or angelic encounters?
- Want to heal your own life as a first step in healing the world?
- Feel compelled to write, teach, or counsel about your healing experiences?

- Know you are here for a higher purpose even if you are unsure what it is or how to fulfill it?

Everywhere lightworkers are awakening to faint memories of
why they came to earth. Like me, they hear an inner calling that
can't be ignored. This call is a reminder that it is now time to stop
toying with material dreams and get to work. Many lightworkers
are discovering innate spiritual gifts, such as psychic communication skills and spiritual healing abilities. These are gifts they vol-
unteered to use to heal both people and the Earth during the
crucial decades surrounding the millennium. Prophecies predicted
our coming, and now it is time for us to fulfill our divine life
purpose. The world depends on us!

That evening I woke up again to a warm loving presence in my
room. I received the message, *"You are to gather the troops of
lightworkers all over the country. You will help them free themselves of
fears and doubts. Work with them to help them fulfill their Divine Life
Purpose."* Scenes were shown to me of my conducting workshops
and signing books. I saw Doreen and myself leading workshops for
many individuals who were called to guide others. There were
scenes of Doreen doing phone classes with the technology I had
learned about through Coach University, and I saw many people
releasing years of pain and fear in those programs.

The next day, I told Doreen some of what I had seen and she
was very supportive. She said we would do whatever we are guided
to do that will serve the highest good of all concerned. She assured
me that we aren't to worry about how all of this would occur. Our
only job was to give it all to spirit. She told me that in her own life
she often received messages that seemed impossible, yet a few
months later all the things would just fall into place. She told me
that she noticed, however, that things moved faster when she fully
released from outcome and attachment and surrendered it all to
God. She said that it was her experience that the larger a person's
mission and the numbers of people they were to impact, the more
fear and obstacles they seemed to create as a delaying tactic. I have

seen this over and over with my own clients. I have also witnessed true miracles when they have finally been moved to fully let go and to become a vehicle for God and the angels. These individuals are highly functioning members of society. They have not given up on themselves or their community. But they live life in a place of awareness that recognizes there is more going on than we can understand within the context of our five senses.

According to Gary Zukav, author of *The Seat of the Soul*, we have been living in an experience he defines as "five sensory." We have lived interpreting our experiences and life situations according to that which seems "logical" according to our five senses. Zukav suggests we are rapidly moving to human beings that are "multi-sensory." A multi-sensory human being operates from an expanded model of consciousness, and lives life through expanded capabilities. These include making choices through intuition and expanding our awareness to connect with higher realms of consciousness.

To the five sensory human, this approach or these concepts are illogical. They make no sense in the framework of what we can physically experience with our five senses. Two hundred years ago microwave ovens, computers, airplanes and the technology that makes these conveniences possible was not "logical." Somewhere along the way we released our belief that this technology was "not possible" and we allowed our collective mind to accept the possibility, and it manifested for us. I suggest you allow yourself to open your mind to the possibilities of new ways of accessing information and making choices; even though at this point the idea may seem illogical, irrational or impractical.

Coaching from Spirit Program

Within the next two months I had received, through Divine Guidance the information about my *Coaching from Spirit* program. I began talking to other coaches about it. In just a month, ten coaches agreed to be a part of the first program. The program has now grown enormously. We are training coaches, healers, therapists, and hypnotherapists how to work with individuals to fully embrace their inner power and uncover and fulfill their Divine Life purpose.

Coaching from Spirit is a term that defines a coaching process. It provides us with a tool box of methods, strategies and approaches that can assist us in making shifts of consciousness from an ego-centered way of seeing the world to a spirit (inner) based approach. This approach is effective with individuals from any religion or personal belief system, and can be incorporated at most levels of awareness.

The worldview shown us through mass media often encourages the belief that we are victims in our society and our own lives. We are portrayed as limited in our abilities. The collective mind tells us through these images that we are powerless. The Spirit view, or multi-sensory model, is that nothing is impossible. Through an expanded source of consciousness we have all the power within us to create anything we want. We innately have the power to create our own realities and the choice to create whatever we truly need and desire in our lives. The old view of victim is based in fear. Spirit view is based only in love. In the *Coaching from Spirit* process, clients and ourselves use tools of transformation to uncover these truths. The connection to higher sources of wisdom is available to us in practical ways. We come in alignment with our divine life purpose. This program supports individuals to live that shift in consciousness in a tangible way.

In the *Coaching from Spirit* process, coaches meet clients wherever they are in their awareness. Using spiritual, metaphysical and energy methods, coaches help clients to un-learn negativity, to truly listen, and to trust their inner guidance. Some examples of these methods include a daily journaling and listening process designed to open a channel for clients to hear their inner guidance and connect with their divine helpers. As a Spirit Coach we then listen to that guidance to help us guide the client in creating what they choose to create in their life. Another tool is to help our clients create an inner temple (space) to get information and guidance. We incorporate this "inner" information in our coaching. Spirit Coaches meditate specifically for each client, before a session or in the morning. They use energy methods (such as controlled visualization) to support the clients' realization of their conscious and unconscious goals. Clients can either believe these tools are a connection with divine realm of helpers, or define them as visualizations. The results are the same — powerful shifts and transformations!

Finding Divine Life Purpose

Susan came to me because she was experiencing some marital difficulties. We soon realized the problems in her marriage were a reflection of her own sense of confusion about her life mission. Susan began journaling. Within two months, she had discovered her mission, to support others in creating spiritual wellness. She began to easily communicate with her angels and learned how to interpret and trust the guidance she received She learned how to tell true Divine Guidance from wishful thinking. Later, Susan was given the message through Divine Guidance that she was to coach individuals on how to incorporate spiritual tools and an intuitive parenting style to create more harmony, peace and prosperity in their lives. Her marriage is now fully transformed into a conscious, loving relationship. She is guided daily in parenting with her two young children. She has begun teaching classes on spiritual parenting, and has recently begun her own coaching practice, focusing on spiritual parenting.

Angels In The Boardroom

John is a CEO of a Fortune 500 company. He is practical and very pragmatic. John heard a talk I gave about learning to listen to and trust your divine guidance. He called me the next day. He told me, somewhat nervously, he had had a dream the previous night. In his dream an angel appeared and said, "She will show you how to fix the sales." He said his company was experiencing lagging sales and he was very concerned.

I worked with John to help him release the blocks to hearing his inner guidance. Energy drains were sapping him. John appeared to be a very angry and withdrawn person. He was holding in a lot of anger towards his parents, his current wife and his employees. We worked for several sessions releasing fears and doubts that stemmed from his childhood. Through his journaling and newly formed practice of going to his inner temple, John soon realized he held a lot of anger toward God. He had been a victim of religious abuse and held deep-seated fears about connecting with his Divine Guidance.

In one session, John felt a tremendous electrical charge in the top of his head as we were doing releasing work. He said he saw a movie, a vision of himself when he was very small. He was talking to an angel! John sobbed as he told me of this remembrance. He said that he used to talk to this angel. When he told his mother, she took him to their preacher to exorcise the demons from him. John said he never again saw or heard the angel again.

The next day he called me. "You will never guess what happened!" he said excitedly. "Last night I dreamt of that same angel from my childhood. She told me exactly what is going on with my company. She said my family made a mistake when I was little, out of fear. She told me I had to fully let go of the anger and hate towards my parents. She would take it away for God to heal. I felt her touch my hand, as she prompted me to let them go and let God heal the past. She then gave me very specific information, and I just know this will turn around our sales!" John continued excitedly, "She told me we have to give back to the community. That is a part of why are sales are lagging! She gave me an idea for a community program I can start."

John's company tripled their sales by year-end, and he received grateful public recognition for his community program.

Affirmation

We must embrace the mystery of the energy of God and the angels and stop trying to put everything we don't understand out of our minds. We need the help of our own Divine Guidance to re-create all we believe, feel and know that is not resulting in love in our lives. The door has been opened for us. God and the Angels stand ready and waiting to help us in every aspect of our lives, but we must ask. These loving beings are real and will assist us in releasing our feelings of unworthiness. They can help us to fully embrace the expanded multi-sensory capabilities we all have. They teach us to accept how truly powerful we are through love. This is powerful work, and the fact that you are drawn to continue reading this chapter is significant. There are no accidents in the Universe. The fact that you reading this chapter is no accident. You do not have to agree with everything presented here, only take what fits for you and your way of being. I only ask that you be open-minded and suspend your rational thoughts and processes to enter an expanded place for you.

As we heal ourselves, so shall we heal the world!

Sharon Wilson lives in the peaceful countryside of Pennsylvania with her husband Bob and daughter Joy. In a cooperative venture with like-minded Spirit coaches, she is the founder of a virtual university called Illumine University. Sharon works with individuals, corporations, and conducts group coaching and classes by phone. E-mail her at joycoach@illumineu.com or visit the site illumineu.com

Recommended Reading

Virture, Doreen: *The Lightworkers Way*. (Carlsbad, CA: Hay House, 1997)

Zukhav, Gary: *The Seat of the Soul*. (NY: Simon And Schuster, 1989)

COACHING THE HIGHLY SENSITIVE PERSON

Sue Pouppirt

When I am out in the world talking to people about coaching, I pause for just a moment before I mention that my specialty is working with highly sensitive people. That pause is a division between the sometimes scripted language about the generalities of coaching, and the beginning of a conversation that is inspired by my passion for sharing my own experience and evolution as a highly sensitive person (HSP). Perhaps the person I am speaking with will have no idea about what I am talking about. However, if the person I'm speaking with is highly sensitive, I can often anticipate the response. Just mentioning that I work with highly sensitive people may elicit a quick emotional reaction; a nervous giggle, a catch of the breath, glistening eyes, or a subtle relaxation as if they can finally put down the burden of pretense. The body language says, "You know who I am." My short pause gives me a moment to prepare myself for a potentially quick, deep connection with a person — a person who is not used to being understood. That is the beauty of my niche. My clients recognize themselves and are naturally drawn to my coaching.

Becoming a Coach

I first heard about coaching when I was contemplating a major career change. I was more than ready to close a successful business, even though logic advised differently. How could I even consider giving up something that I had worked on for so long? After 16 years in business, I had no idea what I would do instead. I was, however, firmly committed to finding work I could love. I went to see a career specialist who told me about coaching. Coaching seemed to be made to order for me. Within a month I registered with Coach University, hired a coach to help me with the transition, and began coaching my first clients. Looking back, I don't know how I moved so quickly, but I'm glad I did.

My HSP Specialty

My next big decision didn't happen as quickly. I needed to decide how I wanted to design my practice. Who would hire me? What special services could I offer? I heard a lot about developing a specialty or niche, but I wasn't sure what that meant for me. I wasn't sure if my niche would be based on who I was, or if it was more about who my clients would be. When nothing compelling came immediately to mind, I thought about how my experiences could lead to a coaching niche. I considered coaching small businesses owners, women, people in mid-life burn out, working moms, single moms, sales people who love their clients more than their commissions, to name a few. Lots of possibilities and topics interested me. Nothing, however, took me by the hand and led me forward. I stopped thinking about niches. I decided instead to coach the clients who came to me, and watch carefully to see who they were. My belief is that if an answer is difficult to find, then it isn't that answer's turn to be found yet. Time and experience have a way of encouraging some of the subtleties of a situation to make their way to the surface if I don't hassle them too much. When it is ready, the decision seems to make itself.

I allowed myself time and immersed myself into the theories, language, techniques, writings and community of Coach University. After all, I was getting used to not knowing lots of things! The Coach University format was very new to me. I had never sent an e-mail or accessed a web site before. And I certainly had never been in a teleclass. My college-aged children were impressed. "Hey, Mom is distance learning," I felt I was technology-disabled. And, yes, I was overwhelmed to the point of tears more than once. Finding a niche seemed less immediately important than finding the Top Ten List that pertained to my most recent field work assignment. I was sure I had saved it, but now only God and Bill Gates knew where it was....

One day I saw an announcement for a class led by Thomas Leonard about Super Sensitive People. It was the first time I had seen that term. I took Thomas' "SSP Self-Test" and found myself perfectly described. Realizing that so much of my life experience was related to my all-encompassing sensitivity created a tremendous change in the way I saw myself. I studied Dr. Elaine Aron's book, *The Highly Sensitive Person*. It was a revelation. I have always had a secret arrogance about my high sensitivity, but I was resigned to the fact that most other people would feel that my sensitivity was mostly a pain in the neck. The more I learned about this trait, the more I understood how I could structure my life so that I could thrive on my own terms. The more I supported myself, the easier my life became. As my confidence deepened, I was able to articulate my personal experience with more clarity, and with that clarity came more respect. I may be different than many, but different can also mean rare and worthwhile. I wanted to share all that I was learning, and I wanted to learn more from other HSPs, which was easy to do. As I opened to the potential of my own high sensitivity, I was thrilled to see that most of my clients were also HSPs. My niche had finally found me. The purpose of my work with HSPs is to bring respect and confidence to a group of unique and vital people who often feel left out of a world that undervalues them. It is a mission that I cannot deny. It is a specialty that, like so many other aspects of my life, is unusual and deeply satisfying.

What Is A Highly Sensitive Person?

What makes someone a highly sensitive person? If you've heard directives such as, "You're too sensitive," "Can't you lighten up?" or "Get a thicker skin," then you can bet you are a highly sensitive person (HSP). In her book, Dr. Aron estimates that 15-20% of the population is highly sensitive, which encompasses physical, emotional, mental, and spiritual sensitivities. Scientifically speaking, the HSP has a greater receptivity to stimulus than most people. What that means is that everything affects the HSP. Environmental issues such as noise, lights, crowds, chemicals, smells, uncomfortable clothing, and stress are exhausting. Think "The Princess and the Pea". You may remember that fairy tale, in which the royal family devised a test to help them identify their lost princess. They stacked mattresses to the ceiling and beneath them placed just one small pea. They knew that their princess would not be able to sleep because of the lump caused by that single pea. She was an HSP, as they knew she would be.

HSPs are perceptive to the moods and emotions of others. Their bodies may be plagued by such things as allergies, chemical sensitivities, chronic fatigue or stomach disorders in response to an environment that is seemingly benign for others. They are like the canaries in the mine shaft and exhibit symptoms of environmental disease well before it appears in the general population. They are more aware of subtle details and deeper significance behind situations or events. They are conscientious, vigilant, perfectionists, and serious. And yet their intuitive and introspective nature makes them extremely creative and they may have a whimsical nature. They think and behave in innovative ways. They may seem both spacey and gifted.

The ideal our society holds for the model of success is not a highly sensitive person. Awareness of this contributes to the low self-esteem and the sense of being flawed that is very common amongst HSPs. But high sensitivity is a blessing that affords the HSP a rich and inspiring world. The HSP offers a fascinating perspective for anyone who takes the time to get to know ᴜᵣ precious quality, unfortunately, is very delicate and easily squashed if not honored and protected. You wouldn't throw a porcelain bowl in the dishwasher, would you?

Benefits Of Coaching For HSPs

My HSP clients tell me that the one most important benefit of working with me is the understanding they gain about what their sensitivity is and how to work with it. We focus on specific strengths and design the lifestyle that best supports them. I encourage them to make changes that might seem selfish or bold to them. I let them know how often I see them as being right on with their impressions, even when others tell them they are over-reacting yet again. I suggest tools to help them organize their abundance of creative ideas and projects. I show them techniques to short circuit the long run of their emotional roller coaster. I encourage their natural, but sometimes hidden, good sense of humor and encourage them to use it when all else fails. And I value them for being the wise old souls that our society needs so desperately. The world is a better place with our HSPs operating at their full potential.

One of the most damaging misconceptions about highly sensitivity people is that they lack strength and are less effective than non-HSPs. Many HSPs have adopted this view and sink into a sort of malaise. This is based upon their belief that they are cursed with a painful life, without the strength or capability to do anything about it. No wonder depression is a malady that plagues HSPs. However, my experience is that at the core of the HSP personality is a quiet determination — even stubbornness — that holds them to standards that are unusually high. Their capabilities are distinct and worthwhile, even superior, but are fragile enough to be easily repressed if treated callously. Reconnecting to their inner strength is essential to an HSP who is struggling with and wondering how they will survive a lifetime of non-consideration and disrespect. Seeing themselves as essential and vital beings allows them to tap into that strength so that they can gently stand up for themselves and confidently argue for an environment that allows them to flourish.

One of my clients dedicated several weeks, night and day, to select her company name. Her process was fascinating. She worked from quotes that were meaningful for her, images that were pleasing, symbols that portrayed bigger concepts, colors, her vision for her work, and descriptive phrases of the services she offered. It was important to her that she find a name that not only presented her new undertaking correctly, but that attracted the people she most wanted to work with. Much love for her clients-to-be and passion for what she had to offer them went into this selection. Even as she wore out from the effort, she stayed committed seeking to the inner sensation she knew would be there for her when the name was perfect. As her coach, I supported her in her search, gave her my honest opinions and enjoyed the process with her. When she became discouraged, I acknowledged her for her intent, wrote detailed commentaries to her about the pros and cons of each of the possibilities she was considering, and let her know that the time she was spending was important. We exchanged e-mails daily and stayed in touch as she went through this process. My message to her the whole time was, "All of these names are lovely. You can't go wrong. I understand your need to feel that you have considered everything before making your decision." There is no rushing a fine wine or an HSP intent on settling for nothing less than divine perfection!

Group Coaching For HSPs

In concert with my own personal experience with high sensitivity, I have learned a great deal through the coaching groups I lead for HSPs by telephone. By putting together the creative and insightful energy of a number of HSPs, we gain an incredible amount of collective wisdom. Often the experience of being deeply heard and completely understood by other HSPs is so new, that they feel as if their lives will never be the same. One very exuberant first-time participant proclaimed, "I've found my people!" I have learned to be extremely flexible with my agendas for these groups, because it is so common for someone to raise a fascinating topic that is important to everyone on the call. Here are some of the surprises:

During one call, I suggested that we discuss relationships. The topic turned to love stories. There is nothing like a beautiful love story told by an eloquent and inspired HSP, but with an all-HSP audience, the moment was sheer magic. My notes regarding the points I wanted to make were out the window. During the first call for another one of my groups, I discovered that every single person on the call had some level of Chronic Fatigue Syndrome or fibromyalgia. Ironically, another woman was interested in joining the group, but her CFS was so severe she didn't feel she could handle the commitment. I was struck by the coincidence and have since seen that Dr. Aron has addressed the connection between HSPs and CFS. Some doctors believe that every patient suffering from CFS is a highly sensitive person. The point I make with my clients is that self care is even more essential for HSPs. This is a wonderful message for any one who can hear it. This seems to be a difficult thing for many HSPs to do.

During a conversation on the topic of what is required of a CFS sufferer in the form of self-care, I asked one of my groups if they could tell me the initial signs of getting tired, as opposed to the final sign which is physical collapse. No one knew the answer. It amazed me that no one in a group of highly sensitive people could describe such a simple phenomenon as being tired! We decided that we were all so used to working through our fatigue that we had learned to not notice it. Perhaps we had all been told too often that we couldn't feel that way, because no one else did. And we worked through our fatigue because we hated being the first one to give up, when it appeared that everyone else was still able to keep going. It is difficult to admit that you are a wimp or in some way weaker than the people around you. However, if we could understand that we actually are not weaker but truly more tired because we are less able to screen out much of the stimuli that others don't notice but drives us crazy, maybe we will be willing to step away and take the breaks our bodies need.

One group participant expressed his inability to tolerate pain the way most other people can. That sounds so dishonorable. I suggested that he rephrase that in a more accurate way. He actually feels more pain from the same experience and reacts the same way anyone would to that level of pain. Again, a slight change in words, but enough of a difference in meaning to allow him a more positive self image.

Another interesting observation from a group member was that after spending a few days with her sister that she actually started to become her sister. She could feel herself seeing through her sisters eyes, moving the way her sister moves, feeling the way her sister felt, etc. When she asked her sister if she had the same experience, her sister looked at her like she was crazy. Most of the people in this group could remember having as similar experience at one time or another. Makes me think that HSPs ought to be pretty careful about who they hang out with! HSPs struggle with a sense of self. It is more difficult for them to distinguish between their own experiences and those of the people around them, especially as children. They are so aware of the emotions and moods of the people close to them. It is important that they learn how to establish strong personal boundaries that protect them from overwhelming experiences, or prevent them from taking on too much responsibility for the well-being of another.

One group member asked for help in supporting her HSP daughter through some difficulties in school. The exercise of returning to our young years in light of our new understanding for our own high sensitivity was very powerful. The question I asked was, "What would have changed your perception about your sensitivity if you had heard it as a child?" Most simply wanted to hear that they were OK; different from many others, but special in some ways because of those differences. Few of us heard anything resembling that sort of support.

Many HSPs are accustomed to protecting themselves from disapproval by pretending to be more OK than they actually feel.

They hide behind walls or masks of their own construction in order to get by. These defense mechanisms can get in the way and block the flow of creative energy that comes with their sensitivity. It is the balance between boundaries and openness that allows us full expression of who we are. We must feel safe to be fully creative. Allowing ourselves the time and space to simply be, and experience the full depth of our emotions is the easiest route to our most creative productivity. It is imperative for the physical as well as emotional well-being of a highly sensitive person to organize his/her life to allow for slack time.

Business And Careers

One of the major ways that coaching can help HSPs is in defining and succeeding in their careers. They are bored unless their work is meaningful, but they are damaged by many high-stress work environments. Dr. Aron describes two types of people: the warrior king and the royal advisor. The warrior king is greatly honored in our society. He/she is the football hero, the award-winning sales person, the rags-to-riches business person, and the savvy politician. These people are aggressive and thrive on competition and winning. Without them, our society would be lost. Highly sensitive people do not last long on the front line. Many of my HSP clients have tried don the armor of the warrior king and have succeeded to some degree, but more often with disastrous results to health and well-being. There is a better place for them that allows their innate talents to flourish and prosper in the role of the royal advisor. HSPs do very well as consultants, coaches, therapists, writers, philosophers, artists, judges and teachers. A huge element of my coaching with HSPs is in helping them to define their strengths and draw boundaries for themselves. I coach them to design a work environment that makes the most of who they are.

The following are some common traits of HSPs in a work environment:

- They thrive in an environment that values quality results over speed.
- They like autonomy, and are less effective with a supervisor breathing down their necks.
- They are creative problem solvers; good at developing innovative systems and coming up with new ways of thinking.
- They are great at handling details but many need help with organization.
- They require quiet, privacy and time to settle down to do their best.
- They are most comfortable with honest, authentic people who understand and respect them.
- They do well with plenty of time for preparation, and also enjoy flexibility and the opportunity to share hunches and gut reactions.
- Unconventional, often self-guided work schedules allow them to keep working when they are immersed in an important project and make up for lost sleep or overwhelm when necessary.
- Clear communication rather than office politics feels safer and more understandable to an HSP.

John

John came to me as another one of his career choices was coming to a sorry close. He had a long history of accepting jobs that required the toughness of a prize fighter to succeed. These jobs fit his image of what he was supposed to do to be successful. He was a delightfully bright, innovative, and dear man with enough energy to convince potential employers that he was up for any challenge. He was, however, starting to run out of steam as he met with one humiliating experience after another. His opportunities were narrowing as his resume collected evidence of short-term commitment. In desperation, he had accepted this most recent job from a company that was, at best, marginal. When we first talked, he was not sure how much longer he could remain associated with a company that seemed unethical and unprofessional. His customers loved him, and he cared about them. He did not want them to buy into his company's program because he knew it was unstable. He did not have to wonder much longer, because shortly after our first meeting, his pay check bounced and he knew it was time to go.

His first instinct was to call about other jobs before the end of the day. He indicated on his client intake materials that he wanted to learn how to take bigger risks! The last thing I wanted to see this man do was to take more risks without first finding out how he was getting all of these black eyes. As we talked about what brought him the most joy and what his ideal job would look like, I noticed a trend. His most pleasurable times of the day were spent quietly alone, in deep thought. He enjoyed getting up early and having time to himself before his family was awake. He loved taking solitary walks, or sitting in a book store with a cup of coffee, brainstorming and jotting down notes. He pictured himself wearing a red flannel shirt and khakis, working from his quiet home in the mountains. His proudest achievements were independently creating innovative new systems. His solutions addressed problems that no one else had even noticed until he solved them.

Since his ideal image didn't fit his borrowed image of success, these projects were only occasional reprieves from John's efforts to fit the tough-guy image of a corporate success. He tried valiantly to model himself after the warrior kings who hired him, but was unsure and uncomfortable in the role. When he fell short of their expectations for him, their judgements felt like red-hot branding irons with the word "loser" written in capital letters. With his emotions storming within him, John expressed himself as best he could — with rage. It was not long before one or the other called it off, and John would be looking for a job again.

With so many years of effort focused on being who he was not, John had lost confidence in his intuition. When I asked him when did he know that his latest job was a mistake, he said, "During the interview." My hunch was that John was a highly sensitive person in disguise. When I shared this observation with him, he was very quiet. As I described the trait in detail he listened intently. When I was finished, he said, "That's it. You just described my life."

John joined a weekly coaching group, and he became one of the most eloquent people in the group. His initial attitude was, "If I was less sensitive, I would be much more successful." In time, he saw how his natural talents were the perfect tools for attaining the authentic success and the life he dreamed of. He decided to go into business for himself as a consultant, with the flexibility to accept diverse projects. Opportunities started coming forward to him at such a fast pace that we had to keep a list to keep them straight. His confidence level grew. People who could appreciate his special talents and style wanted to work with him. The last time I spoke to him, he reported that he was in love with his life and felt better about himself than he ever had before.

Some HSPs struggle financially. They tend to believe that they do not fit the model of a person who can earn a lot of money and often look for something other than financial reward when deciding what they would like to do. Many pursue artistic careers or stay at low-paying positions to avoid the stress of a more challenging job. By focusing on their unique talents and aptitudes, instead of seeing success only in terms of the standard warrior king model, HSPs are very good at developing ways to make money doing what they love and what they are best at doing. Working for themselves supports their need for independence, allows for the creative process to unfold at their speed, protects the introverted HSP and puts them in charge of how they organize their days.

Marnie

The internet is opening up wonderful opportunities for HSPs. Marnie is a self-employed web page designer/writer/HSP. Her vision for herself and her company came from her fascination with the internet. Marnie hired me to coach her on establishing her business, achieving financial success, and maintaining the life style that is comfortable for her introverted, highly sensitive nature. We began our work together by defining exactly what she wanted and supporting the belief that what she wanted was not only accept-able, but the only way she could be successful. We then set out to design the structures and policies that would allow her to build her business so that it fit her unique way of working. Marnie was so used to feeling like an under achiever, that she was thrown by the slightest hint that she was too slow, not correct, or too expen-sive. Rather than focus on those concerns, I asked her to keep her attention firmly attached to the things she did well. When she felt that a client was unhappy with her work, she was so affected that she was ready to close her business. If a client was looking for something different than her strengths, she was happy to refer them to a different designer.

While I supported her in her determination to work with only ideal clients, I also asked her to get clear on what was disturbing her about her interactions with less than ideal cli-ents. I asked how she would like the interactions to flow. I coached her to write to the client with those clarifications. Ironi-cally, most of her concerns were unfounded. Most clients ap-preciated her talents more than she knew, and were happy to stay with her even if she occasionally said "no" to their requests. As she had positive experiences about telling the truth about how she worked best, she learned that most people were more accepting of her style than she expected. Usually her fears of falling short were unfounded. In the meantime, the web sites she created were beautifully designed and technically profi-cient and she was gaining a very satisfied client base. Her abil-ity to understand her clients and to design sites that eloquently represented them brought referrals and more of the sort of cli-ents who appreciate her strengths.

Her business is growing so rapidly that we are now working on protecting her time. She wants to create her own exceptional web sites on topics that interest her. The internet is a better place because of her contributions. If you want someone to slam out a fast boilerplate web site with lots of high-tech bells and whistles, don't hire her. If you want someone who will hear what you say and translate it to a web site you will love, she's just who you want. She does not want to compromise her high standards. Her clarity on that point is enabling her to realize her own definition of financial and personal success.

Relationships

Relationships ain't easy. Relationships with and for HSPs really ain't easy. Most are introverts. They care so deeply about other people that relationships can be exhausting. They dearly want to be sure others are happy and take on more responsibility for that than is prudent. Unfortunately, they are also much more aware of the inevitable conflicts and discomfort that result. If something is bothering you, your HSP friend or family member will be asking you what's wrong, maybe before you know it yourself. Your distress may be bothering them more than it bothers you. Just tell the truth to your HSP friends. Nothing makes an HSP feel crazy faster than sensing a problem and being told that it is not there. The most important strategy for coaching HSPs about relationships is getting them to establish clear and healthy boundaries.

It is essential that HSPs protect themselves from the damaging effects of traumatic personal encounters. Boundaries are the best way to do that, but they are challenging. Unless the HSP will: 1) acknowledge to themselves that they must tell the truth when someone crosses or threatens to cross a boundary, and 2) have a plan of action in place in case the other person does not take them seriously. A person who will not respect the boundaries of an HSP is a person that the HSP can't afford to be around. It's that simple. When the HSP really gets that, he/she will be much more successful at communicating their needs. He/she will most likely find that others will respect them for their clarity and honor their wishes. I tell my HSP clients that this is not optional. Do this or die young. I say to them, "Your creative spirit is destroyed by your unwillingness to take care of yourself!" And I'm not kidding.

HSPs tend to be high maintenance; there's no other way to put it. We are unpredictable, very emotional, easily hurt, unconventional, and hard to hide from. We take everything seriously and have a hard time letting go of the slightest detail. For example, it takes me forever to order a meal at a restaurant. It's exhausting. You can imagine how often I talk about high sensitivity and HSPs around my house. It's incessant, I'm afraid. But the most effective phrase for communicating the point to my husband was: "Everything matters. *E V E R Y T H I N G.*" This is a phrase I learned from Thomas Leonard. My husband thought about that simple phrase. Finally, the light went on. He said, "That's you! That is exactly how you are!" Now he knows I am not purposely trying to drive him crazy. It is just a part of my nature.

HSPs can get carried away by the romantic side of relationships. They are normally very loyal to anyone whom they allow into their inner world. They are more likely to have a few close relationships instead of a large number of acquaintances. Before any decision is made about an important relationship, HSPs need to be sure that they are giving themselves enough time. They need to allow their strong sense of protection, as well as their intuitions about people, to come forward. HSPs often blow it here. Time seems to be the only remedy for the urge to make impulsive relationship decisions.

Kathy

Kathy is a live wire, an extroverted HSP. Her energy flashes from her eyes and fills the room the second she enters. It is impossible for her to hide how she is feeling, and she is always feeling a lot. Nothing ever gets past her, including nuances that are so subtle the sender is not even aware of them. Kathy has succeeded financially in many careers and is very good at what she sets out to do. But she never stays in one place for very long. She has been married twice and engaged countless times, but the relationship and family life she so desperately wants has escaped her. She just started a new job, is already thinking of quitting, and fears that she is about to be fired. She is thinking of breaking up with her current fiancée even though she is very much in love with him. Her cleaning people quit because she is never satisfied with their work. Her assistant told her she is difficult to work with because she expects too much. Kathy is starting to think that is true. Her perfectionism is driving away the people she needs. She wonders what is wrong.

It is not unusual for an HSP to be buried by all of the data coming in from outside sources, as well as the emotional upheaval going on within. They truly cannot see out. If their self-esteem is tied in with their achievements, they can get quite distraught if threatened by someone else's less perfectionist tendencies. They don't really get to know the other's perspective because they are so overwhelmed with their own experiences. Without meaning to, they can appear harsh and unforgiving.

I began coaching Kathy with just one assignment. I knew that she cared very deeply about people, but that very few people understood that to be true. I asked her to start really listening to people and to find an opportunity to say, "You are so right," to as many people as possible. She was reluctant to try this assignment, but she was desperate enough to give it a try. The point of this exercise was for Kathy to step outside her own painful reactions. She had to shift to their perspective enough to see that, from some angle, every person is right, or they wouldn't be doing what they are doing. The first sign of success with this assignment was that she laughed. She shook herself free of years of stress, and laughed hard. Her sense of humor was one of her most endearing features. It allowed her a creative expression that softened the hard edges that were causing her so much distress. That first week, she couldn't get the words out of her mouth, but she thought about them a lot. The fact that they were hard to say, opened her eyes to how tough she was being on people.

I also asked her to clearly define what was causing her so much stress, and why she felt so compelled to perform perfectly. We uncovered some important unfilled needs that were driving her. She discovered that some of her anger with her fiancé was based upon his generosity to his children. Kathy was afraid to ask for that same treatment. I asked her to communicate with him about her needs and allow him to include her in his generosity. She eased her assistant's fears by telling her what she did well and encouraging her to ask questions if she was confused. She also explained how important quality work was to her so that people could understand her intensity.

As she progressed, she was able to see that everyone really was doing their best. If she listened to her intuition, she was especially good at knowing what was going on with others. Her naturally positive personality came to the surface as she met her own needs, and then focused on what she could do to make other people comfortable. She began to attract the very things she had struggled so hard to get. She did end up leaving her job so that she could be with her fiancé. In her exit interview, her boss told her what a pleasure she was to work with and that she could have her job back any time she wanted it. She even held back from her old style of listing her observations about what he ought to do better, and thanked him for his kindness. This un-burned bridge supported her need for extra security by providing her with a standing offer of a good job, if she ever needed it.

Managing Emotions

The emotional aspects of high sensitivity are one of HSPs' greatest challenges. It causes the most disruption to careers, relationships, and even physical well-being. Many HSPs feel enslaved by their emotional highs and lows. They need some practical tools to help them maintain balance under sometimes overwhelming emotional responses. Many try to operate with the only tool they learned as children; squelch your emotions. Most HSPs are pretty good at doing just that, but this technique is very damaging. Not only does squelching block unacceptable emotional responses, it blocks the very acceptable creative flow of the HSP's intuition, perception and artistic nature. This seems to be especially common in HSP men. (You may be surprised to hear that there are just as many HSP men as there are women. Men just "get" this squelching rule better, so they aren't as noticeable.) This practice also happens to be very hard on HSP bodies, and HSP bodies have more than enough to handle as it is. Try as you will, intense emotions have a way of coming out. The leaks may be explosive outbursts or inner destruction. Therefore, I don't recommend my clients repress their emotions.

Some HSPs retreat to a life of varying degrees of seclusion. If this is truly the life that appeals to them, then I encourage them to go for it. If, however, they are hiding from a life that seems too unmanageable to tolerate out of fear of emotional pain or a lack of acceptance for their emotional responses, then they are losing out on a full life. Depending upon the severity, this situation may require referral to a psychotherapist.

So, do we have to stay victims to these seemingly unpredictable emotional storms? Sometimes, I think we do. It's the price we pay for the depth of emotion which is so useful when we want it. However, there is another way to see emotional responses. As just that; responses. Emotions are not a root cause. They are an echo of messages called out by your mind. We choose those messages, consciously or unconsciously. Every situation has an infinite number of views. If you can identify at least three, then you stand a good chance of realizing how your choices rule your emotions. Decide which perspective to take. Decide what to notice. This is a world of opposites. For each negative thought there is a positive thought. Actually, there is also a neutral thought as well, somewhere in the middle, which may really be your best bet. Every time you see a tragic story in the newspaper, you can find one that is uplifting. Which one do you want to read? I know some of you will say that this sounds irresponsible. But what is your definition of responsibility? Mine is maintaining your ability to respond. If you want to read the tragic story, then do, but just acknowledge your decision. Some HSPs feel that they are required to fix the world's ills and identify with the most difficult situations in sight. This is not true. It is also not good for you. Who is to say that by focusing on the negative, you are improving the world one bit? I think you are doing just the opposite. By focusing on the negative, you are causing yourself pain rather than pleasure. I encourage my clients to experiment with this idea.

Spirituality

I cannot imagine a happy HSP who is living a life void of deep inner spiritual connection. It's that simple. I am not here to tell anyone what that spiritual connection must look like or how they are to go about getting to that connection. I am suggesting that it is an essential factor in the care and maintenance of a highly sensitive person. To me, the HSP looks something like this: Perfectionism, impossibly high standards, unrealistic expectations for themselves and others, searching for love and beauty and rarely satisfied, and generally disappointed in the world. It seems as if HSPs are looking for some reality that is higher than the human or physical world can provide. So where might they find this next level? In the spiritual realms.

When I was a senior in high school, my friends and I were very eager to graduate. We were sick of the restrictive routines and the immature behavior of the "kids" in our school. When we wanted to be especially insulting to someone, we would say, "Get out of high school." Please understand, I have nothing against high school. I loved high school while I was there. It was simply that we were bored and ready to move on to a new level of maturity.

That intense sense that I was ready to move on to something bigger is how I experience my highly sensitive clients. It is a powerful shift to go from feeling like you don't fit in because you are less than capable, to feeling like you don't fit in because you are ready for more important things. Few of my HSP clients are fueled by money or material gains. Prestige embarrasses or overwhelms them. Power or control over others offends them. Aren't these the great motivators of the physical plane? No wonder so many HSPs feel as if their lives were meaningless and that it is difficult for them to be excited about things that are essential to others.

So what does interest an HSP? Many talk to me about wanting to touch people deeply through their art, music, words, or presence. They feel that they are here for a purpose, whether that purpose is defined for them yet or not. They speak of love, often spending a lifetime looking for that elusive quality that they know is possible; but they are heart-broken because the love they experience with family and friends never quite lives up to their dreams. Sometimes the picture looks hopeless. What is to become of people who are looking for more love, beauty, truth, serenity and acceptance than the world around them can provide? Time to "get out of high school." Time to move on to a higher, more subtle reality than is available through the physical senses. I am not talking about some mass suicide plan. I am talking about paying attention to the spiritual aspect of yourself and learning how to use your gifts of awareness, perception and insight for what they are so well-suited to do. Bring yourself into contact with the spiritual realm where all that you seek is possible. Anything less will leave you unfulfilled and dissatisfied. When you have a spiritual focus, all of the mundane details of your life fall effortlessly into place. Watch carefully that you place your attention high enough so that you are not distracted by the nonsense that, for you, is beside the point. Seek the answers that you desire. Knowing who you are, and being all of that, is the best way to satisfy those quiet dreams that may have seemed impossible in the past.

As is true of coaching in general, coaching of Highly Sensitive People provides a powerful advantage in a very competitive world. Our society is struggling to find some different ways to operate. HSPs especially are suffering under the old definitions of success and the rigid adherence to limited ideas. Through coaching, HSPs can explore new life designs in order to attain the lifestyle that works best for them.

Sue Pouppirt coaches her clients to succeed on their own terms. She lives in the country, north of Ft. Collins, Colorado with her husband, her youngest daughter, one cat, and a dog. She specializes in highly sensitive people, being one herself. She can be contacted by e-mail: coachsue@frii.com. Visit her web site at http\\www.sensitivepeople.com.

Recommended Reading

Aron, Elaine N.: *The Highly Sensitive Person: How to Thrive When the World Overwhelms You.* (Secaucus, NJ, Carol Publishing Company, 1996).

Holtje, Dennis: *From Light to Sound; The Spiritual Progression.* (Albuquerque, NM, Masterpath, 1995).

COACHING FOR THE THIRD QUARTER OF LIFE

Richard L. Haid, Ph.D.

During a recent third-quarter of life workshop I led, one of the participants said that he felt like he was in a rut. Others nodded in agreement. I asked the group whether they knew what the difference was between a rut and a grave. Upon hearing my answer, "The depth. But the rut usually has one end from which it is easier to get out," they all nodded their heads, and affirmed that they all wanted something more for their lives.

In my work, I have seen persons who have opened up their lives, who are more fulfilled, and who make significant later-life contributions; however, many more miss the potential abundance of the third quarter of life. Many people will leave the full-time work force with adequate financial resources, the gift of good health, and the possibility of 25 or more years of a fulfilling and abundant life. How are we to respond to this gift?

There are those who have the need to move out of the second quarter with its "work addiction" and the emphasis on being productive. These people know that life is supposed to be better but don't know how to get there. Studies show that after persons leave full-time work, little changes for them — other than they no longer going to work. Why? Because they have no model or examples. Simply being busy is not the same as living significantly. The old life maps don't work anymore, and people often need to make new maps. This is where the coaching of people in the third quarter often begins.

Murphy and Hudson, in *The Joy of Old*, describe the seasons of life as Youth, Midlife, and Elderhood. Youth is concerned with one's physical peak, with the slogan of "I am my body." Midlife is concerned with one's productive peak, with the slogan of "I am my work," and "doing" and "having" are common activities of midlife. I divide Elderhood into two parts, the third and fourth quarters. In simple terms, the third quarter is a period of potential growth and abundance while the fourth quarter is a period of decline. Today, there are no specific age markers for these quarters, for much depends on the person and on his or her personal development.

You can see from the diagram that the third quarter can be the largest and the most abundant of all the four quarters. The theme of the third quarter is "being," a more reflective time when we can be more authentic and "more right on." We are more

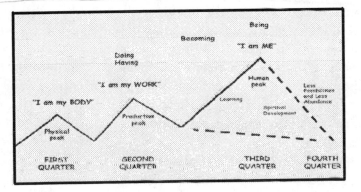

comfortable with ourselves and care less about what others think of us. The activities of the third quarter include engaging with the world on our terms, spiritual development, deepening of relationships and active learning.

Spiritual development may include pursuing questions of faith, the meaning of life and celebration. There may be questions of doubt and leaps of faith. There can also be legacy questions of what we will leave for a better world. These may involve our history, wisdom, and hopes and dreams, as well as property. In the third quarter there is time to enrich and deepen relationships with persons in our lives, including spouses/partners, children, and grandchildren. This includes collecting and sharing our life stories, family history, and wisdom. It is a time of life that embraces reaching out and beginning new friendships.

In the third quarter, learning can occur in many ways other than sitting in a classroom. The continuation and possible acceleration of learning is a great stimulant in the third quarter; it is truly lifetime learning coupled with travel, Elderhostels, the Internet, tutors, tapes, etc. in a setting of new self-direction. You can take charge of your learning, and others can learn with you.

The fourth quarter, which most people don't want to think about, offers fewer possibilities and less abundance, and many people associate it with physical decline. I believe the decline is more than just physical. At the bottom of the graph there is a dotted line, that shows that many people slide through and go directly to the fourth quarter. If a person simply retires, life may not be any different other than not going to work. The decline may have started, the potential abundance of the third quarter missed, and the fourth quarter may be a major portion of his or her life. I believe that the abundance of the third quarter can offer optimum fulfillment and can also postpone passage in to the fourth quarter.

You might ask, how do I get started? To begin with, developing a different way of viewing yourself is most important. One of the signs of maturity is to be able to stand aside from yourself and view yourself. To know that your life can offer more helps to open the door. Second, develop a new map for your life. Assessment is a very important part of getting a perspective of your life and recognizing that there may be skills and interests that are latent and potent, but little developed. Also, what are your values at this point in life? Your priorities may be shifting.

Thinking and reflection may be helpful, but even more beneficial is to make a more formal assessment either as part of group, as an individual or a couple in a mentoring relationship. A variety of inventories, card sorts, and checklists can be used. In these settings, there can be exploration and confirmation; plans can be developed that often involve some form of new learning. Simply being part of a workshop on "How Are You a Legend? What Is Your Legacy?" can open the door for personal growth and abundance.

If you are still part of the full-time or part-time workforce or in a volunteer activity, a simple tool to use is the Career/Life Fulfillment Grid shown here:

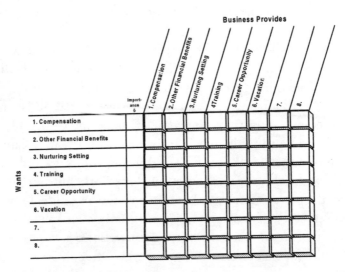

1. Using this grid, some of the typical job "Wants" are shown on the left side of the grid. Fill in additional "Wants" in spaces 7 & 8 that are important for you.

2. Chose a number between 1 and 10, with 1 being least important, to show the *importance* of each "Want" for you. Then enter the numbers in the column on the side under "importance."

3. On the top right side of the grid, under "Business Provides" list the additional "Wants" added in 7 & 8. Now, use the top

of the grid to determine features of your present job, a pro-
spective job, or an ideal future. Be specific in describing what
this job provides.

4. Place a check mark in the small box in the grid where the same
"Wants" and "Provides" intersect, if the "Want" is satisfied by
that job. Notice if another "Provide" also helps satisfy more
than one "Want." An example would be several "Provides" that
may be related to compensation.

5. Now that you have this "snapshot," what changes could be
made to better accommodate your wants or to increase your
satisfaction? Would you change any of the importance numbers? Do you need a redesign or a new job?

In the book *In the Joy of Old*, the authors develop the concept
of "protirement," which is a positive view of how to access fulfillment in the third quarter. Protirement is future-oriented, inner-
directed, and a launch pad for new lifestyles based on emerging
interests and values. Careers are now life-long, and work is blended
with leisure during the full span of our lives. A career can be a
lifetime engagement with the world, using your gifts and talents
as you wish. This engagement can include work, but work should
be on the person's terms, and not the main focus of life. Deal with
the need to be compensated, if there is a financial need, or if it
makes the job more worthwhile. Volunteerism is a wonderful opportunity for engagement with the world. Often, it is very satisfying for people entering the third quarter to use their gifts for the
benefit of others.

Coaching people in the third quarter involves helping them to
make the transition from "becoming" into "being." Our job as a
coach may mean helping them to develop a new road map for
their lives. Usually this shift is gradual, but with the coach's help,
clients can better read the road signs, travel light and enjoy the
journey. A whole new life may open up with an emphasis on learning, spiritual development, and establishing and deepening relationships. This is a time to answer the questions of meaning that

Protirement Coached for You
Second Adulthood

have been left unanswered from midlife. Throughout our lives we have questions about meaning in our lives, and many persons may receive "calls" for a fuller life.

The third quarter of life may be a time to respond to calls or to answer new calls. These calls can lead to the greatest fulfillment of our lives. "Protirement" is oriented toward looking forward to a new life ahead full of possible abundance. Life becomes oriented to all of aspects of our being, not just career. It is a time for individuals to design their lives. As they become more reflective and inner-directed, and they can live more deeply.

Often our parents did not enjoy either retirement or protirement. Both are based on the gift of an extra 25 or more years of life, with all of its potential, as well as its related problems. As a society are just beginning to explore how to use these extra 25 years known as the third quarter of life. It is not surprising that we at first view this extra time as simply an extension of our life and its activities. A more empowering view is to see this as a time available for the third quarter; a surprisingly different stage of life with unique developmental opportunities, and with its own tasks, rewards, and values. Also, the third quarter has a different criterion for success, and its abundance may be greater than that experienced in the second quarter. The possibility that there can be a third quarter is very empowering for many persons. It is an opportunity for a fresh start. Sustained by the gift of this extra 25 years, we can open the door to a deeper, richer life.

There are two books I find helpful for those having difficulty moving on from the second quarter of life. The first, *The Joy Of Old,* holds the belief that joy can develop with the fullness of maturity. The book also contains valuable guidelines for helping persons to become "successful elders." The second book is *From Ageing into Sage-ing* by Schachter and Shalomi, which discusses new concepts of aging and the richness of being a spiritual elder. It also includes helpful ideas about aging and the possibilities for using one's life experience and gifts to become a sage. Schachter-Shalomi describes a sage as, "becoming spiritually radiant, physically vibrant, and developing wisdom that is consecrated as service to the community." These are new concepts for our culture of being valued when becoming older.

This ongoing process transforms aging into meaning and purpose that can crown an elder person's life. The coach who wishes to appreciate the challenges facing those entering the third quarter of life thus will find both these books valuable reading.

Coaching People Entering The Third Quarter.

Generally I meet with all of my clients for a day or more to do an initial assessment. Their spouse or partner may be involved for part of the initial session. Most of the continuing contact will be made using scheduled telephone coaching calls; usually three calls per month. I encourage clients to fax a coaching call sheet to me prior to the call to set the agenda and to take responsibility for the session. My minimum period of time for coaching is three months, with many clients developing their plans over a year or more. Often clients think they are the first to ever experience some of the pain and lack of external energy during a full transition to this period. That I have experienced a full transition in my career and in my life is important to many clients because they value my experience of having "been there."

One of my favorite questions is "What do you celebrate and how do you celebrate?" For some, this is a difficult question, but it leads to looking at their lives in different ways. Some clients have started watching more sunsets, others sow more wildflowers, others tell spouses, children, and friends how much they love them. The also become more patient listeners. A later question is "What else might you celebrate?" These celebration questions have connectedness and thanksgiving themes and help clients find more of their depth and spirituality.

I use celebration sheets, skills and values card sorts, leisure-development inventories, learning-style checklists, achievement-competencies forms, and the Owner/Business Fulfillment Grid.

This grid is an inventory that I have developed for executives to help them learn the degree of correlation between their personal life cycle and business life cycle, and to start them on the planning process to achieve less correlation between these two. For business owners, the Career-Life Fulfillment Grid shown earlier can be modified to become the Owner-Business Fulfillment Grid by using a separate sheet for the owner and another sheet for the business.

I often raise the legacy question by showing a picture with the caption "Who Says You Can't Take It With You?" It is a picture of a hearse entering the gates of a cemetery while pulling a U-Haul trailer. This raises questions about mortality, possessions, and what we leave behind after death. The legacy question is very important to a person who has spent a lifetime building a business. It is also important for persons who wonder how they will be remembered. This may open the question of what else they have to give in addition to material things. Their life story, family history and important experiences are often involved. Also, I ask clients to write "Messages from the Heart," a form of an ethical/values will, which incorporates their history and hopes for future generations. In doing this, they may discover their abundance and what they can pass on.

There is a spontaneous part of me that responds to clients during coaching calls that may raise questions, and also suggest assignments to be completed before the next call. The client has the freedom to accept the assignment, modify it, or devise his/her own. These assignments may vary from making check lists, doing force-field analyses, filling out assessments or reading a small section of a book and browsing the rest of the book. Keeping a journal can also be helpful. From my own experience and learning I recommend a number of books that clients can read to further their explorations. These include books on such topics as management, lifestyle, personal finance, family business, religion, spirituality, volunteering and leisure. I suggest assignments, often to read a specific small section of a book and to respond.

Another coaching option I employ is telephone group coaching, which facilitates reaching many more persons than simply working one on one. In group coaching, participants can learn much from other participants. I have found that some attendees are also more comfortable. Others who have been in an individual coaching relationship can benefit from continued coaching in a group. More formally structured teleclasses also offer an opportunity to customize learning to help people invent new futures.

Summary

During a review that I periodically do with clients, one client told me that I am his "conscience." He is very much in charge of his life and his international business. I keep asking him what he wants to be in his third quarter. I support him in his journey as he assesses and gives of his gifts, including his leadership. For me, coaching is very fulfilling. I am able to use my many years of experience in business and the behavioral sciences to walk with clients as they invent new chapters in their lives.

Dr. Richard Haid is a former CEO of a 115-year-old family business. In answering a call that there were indeed more chapters in his life, he discovered mentoring and coaching. He can be reached at 513-868-1488 or by e-mail at dickhaid@concentric.net

Recommended Reading

www.adultmentor.com

Arnoff, C. & Ward, J.: "Facing the Fears of Retirement." *Nation's Business*, February 1991, pp. 38-40.

Arnoff, C. & Ward, J.: *Family Business Succession: The Final Test* of Greatness. (Marietta, GA: Business Owner Resource, 1992).

Bolman, L., and Deal, T.: *Leading With Soul: An Uncommon Journey of Spirit*. (San Francisco, CA: Jossey-Bass, 1995).

Haid, R.,: "Stepping Down and Stepping Out: A Qualitative Study Of Family Business CEOs Who Have Turned Over The Management Of The Business To Their Families." (Doctoral dissertation, The Union Institute, 1994). Dissertation Abstracts International, 55, 1314, (University Microfilms No. 94-26-975). (Also available as "There is Life after Family Business" Hamilton, OH: Haid Publishing,).

Haid, R.,: How are You a Legend? What is Your Legacy?: Seminar Readings and Supplemental Materials. (Hamilton, OH: Haid Publishing. 1997).

Haid, R.: "There is Life After Family Business For The CEO/Owner: Preparing for a Soft Landing and An Abundant Life." *Estates, Trusts, Pensions Journal*, Spring, 1999, pp. 195-214.

Hudson, F.: *The Adult Years: Mastering the Art of Self-Renewal.* (San Francisco,CA: Jossey-Bass, 1991).

Leider, R.: *Repacking Your Bags: Lighten Your Load for the Rest of Your Life.* (San Francisco, CA: Berrett-Koehler, 1995).

Levoy,G.: *Callings: Finding and Following an Authentic Life.* (New York: Harmony, 1997).

Moody, H. and Carroll, D.: *The Five Stages of the Soul: Charting the Spiritual Passages That Shape Our Lives.* (New York: Doubleday, 1997).

Murphy, J. and Hudson, F.: *The Joy of Old: A Guide to Successful Elderhood.* (Altadena, CA: Geode Press. 1995).

Schachter-Shalomi, Z. and Miller, R.: *From Age-ing to Sage-ing: A Profound Vision of Growing Older.* NY: Warner Books,1995).

THE ETHICS OF COACHING

John S. Stephenson, Ph.D.

Why Ethics Are Important

Jason found Mary to be his most challenging client. At the same time, he felt she was his greatest success. He had worked hard; holding Mary accountable for her actions and helping her to make major changes in her life. Over the year that they had worked together, Mary had received a significant promotion at work. Her personal life, which had not been at all satisfying, became much more fulfilling. She was clear about her future goals.

During a telephone session, Mary said, "Jason, I'm so very grateful for all of your coaching. You've helped me reach many goals I'd only dreamt about. As a kind of 'thank you,' I'd like to make you this offer: A very select group of investors, in which I am included, is buying the rights to an invention. It has tremendous potential. If you would like, I can get you in on the ground floor."

Jason leapt at the chance, and immediately invested $10,000. Six months later, a large corporation filed a patent infringement case against the investors. The project was shut down, and Jason and the others lost all of their investment. The coaching relationship between Jason and Mary was never the same. Shortly after the collapse of the investment group, they stopped working together. They haven't spoken since.

The above fictional example demonstrates how a decision can have implications far beyond what is expected. As we go through life, we are constantly making decisions about our actions. Sometimes we have the time to seek counsel from others. Often, we do not. Obviously, we cannot take the time to ponder every decision we make. We trust on our experience and our moral upbringing. For example, you might have heard someone explain his/her actions by saying, "I wasn't raised that way." Here, the person is relying on the teachings they received in childhood to justify his/her behavior. Over time, these childhood moral teachings become habituated, so we respond almost automatically when certain situations arise. This is beneficial, as it allows us to move smoothly through life.

But there are some problems associated with this kind of moral reasoning. Kitchener (see Recommended Readings) points out that we can't trust everyone to have had a sound ethical upbringing. In other words, we cannot always trust people to make good judgements. Also, we may find ourselves in situations where our past experiences and understandings don't apply. The situation may be so unusual as to make it difficult for us to understand it's ethical implications. Finally, it may be difficult to make a good ethical decision in the immediacy of the situation.

Jason, in the example above, made a quick decision to take advantage of Mary's offer. Both were acting in good faith. In order to take advantage of the offer, Jason had to act quickly. Also, it was a very attractive opportunity. Jason might have remembered the saying he heard as a child, "Strike while the iron is hot." As a result of Jason's decision, the coach/client relationship was permanently damaged.

Clearly, we need something in place which will guide us — a set of rules by which we can judge our intentions or actions. For this reason, professions develop codes of ethics, which regulate the actions of their members. Ethical codes serve to guide and remind people as to what is considered proper behavior. They are created away from the burden of having to make immediate decisions, and are often modified through analysis and debate before being accepted by a professional community. Professional organizations continually update and interpret their ethical guidelines.

Before we get into a discussion of the principles most common to codes of ethics, a few general points: First, codes of ethics are not laws. Jason violated no laws by accepting Mary's offer. Codes of ethics are guidelines for how to act. True, one can be denied membership in the professional organization, but not found guilty in a court of law for violating a particular code of ethics. That said, it is important to know that, should one be sued for harming another person, he/she will be judged by whether or not his/her actions were in compliance with existing community standards. As coaches, if you or I were to be sued, the court could take into consideration whether or not we violated the Ethical Guidelines of the International Coach Federation (I.C.F.). This ethical code could be considered as a standard of behavior by the court whether or not the coach is a member of the I.C.F.

Second, this chapter should not be considered as an absolute list of "do's or don'ts." The ethical principles discussed and their applications to particular situations will vary. It is up to each of us to be aware of the ethical principles governing our coaching, and to make sure we take into consideration the possible ethical implications of our actions.

Professional people make bad ethical choices for one of three reasons: They may choose to deliberately do something illegal or unethical. They may act unethically out of ignorance of the ethical implications of their actions. They may act unethically due to their own emotional neediness. I believe that while deliberate unethical acts get the most publicity, most unethical actions are committed out of ignorance. It is my hope that this overview of ethics will help coaches to raise their "ethical consciousness," so that they are constantly aware of possible ethical issues in their work.

In one of my ethics seminars, someone joked that I was intent on stirring up everyone's paranoia. While I appreciate the humor in the remark, better a bit skeptical and suspicious beforehand, than remorseful later. In *The Clinician's Toolbox,* Zuckerman & Guyett put it this way:

> Ethical education should result in a 'learned queasiness.' This sense of vulnerability, complexity and multiple perspectives is almost an operational definition of an ethical consciousness. The anxiety is inescapable and should motivate thoughtfulness, consultation, conservatism, foresight, contingency planning, and empathy. (Pg. 39)

Part of being "professional" is holding ourselves to the highest ethical standards. We should ask no less of ourselves, or of our fellow coaches. The unethical behaviors of any coach reflect negatively on us individually and on the whole profession.

Some Principles of Ethics Important to Coaches

This chapter does not seek to define all of the ethical criteria affecting coaches, but to concentrate on a few key principles. The principles of autonomy, confidentiality, conflicts of interest, and competence are considered in most major professional codes of ethics, and we shall consider each below.

Autonomy

The principle of autonomy holds that people have a right to decide for themselves. This means people have the right to decide what information about themselves is private as well as what values they choose to live by. This principle implies that we as coaches need to respect the differences, the uniqueness, of each of our clients. We need to respect their right to make decisions which affect their lives, *regardless of whether we agree or not.*

May we share with the client a different perspective? Of course. But it would be unethical to attempt to manipulate a client into

accepting our values or beliefs. The danger lies in becoming pater-
nalistic, whereby we make all of the clients' decisions for them.
This undermines the autonomy and growth of the client. At the
same time, it encourages the client's dependency on the coach.

Confidentiality

One of the values we considered under autonomy is the right to
privacy. As coaches, we need to hold in strictest confidence the
information that clients share with us. To do otherwise may harm
the client and damage the coach/client relationship. Who would
want to share the vulnerable parts of their lives with someone they
couldn't trust? Remember, the very nature of coaching involves
the private parts of a client's life. Therefore, everything, including
even the fact that you have a coaching relationship with someone,
is confidential information.

While we have a duty to protect the confidentially of our clients, we also have an ethical responsibility to the community. What
this means is that, if a client shares an intention to harm him/
herself or another, we are not bound by an ethical imperative to
keep that information secret.

Conflict of Interest

There are several implicit understandings involved when we agree
to work with a client; one of these is that the interests of the client
are paramount. Also, that as coaches we approach the relationship
with objectivity and clarity of judgement. We are not there for our
personal gain, nor do we have any kind of a hidden agenda. We are
there to help the client.

One of the ways in which the relationship with a client can be
damaged is through engaging in dual relationships. Recall the story
of Jason. His relationship with Mary was a coaching relationship.
After he invested the money, he also had a relationship with Mary
as a fellow investor. The "fall out" from the financial failure con-

taminated the coaching relationship. Jason's interest in his client became tainted by his interest as an investor. Had he not gotten involved as an investor, he might have continued his coaching of Mary. (And he'd still have his $10,000!)

The danger in dual relationships is that they cripple our objectivity. Our judgement can be distorted by our own self-interest. Does this mean that all dual relationships are inherently unethical? I don't believe so. However, their capacity for being damaging is immense. In other words, they are potentially dangerous and most often not worth the risk. Entering into financial dealings, becoming close friends, or developing some other form of a personal relationship with clients, while also serving as their coach, can easily constitute a conflict of interest.

The I.C.F., in its "Ethical Guidelines," says it well: "The Coach will not only communicate, but will continuously demonstrate, that the intended outcome of an exchange of information, discussion, referral, or recommendation is the Client's growth and well-being, and not the promotion of the Coach's self-interest."

Competence

When a profession first emerges, it is usually not clearly defined. Today, anyone can decide to go into the coaching business. There are no legal requirements to be a coach. I believe that we have a responsibility to be well-trained coaches. Our clients come to us seeking professional help. They believe that we are competent to provide what they need. This does not mean simply going through a recognized coach training program. It includes maintaining ties to the professional community of coaches, continually seeking to upgrade our skills and knowledge base, and maintaining a relationship with peers and mentor coaches to whom we can turn for their professional insights.

Competence also involves knowing one's limitations. Don't attempt to practice outside of your area of expertise. If you are giving advice about health, make sure your client knows you are not speaking as a physician. The same thing applies to other fields. Do only what you do well.

The above principles underlie some of the major themes one finds in professional codes of ethics. They are not inclusive of all ethical situations or values. This discussion is intended to highlight the importance of ethical principles in the daily conduct of coaching. In the following sections, we will examine two important questions around ethics: First, what to do if one becomes aware of another's unethical behavior, and second, how to protect ourselves from acting unethically.

Responding to Unethical Behavior in Others

In conducting seminars on professional ethics, I present vignettes similar to the one with which I began this chapter. Some of them involve the discovery of unethical behavior by another professional. When I ask the attendees what they would do in the situation, they often reply that they would confront the individual directly. I would urge you to use caution in taking this course. Accusing someone of unethical behavior may result in, among other things, a slander suit against you. Before taking any action, you may want to consult with a mentor coach or professional colleagues, as well as a lawyer. If the person is a member of a professional organization such as I.C.F., or is a licensed professional, there are specific guidelines in place for you to follow. Contact the relevant professional organization or state office for information.

Boundaries

This section draws on the work of Marilyn Peterson. In her excellent book, *At Personal Risk*, she presents a strong argument for maintaining strict professional boundaries. Peterson points out that our clients come to helping professionals in need. They have problems that they do not think they can solve without help. In disclosing the problem to us, the client makes him/herself vulnerable to us. We as coaches become the more powerful person in the relationship. In order to protect the client/coach relationship, clear boundaries need to be in place.

When we minimize our power in the coaching relationship, we are opening the door to boundary violations. In cases involving ethical errors, I have heard professionals claim, "All I did was make the offer. She was free to say 'no'." I disagree. Clients often feel that their freedom of choice is diminished. They often fear that the relationship may cease if they decline to respond positively, thus their "freedom" to decline is decreased.

Once the coach substitutes his/her own agenda for those of the coaching relationship, then he/she is acting unethically. The coach's needs are then more important than the client's needs. The client, being more vulnerable, feels pressured to condone the unethical behavior of the coach.

It is clearly the coach's responsibility to define the relationship, and to maintain professional boundaries. Our clients expect this of us, as do the I.C.F.'s "Ethical Guidelines." We also need to remember that we are modeling behavior for our clients. If we cannot maintain appropriate boundaries, how can we ask them to?

Rules for Inoculating Yourself Against Ethical Errors

Rule 1: *In situations involving an ethical question, always consult with other relevant professionals.* In my experience in varied professional situations and working directly with persons who have behaved unethically, the problems are almost always very complex. Often, one ethical principle will be in conflict with another. It can be difficult to sort out which action is in the best interests of the parties concerned. Get the input of others that might help you arrive at a good decision. Always document with whom you consulted, and how and why you arrived at your decision.

Rule 2: *Ignorance may be bliss, but it is no excuse.* Keep yourself knowledgeable concerning the ethical requirements for your work. Don't just have read through standards related to your conduct;

have an understanding of how to apply ethical principles every day.

Rule 3: *Never need your clients more than they need you.* When professionals seek to get their personal needs met through relationships with their clients, the relationship is no longer professional in nature. Always keep in mind you are engaging in a coaching relationship to serve the needs of the client, and not your own. Have a life away from your practice.

Rule 4: *Your actions have two meanings; what you intend and how they appear to others.* This fact of life often angers people. They want to be judged on their motives. Unfortunately, it can be difficult to "prove" our intentions. Based on how our behaviors might appear to others, we are vulnerable to being accused of unethical motives.

Rule 5: *Listen to your intuitive self.* Often, an intuitive sense of unease indicates an underlying ethical problem. Before you dismiss the feeling, check it out. Be your own devil's advocate, or ask a colleague to act in that capacity. For example, if on the surface an act you're considering seems ethical, yet you have a some inner sense of concern, try proving to yourself why your choice is free from any possible ethical errors.

Rule 6: *Know your limitations.* This applies not only to your professional expertise, but your personal and emotional limits as well. A stressed-out, overworked coach cannot provide excellent services to clients.

Rule 7: *Develop a strong ethical position in your practice.* Working from a strong ethical code is a part of being an excellent coach. Having a strong, well-thought out perspective on ethics is the best defense against ethical mishaps. And, you sleep better.

Rule 8: *Maintain your boundaries.* Our clients expect us to define the professional relationship. If we do not, they will, and this often leads to confusing roles and an ineffective, if not unethical, relationship.

Rule 9: *Remember, you never win a malpractice suit.* You may get a judgement in your favor, but the damage to you and your professional reputation will continue, and may be irreparable.

Conclusion

Being a "professional" is a privilege in our society. We are recognized as having the ability to use our own discretion in our work. If we as coaches do not hold ourselves accountable for our ethical conduct, we will soon find the state stepping in to govern us. Acting ethically is not just about staying out of trouble. It is also about being good at what you do. There are many brilliant and capable former professionals who lost sight of that concept. Keep in mind that your actions reflect not only on yourself, but also upon the entire field of coaching.

Simply put, we owe it to our clients, ourselves, and the profession to subscribe to and live by the highest ethical standards.

Dr. John Stephenson is a former university professor and psychotherapist. A graduate of Coach University, and a Professional Certified Coach, he specializes in personal coaching and mentoring new coaches. He can be reached by e-mail at: drjohn@maine.rr.com, or phone 207-741-2892. Visit his website, www. coachingdoc.com.

Recommended Reading

Hass, Leonard J. & John L. Malouf: *Keeping Up the Good Work.* (Sarasota, Professional Resource Exchange, 1989)

International Coach Federation: *Ethical Guidelines.* Available at the I.C.F. website, www.coachfederation.org.

Kitchener, Karen S.: "Intuition, Critical Evaluation and Ethical Principles." *The Counseling Psychologist,* 12(3) pp 43-54.

Peterson, Marilyn R.: *At Personal Risk.* (NY: Norton, 1992)

Van Hoose, W., & J. Kottler: *Ethical and Legal Issues in Counseling and Psychotherapy.* (San Francisco, CA: Jossey-Bass, 1977)

Zuckerman, Edward I. & Irvin P. R. Guyett: The Paper Office (Pittsburgh: The Clinician's Toolbox, 1992)